Those Words I Dread

Tales of the Tuath Dé
Book 1

Tess Barnett

ALSO BY TESS BARNETT

Tales of the Tuath Dé
Those Words I Dread
Because You Needed Me
To Keep You Near

Devil's Gamble

Starbound

Domesticated: A Short Story Collection
In collaboration with Michelle Kay

AS T.S. BARNETT

The Beast of Birmingham
Under the Devil's Wing
Into the Bear's Den
Down the Endless Road

The Left-Hand Path
Mentor
Runaway
Prodigy

A Soul's Worth

Those Words I Dread

Tales of the Tuath Dé
Book 1

Tess Barnett

Pensacola, FL

Cover Art by Jasmine Monterroso
kikissh.com

His Princely Delicates
An Imprint of Corvid House Publishing
Fantasy and Science Fiction Gay Romance Novels

Pensacola, FL
http://www.hisprincelydelicates.com

ACKNOWLEDGMENTS

Thank you to Kaylyn, who is always ready to indulge my need for handsome boys who touch each other.

1

The rain was more of a hindrance to Julien than the fairy's glamours. He weaved through people on the street, shouldering his way between couples and upsetting more than a few umbrellas, but he always kept the creature's back in sight. It was slow; the wound in its gut made it limp down the sidewalk, perhaps unseen by anyone but Julien himself. He would need to chase it until he could force it into a less public location. His boot sunk into a puddle as he was forced off the curb by a cluster of people, soaking his sock, and he cursed as he wiped the plastered hair from his forehead.

Ahead of him, the fairy ducked into a building, and Julien picked up speed, taking the front steps two at a time and flinging the glass door open to keep the creature in view. He moved to follow it through the lobby and was stopped by a quick shout and a hand on his chest.

"Afternoon, sir," the doorman said in a tone less friendly than his words. "Can I help you?"

Julien looked past him to the fairy in the corner, clutching its stomach and watching him with a wicked grin. The guard couldn't see it. As big as a man and standing two feet from him, laughing—and he couldn't see it.

"I'm here to see someone," Julien said as calmly as he could, glancing briefly at the man in front of him. He couldn't exactly tell him the truth.

The doorman looked over his shoulder a moment to follow Julien's gaze, but he only saw the elevator doors and the tall potted fern in the corner of the lobby. "And who's that?" he asked, turning back to the taller man with a more skeptical eye.

Julien grit his teeth at the fairy's snickering grin. The creature looked up as the elevator beside it let out a soft ding, and it slipped inside, wiggling its fingers at Julien in a taunting wave as the doors slid shut between them.

"Sorry," he ground out. "Wrong building." He watched the numbered lights above the elevator go up and up, but he had to turn and leave before he saw them stop.

Julien let out a curse as he stepped back out into the rain, pushing his wet hair back from his forehead as he craned his neck to look up at the building. He hadn't anticipated the fairy having a home. Maybe only a hideout. He took a look up and down the street, as well as he could see through the pouring rain. Nothing but housing. He would just have to wait, try again in the morning with a different doorman.

He hunkered under some scaffolding and dug in his pocket, retrieving his small brass compass and clicking it open. The makeshift screen inside still lit up green, confirming that a magic creature was still nearby. The compass case had made a convenient receptacle for the magic tracker he had cobbled together years ago. The fairy had been killing women around Vancouver for months, and now that Julien finally had it in his sights, he didn't plan on letting it slip away from him. He shut the compass and dropped it back into his pocket, then settled under the scaffolding and lit a cigarette. He could wait.

Ciaran leaned his head against the back of the elevator and took a few long, slow breaths before looking down to check the seeping wound under his hand. Black blood had smeared across his palm and soaked his shirt where the hunter had cut him, and the open gash burned from the iron blade's touch. He felt lightheaded. Damn that man. Who did he think he was?

The elevator rose up to the top floor of the building, as he had requested, but a sick turning in his stomach made him punch the button marked '19' and stop it one floor early. He needed somewhere to hide, and that tugging feeling in his gut told him this was it. The door was locked, of course, but it only took a turn of the knob to click it open. He put his hand back to his stomach as he entered, leaving a coating of pitch-colored blood on the door knob.

The apartment was spacious and sparsely decorated, with cool stone floors and tall windows. There was hardly any color anywhere—only a black leather sofa and the cold stainless steel of the kitchen fixtures. Ciaran spotted the source of his unrest in the octagonal mirror on the wall, the round convex glass surrounded by black, red, and yellow markings. He couldn't read them, but he knew a talisman meant to keep evil spirits away when he saw it. Luckily for him, he wasn't an evil spirit. At least, he didn't mean this particular resident any harm just now. He peered at his distorted reflection, one green eye growing large as he leaned close to the polished surface. He looked as pale as he felt. He wiped his brow with the back of his hand, only smearing the gathered sweat. He could barely breathe.

He walked through the open dining area and living room, pausing by the kitchen and taking a few sniffs near the pantry door. He helped himself, though the skim milk in the refrigerator was a disappointment, and the blueberry muffin he stole from the counter was a bit stale. He eased himself down onto the sleek leather sofa near the balcony doors and sighed, wiping a few remaining crumbs from his mouth. He could feel the iron in the heavy wooden armoire nearby, no doubt hiding some other collection of spiritual goodies. What sort of person lived here? Whoever it was, the magical trinkets would doubtless help to hide him when that hunter inevitably came calling again.

Ciaran curled up fully dressed on the sofa, his hand covering his tender injury, and he slipped off to sleep with his belly not quite as full as he would have liked.

By the time he woke up, the lights in the kitchen were on and the double doors near him had been opened, showing the office inside. A man sat at the desk chair with his back to the door, typing something on the laptop in front of him. Ciaran sat up and lifted his shirt to inspect the crusted injury on his belly. It was still open, but the bleeding had stopped, at least. He wiped idly at the dark stain left on the sofa seat and stood to approach the office door with an unsteady step.

The man at the desk didn't notice him, of course. No one ever noticed him unless he wanted them to, or unless they were unfortunate enough to stumble onto something they shouldn't. It was just the nature of his kind.

Ciaran sat on the desk beside the open laptop to catch his breath. Damn the iron. The short walk from the sofa to the office had winded him. He would have to think up something truly unpleasant for that man the next time he saw him.

The man beside him now, however, was a bit of a surprise. He was very young, and Chinese—which Ciaran supposed explained the mirror by the door. A handsome kid, with soft black hair just touching his ears, and deep brown eyes that narrowed as they peered at the computer screen through rectangular half-frames. The apartment was quiet except for the ticking clock in the living room, and as Ciaran leaned forward to see the screen for himself, he found nothing interesting there. Just a bunch of figures and charts. He wished he hadn't made the trip from the sofa just for this, even if his unwitting host was good-looking.

The man rose at a distant knock on the door, and Ciaran made his way back to the couch to listen. A boring conversation with a maintenance man about the blood Ciaran had left smeared on the knob, and the open door itself—oops. He hadn't even bothered to make the place look burgled. Except for the muffin. Speaking of muffins.

Ciaran pulled himself away from the sofa with a squeak of leather cushions and went into the walk-in pantry, pulling down boxes of pasta, bags of potato chips, and tins of nuts. He let them fall to the floor as he dug through the shelves looking for anything that might satisfy him, and he heard the front door shut. He turned his head when his host appeared in the pantry doorway, a bewildered look on his face as he took in the scene. Ciaran had to steady himself against the shelves from the exertion of standing, and he took a slow breath as he let his forehead rest on a beam. Damn that man.

He heard a short gasp from the door and looked up to find the young man a step closer to him, staring straight into his face with

4

narrowed eyes.

"Who's there?" he demanded, seeming to have lost sight of Ciaran in a moment. His glamour must have slipped in his weakness. The man moved past him to look around the corner of the pantry, then scowled back toward the door when he found nothing. Well, now Ciaran had two options. Explain himself, which would be boring and repetitious but might give him a chance to rest, or keep hidden and risk drawing the attention of some sort of hired exorcist or medium. That had happened before. Catholic priests had little power over him, of course, but it was a nauseatingly drawn-out endeavor that made it hardly worth staying.

So, the fairy reached toward the younger man, and with a quick whisper, found himself eye to eye with his unknowing benefactor. The young man jumped back in a start and swore as his back hit the wall.

"Easy, boy," Ciaran said, holding out one hand and letting the other rest over his aching wound. "I didn't come to give you no trouble." His voice was quiet and deep, with a smooth brogue that went well with his impish smile. The long-sleeved shirt he wore was ragged and stained, stretched out of shape and hanging loosely over his jeans.

"What the hell are you doing in here? How long have you been here? Why couldn't I see you?" The man inched toward the pantry door without turning his back on Ciaran.

"Fair questions, all," the fairy admitted. "But ones that might take a bit of explaining."

"How about what you think you're doing to my pantry?"

Ciaran glanced over at the shelf to his right, which held a tantalizing bag of sugared candies.

"Forget it. I'm calling the cops."

"Won't do you no good," Ciaran called after him, and he let the man turn to see him in the pantry door before vanishing and reappearing on the sofa a moment later, candy bag in hand.

The young man stopped with his hand on his phone on the kitchen counter, and he looked between the sofa and the pantry door once or twice before settling his frowning gaze on the interloper eating his candies.

"What the hell is going on?"

"Fairy magic," Ciaran said simply, slurred by a candy. He waggled his fingers for effect, but the other man didn't seem impressed. "See, I've been in a bit of a scrap, and this spot here was nearby enough and has just enough magic in it that it should hide me away decent enough. So I'll just be staying a few days and I'll be on my way."

"The hell you will."

Ciaran shrugged. "Call the police as you like, boy, but they won't find nothing here but a ranting lad and a messy larder. You stay out of my way and I'll stay out of yours, and as soon as I'm well, we can happily part company."

"Stay out of *your* way? You're in my house!"

"Aye, and it's not the coziest of spots, is it?"

"So sorry it's not up to your standards, crazy," he answered with a sneer.

"Hey now, there's no call for any of that. You're the one what sees strange disappearing men."

The young man took a deep breath, and he took his hand away from his cell phone, stepping closer to lean against the kitchen island and fold his arms over his chest. "You're the one that left that black shit on my door?"

"Blood, aye. Sorry I was busy bleeding to death; didn't think to clean up after myself."

"That's blood?"

"Fairy blood. Slightly different."

The man snorted at him and only stared for a long moment, the crunching of candies echoing through the apartment between them. "So assume I believe at least that you're on the run," he said at last. "I'm supposed to believe the rest of it is 'fairy magic?'"

"Aye. Don't you believe in fairies, boy?"

"Stop calling me boy. And no."

"Don't you know whenever you say that, somewhere a fairy drops dead?" The other man sighed through his nose without answering. "You're right; that's probably not true at all. At any rate, you saw what you saw, hm? Believe yourself if you don't believe me."

"Why here? What the hell did I do to deserve having you show up here?"

"Well you've got a fair bit of magic in this place, as I'm sure you know."

"What are you talking about?"

Ciaran gestured toward the entry hall. "That mirror, for one. Don't get many bad spirits in here, do you? There's other things; I haven't exactly been searching the place."

"That stuff isn't magic; it's just old."

"Magic and old are frequently one and the same, lad," the fairy smiled.

"Why should it matter if it's magic or not anyway? No—you know what? I don't even care. It doesn't matter. Magic or not, you're not my problem. Get out."

"Well that's pragmatic," Ciaran chuckled. He pushed himself off of the sofa and stepped closer to the young man, setting the candy bag on the counter beside him and smirking to himself as the young man straightened, clearly wary of their proximity. "Let's try this again." He offered the other man his bloodstained hand. "Name's Ciaran. What's yours?"

The young man sneered down at his hand without reaching for it, so Ciaran slowly moved it forward until his fingertips touched the other man's stomach.

"Don't be rude, lad," he murmured as he lightly prodded his belly, a smile touching his lips at the man's slight squirm.

"Trent."

"What's that, boy?"

"My name is Trent," he said again, and he scowled as he took Ciaran's hand in his and gave it the briefest of shakes. "And stop calling me boy. What sort of a name is Ciaran, anyway?"

"Keer-an," the fairy corrected him.

"Whatever." Trent pried his hand away and slid out from between the counter and the other man.

"The way of it is, Trent, I'm not in top form," Ciaran said, wincing a bit as he lifted his arm to let the younger man see the black stains on his shirt. "There's a man after me, and I'm in no shape to run. I'll be staying until I am."

"What did you do?"

Ciaran seemed hesitant to answer, so Trent snatched the open bag of candies away when the fairy reached for them.

"What did you do?" he asked again.

Ciaran sighed. "It's a bit complex."

"I'm a smart guy."

The fairy pondered, glancing between the candy bag and the other man's face. "All right. Let me sit down."

Trent sat across the L-shaped sofa from his unwelcome guest, letting him settle and shift until he was comfortable, and then Ciaran took a deep breath and let it out with a puff of his cheeks.

2

"So, I'm what they call gean cánach," Ciaran began, pausing to peel the sticky shirt away from his wound. "People end up dead because of me. It isn't out of malice, you understand; in fact, I don't even rightly kill them at all."

"Kind of you," Trent scoffed.

"Do you want an explanation, or do you want to be a shite?" Trent scowled at him. "Stuff it then. At any rate, I don't kill anyone. Quite the opposite. It's a bit awkward to explain, really. This is why I don't tell people. You see, gean cánach, we have a bit of...what would you call it, a toxin? In the skin, see."

"You're poisonous?"

"Eh, not quite. More like addicting, right? I'm sure you know, everyone has urges, don't they, and so, when I give in to those urges, as it turns out, the women can't get enough. When I leave, as I eventually do, they pine away and die for want of me. It's flattering to start, but it gets a bit worn out, as I'm sure you can imagine."

Trent gave him a deadpan stare. "You're telling me that you're being hunted because you're a fairy who is so good at sex that the women literally die when they can't have you anymore?"

"They stop eating, don't they?" He shrugged, rubbing a hand over the dark, messy hair on his head and showing the tips of slightly pointed ears. "They don't do a thing but seek me out, but I'm nowhere to be found, of course—"

"Get out."

Ciaran paused. "What's that?"

"I said get out. This is bullshit, and I don't have time for bullshit." He stood and walked back to the kitchen island, scooping up his cell phone. "I can't believe I even listened to this. Fairy magic," he grumbled, flicking his thumb to unlock his phone's screen. "You're a crazy person with some kind of blood disorder, and I need to get better sleep at night."

"Shall I prove it to you?"

"Prove to me that you're some sort of sex fairy?" Trent muttered without looking up.

"Well, not that bit. It don't work on men."

"Convenient."

Ciaran sighed, and with a slight wave of his hand, the phone in Trent's hand twisted into a hissing snake. Trent dropped it to the floor with a short cry and stepped back from the snake's exposed fangs.

"Mind your screen, lad. You'll break it that way."

"What the fuck is this?" Trent demanded, not taking his eyes away from the thing's rattling tail.

"Didn't you say you were smart? It's a snake."

"I know it's a fucking snake; why is my phone a snake?"

The fairy snapped his fingers, and the snake vanished in a small puff of smoke, leaving Trent's phone upside down on the stone floor. "It's only a glamour. An illusion."

The young man tentatively reached down for his abandoned phone, half expecting it to hiss at him, and he clicked his tongue as he turned it in his hand. "You couldn't have done something that didn't crack my screen?" He stood and weighed the phone in his palm as he watched the man on his sofa. He looked homeless. But a normal homeless person wouldn't have been able to get by the doorman, and definitely couldn't have turned his phone into a snake. "What is it you want from me, exactly?"

"Like I said, a place to stay whilst that hunter's after me. Once I'm healed up, I'll be on my way, and you can do…whatever it is you do in peace." He shrugged. "Honestly, it's happening regardless of what you say, so you might as well be hospitable about it."

"Hospitable?" Trent echoed with a slight sneer.

"Or whatever approximation you can manage."

"And what happens if I say this still isn't remotely my problem, and I let this hunter have you?"

"Well, aside from that being extremely rude, you'd have a bit of blood on your hands, wouldn't you? He isn't exactly trying to give me a slap on the wrist, you know."

Trent let out an irritated sigh through his nose and set his phone back on the marble counter. He didn't want this person in his house or in his life, but on the off chance that it was all true, he didn't really want to deal with a dead supernatural something on his conscience or on his rug. At least if he cooperated, Ciaran had promised to leave. He gave another small sigh. "For how long? Precisely."

"Hard to be precise." Ciaran lifted his shirt to inspect the wound in his stomach, cringing as he exposed it to the cool air. "That iron is nasty business, you see. A few days, a week or two at most."

"A week or two?" Trent echoed with a scowl.

"You'll hardly notice me," he assured him. "Just carry on as you will, hm?"

"Sure. With a fairy in my house. Don't you have your own place? Or you're some sort of hobo fairy?"

"What fairy have you ever heard of what had a house? I'm transient by nature, lad. Part of what makes me such a good house guest."

"This is being a good house guest?"

"Comparatively, sure," Ciaran chuckled.

Trent almost laughed in disbelief, and then he gave a small gesture of resignation. "Fine. Whatever. If you can stay out of the way."

"It's an agreement, then?" Ciaran pressed. "You'll show me hospitality?"

"Or whatever approximation I can manage," Trent said with a slight sigh. He shook his head and started the short walk back to his office, but he was interrupted by Ciaran's conspicuous throat-clearing. He paused to look at him, and the fairy had one arm reached out over the back of the couch, gesturing with his hand and glancing pointedly at the bag of candies. Trent's lip curled, but he tossed the bag into the other man's waiting hand, earning himself a short laugh in place of a thank you.

"Clean up the pantry," he ordered on his way by.

Trent left the doors to his office open while he took his place at his desk, not trusting his intruder enough to leave him completely unsupervised. He had school assignments to do, and he wouldn't be able to use "fairy houseguest" as an excuse for late work. Every crunch of hard candy behind him grated on his nerves, but he refused to pay the man any attention. Green eyes and high cheekbones scattered with freckles would not be enough to distract him from the insanity that Ciaran had brought into his house. He kept his focus when he heard the fairy stirring behind him, relaxing ever so slightly as the pantry door opened and closed in the distance. Maybe he was actually picking up after himself.

Trent pointedly kept his gaze ahead of him when he finally emerged to cook dinner, breezing past the reclined figure on his sofa and opening the refrigerator. He paused. "Did you drink all of the milk?"

"Aye, and I was a bit let down, to be frank," Ciaran called across the room. "Why don't you have whole fat?"

Trent snatched up the empty jug and held it out accusingly. "And you put it back like this?"

"Where should I have put it?"

"Literally anywhere else."

Ciaran climbed over the back of the sofa and limped across the living room to stand in front of him, then took the empty jug from his hand, lifted his eyebrows in acknowledgment, and immediately set the jug on the counter directly in front of him.

Trent's eyes narrowed at the fairy's teasing grin, and he let the fridge door drop shut behind him.

"So, what's for supper?" Ciaran asked, not seeming to notice the other man's agitation.

"Didn't you just eat an entire bag of candy?"

"And now I'm asking you what's for supper."

"I don't know what you're having. Didn't you say we were going to stay out of each other's way?" He leaned an inch closer to the fairy's face, urging him to move out of the kitchen. "So stay out of the way."

"You wouldn't leave a person to starve," Ciaran objected, though he obediently stepped aside to let Trent go by him to the pantry.

"*If* you want what I'm making, and *if* I happen to make too much, then you can have some." He opened the pantry door and clicked his tongue at the misplaced items on the shelves. He supposed an attempt was better than nothing at all. He picked up the large container of rice and set it on the counter when he emerged, ignoring Ciaran's chin very near his shoulder as he prepared the rice cooker.

The fairy lingered much too deep into Trent's personal bubble the entire time he was cooking, obviously having no intention of being unobtrusive or staying out of the way. Trent hesitated with his hand on the cabinet door, but with a small huff, he took down two plates instead of one and spooned out the mixture of rice and vegetables equally between them.

"You've a tender heart, a chara," Ciaran chuckled, snatching away the plate before the other man could change his mind.

Trent only brushed past him on his way back to the office, leaving him alone in the kitchen and returning to his school work. In the time it took him to glance down at the open book beside his laptop, Ciaran had somehow appeared beside him, plate in hand and feet swinging as he sat on the corner of the desk. Trent jumped, but the fairy didn't seem to notice.

"So, this is a posh place for someone so young," Ciaran noted as he poked at the rice on his plate with his fork. "You some sort of boy genius, are you?"

"It's my parents' place," Trent muttered, returning his attention to his screen.

"They accustomed to you having houseguests, then? Won't be a rude surprise for them?"

"They're in Hong Kong. Don't you have a toadstool to sit on somewhere?"

"Starting right in with the racial stereotypes, are we?"

"Go away."

"Bit rude, is all I'm saying."

"Go. Away." Trent looked up at him over the black rims of his glasses, his lips pulled down into a tight frown.

Ciaran felt a momentary urge to bite that scowl off of the other man's lip, but instead he only dropped his half-eaten plate on the desk with a heavy clunk and slid back to the floor, leaving Trent to brood at his computer in peace. He curled up on the sofa again, comforted by the slight weight of his hand upon his wound.

By the time Trent emerged from the office and put away the dishes, his guest was sound asleep on the sofa, one arm over his stomach and the other having long ago slipped off the side of the cushions. He paused on his way by, watching the other man breathe for a few moments. His head had fallen to the side, his lips parted to let out his slow, even breaths. Trent hesitated, biting the inside of his cheek and silently cursing the way the lights of the city shone through the balcony doors onto the fairy's freckled nose. It would be a tousled, smirking one that showed up in his house and claimed to be a fairy. He shook his head. It hadn't been so long that he was going to let this person intrude on his solitude just because he had a pretty face.

He reached down to shake Ciaran's shoulder. "Go and get in the spare bed," he said brusquely, so that the other man wouldn't mistake it for friendliness. "If you bleed on that, at least I can clean the sheets."

Ciaran's brow furrowed as he shifted away from the touch, tugging his shoulder away and curling up on his side. Trent huffed at him and tried flicking him in one pointed ear, but that only drew an irritated grunt from the sleeping man.

"Fine." Trent walked around the sofa and pulled on Ciaran's arm, shaking it in an attempt to wake him. When that didn't work, he gave a short sigh and bent down, slipping his arms under the other man's knees and shoulders. He braced himself as he moved to lift him, but Ciaran was so light that he nearly stumbled backwards into the glass coffee table. Trent paused, looking down at the sleeping face against his shoulder, and snorted.

"You're pretty light for someone so full of shit."

He carried Ciaran into the guest bedroom and dropped him onto the bed, not bothering to pull down the blankets. The fairy settled into the soft mattress with a contented sigh, and Trent hesitated beside the bed, his eye focused on the other man's stained shirt.

Keeping an eye on Ciaran's sleeping face in case he stirred, Trent reached down to pull up the hem of his dirty t-shirt. The wound underneath was a black blemish on the otherwise smooth, tanned skin of Ciaran's stomach. The edges of the cut were an angry, infected red, and dark veins were visible around the perimeter of the open wound. At least he was telling the truth about being injured.

Trent released the shirt and shut the bedroom door behind him as he left the room. He hoped there wouldn't be a dead body there in the morning.

3

To avoid checking on Ciaran in the morning, Trent took a long shower and surfed the internet while eating his breakfast, then packed his laptop back into his messenger bag and set it on the sofa, ready for his commute to university. He wasn't looking forward to leaving the stranger alone in his apartment, but if the worst he did was leave food on the pantry floor, he supposed it wasn't so bad. He replaced the bottle of orange juice and shut the refrigerator door, sucking in a sharp gasp as Ciaran's face appeared behind it.

"You need to stop doing that," he growled, scooping up his glass of juice on his way by the other man. Sometime in the night, the fairy had apparently made himself comfortable, as he now stood in Trent's kitchen barefoot and naked from the waist up. A gold amulet hung around his neck by a simple leather thong, the coin-sized circle stamped with a swirling, knotted cross. The wound on his stomach had closed, but it still looked tender and black, and Ciaran idly prodded it with his fingers as he watched Trent move to the sofa.

"Did you eat breakfast without me?" he asked.

"What do you think this is?" Trent countered without looking up from his phone. He scrolled through the news headlines as he sipped his juice. "It's not a B&B. Get your own food."

"I'm in no fit state to go out," Ciaran objected. He walked over and leaned his elbows on the back of the couch, his face far too close to Trent's for the other man's liking. "That's the point of hiding out, boy. Have a heart; go and get me something."

"Eat what's here if you have to. I'm not your servant. And if you call me boy one more time, you can forget this whole stupid arrangement."

Ciaran let out a dramatic groan. "But I'll waste away on the food you have here," he complained.

"What's wrong with it?" He looked up at the man at his shoulder, tensing slightly at the proximity of their faces. At this distance, he could count the dark freckles dusting the fairy's nose and cheeks. He thought for just a moment that Ciaran paused too, but then the fairy pushed up onto his hands and huffed out a sigh.

"All you've got here are vegetables. Dry bread, water, skim milk, sour fruit. You haven't even got any maple syrup, you failure of a Canadian. How do you live like this?"

"With low cholesterol."

"I need better food than this. Look," he added, "I'll give you some money, right? You'll just be out a quick jaunt to the grocer."

"What is it you want that's so much better than the food I have?"

"Does that mean you'll go then?"

Trent frowned, then drained his glass of juice and stood. "I need to go to class. If you want food, go get it yourself."

Ciaran folded his arms and stared after Trent like a child denied a cookie while the younger man picked up his school bag and slung it over his shoulder. "You'll change your mind," the fairy muttered. "Mí-ádh."

Trent paused as he felt a cold prickling at the back of his neck, and he turned to glare across the room at Ciaran, but the other man had already contented himself with the last stale blueberry muffin.

"Have a good time at school, a chara," he said cheerfully. Trent eyed him warily for a moment, but then frowned and stepped toward the front door, deciding he was being paranoid.

When he arrived at the elevator, he saw a sign taped to the doors informing him that it was out of order. With a sigh, he pushed open the door to the stairwell and began his trip down the nineteen flights of stairs. It wasn't as difficult as going up, but he was still irritated by the time he got to the lobby. He walked the four blocks to his bus stop, scowling at the other pedestrians who bumped his shoulder on their way by, and stood to wait with his eyes on his phone screen. It was easier to avoid talking with people than it was to get the image of Ciaran's smirking lips out of his head. He imagined they were sweet.

He let out a scoffing sigh and put his phone in his pocket, unable to focus on the words on the screen. Trent wasn't interested in a boyfriend, especially one who could apparently do magic and was being hunted by some kind of fairy-killer, which sounded ridiculous even in his head. He liked being alone just fine—it was the appeasing alternative he had settled on after his mother had cried when she discovered him with his high school boyfriend. He could take care of himself, and a boyfriend wasn't worth the lecture from his father he would have to sit through on the off chance he ever met anyone worth bringing home.

He took off his glasses to clean them with the bottom of his shirt as the bus pulled up to the stop, slipping them back onto his nose before he climbed aboard. He took his place near the back exit and sat with his head turned to the window. He had spent the great majority of his time alone for as long as he could remember, and he was in no great hurry to change that now, regardless of freckles on noses.

A woman smiled at him when she sat beside him a few stops later, but he ignored her. He rode along in silence, silently scolding himself whenever he pictured the smooth taper of Ciaran's hips disappearing beneath the frayed waistband of his worn blue jeans. He would be a bad decision, even if it was unattached. Better to pay him as little attention as possible until he could heal up and leave, then forget the entire thing had ever happened.

Before the bus reached his stop, it shuddered to a halt with a black smoke billowing up from under the hood. They were all herded off of the bus with apologies and promises of refunds, but Trent only clicked his tongue in irritation and checked his watch. He was going to be late. With no other choice, he set off at a brisk pace down the street, keeping his eyes open for any taxis that might get him to campus faster. There wasn't a single yellow car to be seen; the entire industry seemed to have taken the day off. Trent swore under his breath and sped up to a light jog, holding his messenger bag against his side to avoid jostling his laptop too much.

He arrived at his lecture hall panting and red-faced, with a film of sweat that made his shirt stick uncomfortably to his back. He tried to slip into the room quietly, since he knew he was late, but the door swung open faster than he anticipated and hit him square in the nose. He put a hand to his face and cursed as he stepped inside, glowering at anyone who dared turn to look at him. He took a seat the back of the room to avoid making more of a disturbance than he already had. He opened his laptop with a huff as he caught his breath, but the battery was dead. He frowned down at it. He was sure he had charged it overnight. He took a quick glance around him, but there were no outlets to be found, so he shoved the laptop back into his bag and took out a notebook and pen instead.

He acknowledged Hannah, the girl who always sat beside him, when she turned to look back at him. He was almost glad that he was late, so that he wouldn't have to listen to her idle chit-chat before class started. He had had enough social interaction. Hannah was pleasant enough in general, quiet and focused, and he had known her since high school. Sometimes they ate lunch together after class let out, but today he couldn't bring himself to pretend to care about her. He could barely care about the lecture, as irritated as he was.

The entire class, his arm hung awkwardly over the edge of the desk while he attempted to keep up with the professor's lecture, as the desk was meant for the right-handed majority and he wrote with his left. He continually hit his elbow on the sharp corner of the wall, since the desk he had been forced into was in an awkward spot at the edge of the classroom. He would set down his pen to check his previous page of notes, and it would roll off of the desk as though it had a mind of his own. When he bent to pick it up, he cracked his head on the bottom of the desk despite the fact that the thing was only about a foot across. The professor scolded him for being disruptive, which only made him angrier, but he scowled down at his notebook rather than argue.

As soon as the lecture was over, he gathered up his things and attempted to leave the room quickly, but he stumbled on the top step of the lecture hall and had to catch himself on an unsuspecting classmate's shoulder. She flinched away from him out of reflex and laughed as he straightened himself. He refused to look at her or apologize; he only left the room as fast as he could without hitting himself in the face again. He didn't believe for a second that Ciaran's spite had nothing to do with his sudden, inexplicable clumsiness. He had been too friendly just before Trent left. Who knew what kind of magic the fairy was capable of, and he used it to make Trent drop his pen during a lecture? Irresponsible and childish.

Hannah caught up to him outside as he huffed in frustration, and she hid a smile as she shifted her backpack on her shoulders. "You okay?" she asked with a tilt of her head. "You don't seem to be having a very good time today."

"I'm fine," he said, looking across the courtyard rather than at her face.

"You sure? You're very frowny and distracted. Something on your mind, or are you trying to turn me on?"

"What—" His gaze snapped back to her, but he snorted out a sigh when he saw the small, teasing smile on her face. "It's nothing important. Just some...company from out of town that I wasn't expecting."

"Company? As in, somebody's staying at your place?" She let out a soft chuckle. "And they're still alive?"

He grunted in response. "I'm not that bad."

"Trent, I've known you for three years, and I've never even been inside your building."

"Why would you?"

She smiled at him. "Exactly."

Trent glanced down at his watch with a quick sigh, not really listening to Hannah anymore. She liked to tell him about various happenings in her life that she imagined were interesting, such as which of her cats was the bigger jerk, or the new tea infuser she just got that looks like a sloth. She was usually satisfied with his noncommittal answers and half-hearted agreements. She just liked to have someone to talk at, he imagined. He didn't mind; he could mostly tune her out by now. By the time he started listening again, she was telling him goodbye, so he answered in kind. She gave him a brief wave and moved on to her next class, while he had little choice but to return to his apartment.

He felt a strange, unwelcome anxiety in his chest as he walked back toward the bus stop, despite how flustered his trip so far had made him. He knew Ciaran would be at the apartment waiting for him when he returned. Well, probably not actually waiting for him—but he would be there. Trent wasn't sure he liked the feeling of coming home to an apartment that had someone in it already. It was a reminder of the times his parents came back, only ever long enough to maintain their citizenship. Ciaran wouldn't be waiting with a lecture or with pressing questions about his GPA, but it would doubtless be just as uncomfortable.

He managed to make it back to his building without his bus breaking down, though the car was much more crowded than usual, so he found himself pressed between a sweaty man's back and a woman with a low-cut shirt who seemed to be trying to make a career out of pressing her breasts into his chest and smiling up at him. He kept his eyes facing staunchly forward for the entire ride home and eagerly pushed by her when the bus reached his stop.

Trent acknowledged the doorman, who apologized for the elevator still being out, and let out a resigned sigh as he started the slow climb back to his floor. When he finally reached his door, his legs heavy from exertion, he stopped in the hall with his hand on the door knob. Inside, there would be a man—a fairy—who was handsome enough to trouble him and almost troublesome enough to negate the handsomeness. Not almost, he told himself. Definitely. He gave a brief sigh and turned the knob, letting himself into the apartment.

The kitchen had been torn apart. Everywhere, torn plastic wrappers sat abandoned on countertops or on the floor, muffins were half devoured and left in their paper cups, and his bottle of orange juice, now empty, had been upended and left to drip its remnants on the marble counter. Ciaran was asleep on the sofa with the television on, his arm dangling over the edge of the cushion.

"I was gone for three hours," Trent muttered, and he noisily banged cabinets in the kitchen as he picked up after his guest. Nothing seemed to wake him, so he finished bagging up the garbage and dropped down onto the sofa beside him, knocking the fairy's arm out of the way as he went by.

Finally, Ciaran snorted himself awake. He sat up too quickly and put a hand to his sore stomach, hissing through his teeth.

"Enjoy yourself?" Trent asked, glancing at him out of the corner of his eye. He still hadn't put a shirt on.

"Aye, a bit," Ciaran chuckled. He leaned forward to give the younger man a sly smirk. "How was your class? Everything go well, did it?"

"Ugh," Trent scoffed. "I knew it was you. Whatever you did, just undo it already."

"Will you go to the store and fetch me something real to eat?"

Trent glared at him, but the fairy only smiled, his smug expression putting a slight, wrinkle at the corners of his eyes. "Fine. I'll go. If you stop complaining, and if you give me money."

"Good."

"And you have to undo whatever it is you did."

"Of course, a chara," Ciaran purred, and he let his fingertips brush down the other man's cheek, causing him to freeze under the gentle touch. "Tá tú sábháilte," he whispered, and Trent thought for a moment that it almost sounded like a promise. He took a purposeful step backward to pull himself out of the fairy's reach.

Ciaran wrote a list on a scrap of paper and gave Trent a bit of money, as agreed, so the younger man went on his way with only a little grumbling. Miraculously, the elevator seemed to be working again. Trent spared a glare back at his front door as he mashed the down button.

The list the fairy had written made him sick to his stomach to imagine, but he walked the couple of blocks to the grocery store and gathered the requested items. It was a wonder Ciaran wasn't the size of a house, eating like this. More fairy magic, he supposed. When he reached into his pocket for the money Ciaran had given him, he found only a handful of leaves and let out a curse. He almost went back empty-handed just to spite him, but he didn't trust Ciaran not to retaliate—or the state he'd find his apartment in if he forced the man to dig through the pantry again.

At the door to the apartment building, Julien stood waiting and watching, a half-smoked cigarette in his fingers. He hadn't yet been able to make his way past the doorman, but he had seen his compass flicker green as Trent had passed him on the way out. The fairy couldn't hide his true form—not from him—but this person had had a recent brush with magic.

Julien saw the young man approach, arms laden with plastic bags, and he put a hand on his arm to stop him, leaning in to take a long, slow breath despite Trent's recoiling sneer. He had his trinkets, his makeshift devices, and his talismans, but nothing told a story better than the simple smell of magic. Julien knew this scent by now, musky and grey like a storm. He had smelled it on every corpse the fairy had left behind, and he had smelled it on Vivian Holk just three months ago, before the creature's poison finally took her.

"How was your evening, mon chum?" he asked the stranger, watching him for any sign of alarm. The fairy had chosen this building for a reason, he knew. An accomplice was good enough. But was the boy a witting one?

"Get your hand off me," Trent said instead of an answer. It had been too long a day for him to be willing to deal with street people.

"That's quite a load you have there," Julien said, tilting his head to get a look at the contents of the grocery bags. He knew almost before he looked what he would find. Fairies were notoriously finicky about their food. "Heavy cream, sweet breads, honey, cakes, ice cream...you're either having a party or you've had a very messy breakup."

"Get your hand off me," Trent said again, slower this time and threateningly low.

"I'm here to help you. Do you know why I stopped you?"

"I don't care." Trent jerked his arm free of Julien's grip, jostling his grocery bags, and started up the front steps of his building.

"That creature is a killer," Julien called, hardly feeling he was taking a risk by exposing his true purpose. Trent paused at the top step and glanced over his shoulder. "If you help it, you're putting more people at risk," he went on.

"Creature?"

"Ben là! You know what I'm talking about, don't you? You have a guest."

Trent frowned at him. "You're the one he's hiding from?"

Julien offered him a friendly smile. "That's right."

"And if I help you? You'll kill him, right?"

"Ouais, I will," Julien answered honestly.

Trent stood still a moment, looking down at the grocery bags in his hand. He glanced back at Julien and shrugged one shoulder. "Then I guess you're shit out of luck."

Julien swore as Trent pushed open the front door and disappeared inside. At least now he knew that the fairy had a friend.

4

Trent pushed his apartment door closed with his heel, spotting Ciaran on the balcony with his hands on the railing. Trent set the bags down on the counter and watched the other man's back for a moment, frowning. The fairy seemed to be looking for something, though what he expected to see nineteen stories up was anyone's guess. He definitely wouldn't have been able to see his exchange on the steps. When Trent opened the refrigerator door, Ciaran jumped and turned to look at him with a bright smile.

Ciaran stepped around the sofa and immediately began to dig through the bags. "Oh, grand. You're a blessing, lad."

"That's me," he muttered. "What were you doing out there?"

"Just a bit of precaution, lad. Never you mind."

"If you're doing weird fairy magic in my apartment, I want to know about it."

"I was sending a message to a friend."

"You're not inviting anyone else to stay here."

Ciaran waved away his concern. "I won't strain your hospitality, don't you worry."

Trent made a face as the fairy poured himself a glass of whole fat milk and emptied a solid third of the honey bottle into it, but Ciaran swallowed it down without hesitation. "Wow," Trent said as the other man set down his glass with a satisfied sigh. "That was truly disgusting."

"Never had honeyed milk?"

"No."

"You don't know what you're missing."

Trent pulled the rest of the food from the bags and gathered them up for recycling. "I ran into your friend downstairs. The one you said was after you."

Ciaran paused. "Did you, now?" he asked warily.

"He knows you're here. With me."

"Damn him," Ciaran sighed, absently reaching up to touch his wound. "What did you tell him?"

"Nothing," Trent admitted after a moment. He hesitated before bending under the counter to put away the ball of plastic bags. "We had a deal, right?"

Ciaran's brow furrowed. "We did," he answered quietly. "Not that I would've blamed you for not keeping to it." He slipped around the kitchen island to stand in front of the younger man. "I wouldn't have been your problem," he said. "You could've brought him straight to me, and there'd have been nothing for me to do about it."

Trent frowned, refusing to back away as Ciaran inched closer to him.

"But you didn't," Ciaran went on. He tilted his head as he looked up at the other man with a pensive frown. He knew where it was leading. Trent was doing him a favor, and would be well within his rights to ask for something in return. It may not even be true that he saw the hunter outside. It would be typical. He might not even have minded doing something for him in thanks, but he resented being treated like an idiot.

"Why?" Ciaran asked. Trent frowned at him, and a taunting smirk curled the corners of the fairy's mouth. He could practically feel the coiled tension in the other man, and he had to restrain himself from reaching out to touch him. He had to admit how soft his hair looked, and how his frowning put a pleasant little crinkle in his brow. He would ask for something, definitely, and Ciaran could guess what it would be. "Why keep quiet? You see something you like, lad?"

"Shut up and eat your stupid food," Trent said instead of an answer. He pushed Ciaran away by the shoulder and moved by him, dropping onto the sofa and turning the volume down on the television. He rubbed idly at the sore spot on his cheek where the door had hit him. "That guy shouldn't be able to come up with the security downstairs, so I don't think we need to worry about him. Unless you get too annoying and I decide to kick you out. Which seems pretty likely actually, so maybe you should worry."

"You're a kind and gentle soul, a chara." Ciaran helped himself to the food Trent had brought, devouring an entire pack of cheap, pre-packaged brownies and washing it down with a second glass of milk. He sat on the couch near Trent with a bag of miniature powdered donuts, pressing his hand to the sore bruise on his stomach as he settled, and he let out a satisfied sigh.

"You're still eating?" Trent observed with a slight sneer.

"Aye, and I'm feeling much better. Except in the stomach area," he added, lifting his palm to look at the spiderweb of black veins.

"Maybe you shouldn't have stuffed it with so much garbage."

"A fairy's insides are delicate, lad. You have to put the right things in."

"Like donuts?"

"Aye, like donuts." He reached across Trent's lap to take the remote control from the coffee table, pressing his shoulder against the other man's arm. He seemed pleasantly solid, and Ciaran momentarily considered touching the smooth skin where his shirt showed his collarbone. A silver chain hung around his neck, his shirt barely hiding the simple ring pendant of softly mottled jade. He would likely get snapped at if he touched it, but it might be worth it to see the angry flush on the other man's face. He restrained himself for now, and for a few moments, only the crinkle of the donut bag and the shouting voices from the television filled the room.

Ciaran could feel Trent breathing beside him. He shifted to cross his legs under him, and the other man didn't move when the fairy's knee came to rest lightly on his thigh. They sat quietly for a while, watching the shrieking women on the television. Ciaran let out a short curse as one of the donuts slipped out of his fingers and rolled underneath them. He bent to try to reach it, but when he couldn't, he stood and moved to the end of the sofa, lifting it with one hand so easily that Trent almost slid off of the other end.

"What the hell?" Trent said, stumbling to his feet as the couch rose to too high an angle to sit on.

"Don't worry; I'll get it." Ciaran held the sofa with one hand and stretched underneath it, snatching up the rogue donut and checking it for dust before popping it in his mouth. He let the end of the sofa back down to the ground with a soft clunk and took his seat again, oblivious to Trent's stare.

Trent stood warily for a few moments until Ciaran looked up at him in confusion. Trent had moved that sofa before; it wasn't the heaviest piece of furniture around, but it definitely took two hands, and he definitely couldn't have lifted it over his head. Just when he started to think that it felt normal to be around the fairy, he reminded him how decidedly un-normal he was. Trent didn't know anything about what fairies were really like—but he at least knew now that they were light, strong, and had black blood. Not exactly the image he'd had before Ciaran had shown up.

He scolded himself for wondering how easily Ciaran could have lifted him if he really wanted to, and he took his place beside him again with a small frown. Ciaran settled in as though nothing had happened, chewing on his small powdered donuts with his knee pressed against Trent's thigh.

"What is this, anyway?" he asked eventually around a mouth full of donut. "That one's not half noisy, is she?"

"*Bridezillas*," Trent answered with more than a hint of disdain. "They find these women who are getting married and think that entitles them to be loud and obnoxious, and then they follow them around and film them being loud and obnoxious. It's 'reality' television," he finished with a half-hearted set of air quotes, resting his arm on the back of the sofa behind Ciaran rather than squeezing it back between them.

"Isn't that charming," the fairy snorted. "Nothing like true love to warm the heart, eh?"

"More like a paycheck," he scoffed. "Make a fool of yourself on television and let the world believe you're insufferable, but it's money toward that white wedding she so desperately wants, I'm sure."

"Don't forget the free movie of the wedding day," Ciaran pointed out. They watched for a while longer, until the bag of donuts was empty and Ciaran was forced to lick the powdered sugar from his fingers. "Why do they stay, do you think? If these women are half as bad as they seem, how on Earth did they find men to marry them?"

"There will always be people who like to be ordered around, and there will always be someone willing to order them. I don't understand the dynamic; treating your spouse like a servant just to make yourself feel important." He shook his head while Ciaran scoffed.

"Get a dog," they said together, and they both paused. A faint smile threatened to touch Trent's lips, but he cleared his throat and returned his attention to the television.

"Anyway, it's ridiculous," he said. They kept watching it anyway.

Ciaran managed to behave himself while Trent got his school work done, even if that meant spending most of the afternoon dozing on the couch. When Trent emerged from the office to make himself dinner, he found the fairy sitting on a stool at the kitchen island, a cup half-full in front of him as well as a plate holding a large slice of apple pie.

"What is it you're studying so hard, at any rate?" he asked before Trent could comment on his food choices.

"Finance," he answered, unable to pull his eyes away from the thick residue on the side of the glass as the fairy drank from it.

"Sounds exciting," Ciaran snorted. "What, banking and things?"

"Sure. Banking and things. Is that milk, or are you actually just drinking the heavy cream?"

"Well I have to have something with the pie, haven't I?"

"You're disgusting. How are you not fat?"

"Fairy magic," Ciaran chuckled with a mouthful of cake.

"What kind of stupid magic just makes you want to eat cake all the time? And you still owe me money for all this crap," Trent added, ignoring the non-answer. "Don't think I've forgotten that fairy bullshit you pulled with the leaves."

Ciaran shrugged, taking a large bite of pie and talking around it.

"So what do you want to work for a bank for? System never made much sense to me. 'Here, take my money so that you can loan it to other people and make a profit, but don't worry, I won't expect to see any of the money from it.' Why bother?"

"Because it's better than keeping gold boullion under your bed?"

"Is it? I can scarper with my gold boullion whenever I like, but I understand it's a bit more difficult to get all of your money out of a bank whenever you like."

"I guess when you're a fairy you don't have to worry about taxes."

"Can't say that I do, no. So you're in it for the money, then? Them bankers do quite well for themselves, eh?"

"It's a family business," Trent said, turning his back on Ciaran to search the fridge for food other than pie. "My father works for HSBC in Hong Kong. That's a bank," he added over his shoulder.

"Thanks, I gathered."

Trent shrugged one shoulder and picked a plastic container of leftover white rice out of the fridge, then set a deep pan on the stove to heat up. "How do I know what you learn frolicking in your fairy garden?"

"Do I look like I spend a lot of time flitting my dainty wings, a chara? You need an education."

"I'll pass." He gathered a few vegetables from the refrigerator and set them near the warming pan. "And what's that you keep calling me? A car?"

Ciaran drained the glass of heavy cream before he answered. "What, a chara? It means friend, mate. I don't mean anything by it. Just a habit."

"It means friend in what, fairy-speak?"

Ciaran gave a short sigh through his nose as he stared across the island at the younger man. "Or, you know, Irish. Shall I let you get all of this out of your system, so that we might move on from the race issue?"

"You can't tell someone that you're a fairy and not expect them to have a few preconceived notions." Trent dripped a bit of oil into the hot pan and dumped his chosen ingredients in along with the rice.

"Aye, so I've learned," he muttered, wiping up the last of the crumbs on his plate with one finger and licking it clean.

Trent paused in stirring his fried rice to look over his shoulder. "*Do you have wings? I mean, are you hiding them, or something?*"

"Aye, but I only show them to the people lucky enough to visit me in my wee glen, where I live in gentle harmony with the little creatures of the forest *in downtown Vancouver,*" Ciaran finished with a deadpan stare.

"You know, that's another thing," Trent said, apparently choosing to ignore the fairy's sarcasm. "Shouldn't you be off bothering Stonehenge tourists or something? What are you doing in Canada?"

"First of all, Stonehenge is in Wiltshire, which is in *England,*" Ciaran pointed out. "I'm from the Brú na Bóinne."

"That means so much to me."

"Ireland, is all you need to know. Can't a man travel, see a bit more of the world than where he was born?"

"A man can. I'm not clear on the rule for fairies. Don't you have a forest clearing to protect?"

"At least change it up a bit," he muttered. "And anyway, Chinese folk literally making fried rice in front of me shouldn't throw stereotype stones."

Trent frowned at him. "There was leftover rice," he grumbled, turning his back on the fairy to focus on his cooking. When he was finished, he scooped the mixture into a bowl and sat cross-legged on the sofa with it, doing his best not to notice Ciaran's lean torso as the fairy stretched nearby.

"Is that bed in there mine, then, or shall I find a nice corner of floor to curl up in?"

"I literally could not care about anything less than I care about where you sleep."

"It's so strange how you live here alone and don't have any friends." Ciaran ruffled the younger man's hair on his way by the sofa, causing a growling protest and a swat at his hand, but he only smiled and stepped into the guest bedroom without shutting the door behind him.

Trent sat still and listened to Ciaran settle into bed in the next room, letting out a small sigh only after he was certain the other man was asleep. His inclination was to turn the television up loud and put on an action movie, but it was in his best interest to let the fairy rest and get gone—the sooner the better.

5

Julien climbed the worn stairs to his apartment, pausing at the open landing when he saw a familiar figure leaning on the guardrail.

"Hey, you're clean today," the man chuckled as he glanced over his shoulder.

"Hello, Noah," Julien answered without much enthusiasm. Noah was younger than him, only twenty-six, with a slender frame and a pretty face that made him look even younger than he was. His dark hair was too long in the front, always in his face and rarely combed, and his clothes were always well-worn and a week late for the laundry. He had silver piercings in his left ear and at both corners of his bottom lip—snake bites, Noah had called them. The hunter leaned against the railing beside him and lit a cigarette, pausing a moment until Noah nudged him for a handout like always. The younger man tucked the cigarette into his lips and leaned over to light it from the burning end of Julien's, then returned his elbows to the rail and stared out over the rooftop below.

Noah had been an unexpected asset during Julien's stay in Vancouver. They had met only a few days after Julien moved into the cheap apartment building where Noah lived. Noah had caught him coming home late at night with his torso covered in iridescent green muck, and instead of panicking or calling the police, he had touched it and smeared the blood between his fingers. "Is that from a *lamia*?" he had asked. "I didn't even know there were any here." He had smiled while Julien stood stunned, then immediately demanded to know all the details of his encounter with the monster. Julien had found a fast friend in him, and Noah had been helpful to his hunts on more than one occasion. He had a fascination with monsters of all kinds and an encyclopedic knowledge of the traits, habits, and weaknesses of more varieties than Julien could count.

It was true the boy was a witch, and Julien was still adjusting to the idea that magic could be used for purposes other than evil, but so far Noah hadn't given him any reason to be concerned. He kept to himself, never did magic in front of people, and had never shown any indication that he was dangerous. He was even a vegetarian. Still, Julien found his eyes frequently moving to the wine-colored birthmark just below the younger man's ear. The stained skin was a common hallmark of a witch, said to feel no pain and shed no blood when stuck. He hadn't had to test it on Noah, since he'd announced himself, but the mark was a constant visual reminder of who Julien was associating with.

"Work hard today?" Noah asked him as he exhaled a breath of smoke.

"Surveillance," Julien muttered. "Whoever the fairy is staying with is helping it."

"Not a woman, right?"

Julien shook his head. "No. Some Chinese kid."

"Well that's helpful, I guess." He looked over at the hunter beside him, watching the pensive frown on his face as he pushed dirty blonde hair out of his eyes. Julien scratched at the stubble on his jaw and leaned back against the railing without looking back at him. "What are you going to do?"

"Think. And watch some more. Something will come to me."

"What," Noah smiled, "you're actually taking the night off? We should do something," he pressed, nudging the other man with his shoulder. "You don't relax enough. We could order take out, watch a movie, go to a bar—"

Julien didn't seem to be listening. "If I break in by force, I'll get police attention, and I don't want to get the kid in the middle of it more than he is, if that's possible. I'll need to wait for the right moment."

Noah deflated slightly, but a soft smile touched his lips as he listened to the other man plot. Once Julien put his mind to something, it was difficult to get him to focus on, or even talk about, anything else. That would have been fine, even a quality that Noah admired, if only it hadn't meant that the older man had somehow completely missed the fact that the witch had spent the last few months falling in love with him.

It was completely stupid, of course. The man had devoted his life to killing people not very different from Noah himself, and didn't seem to be very broken up about his body count. Julien was manipulative, he kept secrets, and he was obsessed with this fairy he'd been tracking. But Noah had seen the small smiles on the hunter's face when he made just the right joke, or when he brought dinner after a long day of chasing shadows and asked nothing of him but his companionship. He thought Julien was probably very lonely, and Noah was glad to be his company, even if it meant he had taken up smoking again just to have an excuse to sit around outside with him. He didn't even know if Julien was attracted to men—every flirtation and advance Noah had made seemed to have gone entirely unnoticed. Though he admittedly had been extremely subtle, only testing the waters for fear of scaring the other man off. He would almost have preferred an outright rejection to the complete indifference the hunter had shown him thus far. It didn't sit well in his stomach.

"Well, I'm sure you'll figure it out." He listened to Julien talk to himself until he finished his cigarette, and then he turned to lean his back against the railing, tilting his head in an attempt to catch the other man's attention. "Did you eat? Since yesterday, I mean."

"I'm fine. I thought you were working?"

"I'm heading out in a bit. Those housewives aren't going to stretch themselves." Noah waited for some indication that Julien was listening, or perhaps even meant to speak again, but the older man only stared out across the street with the dying end of his cigarette between his dangling fingers. "Well," he started after a few long moments, "just let me know if there's anything I can do, Julien."

Julien heard Noah leave behind him, but he didn't look back. When the younger man's door was closed, Julien gave a short sigh and pushed away from the railing to return to his own apartment. What he wanted to do was force his way past the doorman, break down the door to wherever the fairy was staying, and kill it while it was still weak, before it could do anymore harm. But that would only get him thrown in jail, and he definitely wouldn't be of use to anyone there. The only person he even knew in Vancouver was Noah, and the yoga instructor wasn't likely to be paying anyone's bail.

He opened the window in his sparse living room and spread a black sheet on the floor, then set about arranging his small collection of handguns and sawed-off shotguns. He hadn't cleaned them in some time. He sat on the floor and systematically took each gun apart, wiping the parts with a soft cloth and adding just a few drops of oil. He checked each as he finished them, satisfied with the click of the empty chamber, and began to reload them.

When he paused to have a drink and smoke a cigarette, he heard a soft scraping at his apartment door. He stood still to listen, and the scrape stopped, only to be replaced by a knock a moment later. Julien scooped up one of the handguns he had finished loading, tossed the excess sheet over the rest, and tucked it into the back of his belt on his way to the door. He put his eye to the peephole and saw a woman standing at his door, dirt smudged on her face and hugging her arms protectively around herself.

With a wary frown, Julien flipped the deadbolt and pulled open the door just enough to address the woman in the hall.

"Hello sir, I'm sorry to bother you," she said in a weak voice. She looked up at him with wide, heterochromatic eyes—one brown, the other a yellowish red. Julien's brow furrowed; that certainly didn't look natural. "I live just above you, and my boyfriend kicked me out. Could I use your phone? I need to get to my mum's but I don't have any money for the bus."

Julien hesitated. "I'll let you use my cell phone. You don't come in."

"Oh, thank you," the woman said, half sobbing, and Julien shut the door and turned to pick his phone up from the floor where he'd been cleaning. When he looked back to the door, the woman was standing just inside. Julien's hand automatically went to the gun in his belt.

"I told you to stay outside."

"I'm sorry," she whimpered. "I saw my boyfriend coming down the stairs, and I just—"

"No. Out."

The woman gave a dejected sigh, and her meek façade seemed to fall away as she let her arms drop to her sides. "So suspicious," she murmured. Her voice had taken on a strange, guttural quality it hadn't had a moment before. "Smart boy."

Julien's hand tightened around the grip of his gun, and the woman in front of him melted away, her skin sloughing off in a fleshy heap to reveal a heaving animal covered in thick black fur. The dog almost filled the entire living room, baring its glistening teeth and watching him with one bright red eye.

"Ní bheidh tú teagmháil mac an cneasaí arís," the creature promised in a ghostly, growling voice that sent a shiver up Julien's spine.

The animal leapt at him, paws the size of dinner plates scattering his guns across the floor and crashing through his cheap sofa. Julien scrambled to get out of the way of the beast, feeling its hot breath on his back as he stumbled over a small side table. He wasn't eager to fire his gun in his apartment, and he couldn't be sure it would do any good. He had silver-tipped bullets loaded in it, but this wasn't a werewolf. He watched the creature's one red eye, waiting for it to snap at him, and he rushed forward to slide underneath its massive body toward his kit across the room. The dog turned after him in an instant. Julien snatched up a vial of holy water from his open bag and threw it in the animal's face, but it was only a momentary distraction with none of the burning and howling the hunter had hoped for. Not a demon, either, then. That only left one option, under the circumstances. The iron blade.

Julien barely got hold of the knife in his bag before the beast's jaws clamped down on his thigh, dragging him backwards and dropping him to the floor at its feet. The dog put one heavy paw on his chest to keep him still. Through the pain, he vaguely heard a thumping on the floor below him, followed by his downstairs neighbor shouting at him to keep the noise down.

"Anois tú bás," the dog hissed, cold and empty, but it stopped short as it lunged at him, held just out of reach by Julien's iron blade stuck deep in its throat. The creature snapped at him twice more, dripping saliva and black blood on his face before Julien twisted the blade and pushed it to the hilt. The dog went still, dropping with a final groaning sigh and trapping the hunter's legs under its weight.

"Câlice," Julien swore, wincing as he sat up and attempted to roll the dog's body off of him. At least he had been right about the iron. He growled in pain as he pulled his leg out from under the heavy corpse, then took a quick breath and removed the knife from the animal's neck. That deadly a reaction meant that this creature was sent—it was a warning. The fairy might be wounded, but he wasn't idle. He didn't know the language the dog had spoken to him, but that red eye stood out in his memory.

The corpse didn't seem to be disappearing, which was problematic. Some monsters turned to ash when they died, or mist, but this creature remained, a massive mound of muscle and fur in his living room. Julien wiped the dog's black blood from the blade with his shirt and slowly pulled himself to his feet, gingerly putting weight on his injured leg and regretting it. He limped across the room to his bathroom and bent to reach under the sink for his first aid kit.

A knock on the door made him go still, and he cursed under his breath, gathering up his gun and his knife and taking the few hobbling steps back to the door. He kept his knife in his belt and his gun in his hand as he looked through the peep hole, then let out a sigh as he saw Noah standing in the hall in a worn tank top and yoga pants. He opened the door and stepped back with a grimace.

"Hey," Noah began with a smile, "I know you said you were fine, but you never eat, so—" He stopped and almost dropped the bag of food in his hand as he took in the state of the man in front of him. "What the hell happened to you?"

Julien thumbed over his shoulder at the massive black dog on his living room floor. "Come in or get away from the door."

"Holy—" Noah slipped inside in a hurry and let Julien shut the door behind him. "What is it?" He looked back at the hunter and frowned as he noticed the blood seeping through the leg of his jeans.

"Did it do that?"

"Ouais. I don't know what it is; it showed up here looking like a woman."

"A woman?" Noah set down his plastic bag and bent down to peer at the wound on the other man's leg. "That doesn't look great."

"Doesn't feel great."

"Hang on. I'll be right back." Noah darted out the front door and back to his own apartment down the hall. He opened the box on his dresser, quickly sorting through the multitude of small Ziploc bags full of various herbs and resins and picking out the ones he needed. He scooped up the mortar and pestle from his kitchen, then rushed out again and let himself back into Julien's apartment with supplies in hand.

He stepped over a large dog paw as he looked for the hunter, pausing near the bedroom doorway at the sight of him sat on the bed. Julien had stripped his bloodied clothes and left them in a rumpled pile on the floor, and he sat at the foot of the bed in only a pair of boxer shorts as he opened the first aid kit beside him. Noah paused a moment to look at him.

The hunter's torso was littered with scars of every shape and size, from what seemed to be a wide variety of causes. There were claw marks and knife wounds and even a scar that looked like a bite where his neck met his shoulder. One long, trailing line went all the way from his chest and down his stomach, disappearing under the waistband of his shorts. Noah hesitated, taking a moment to remind himself that Julien was injured and probably exhausted, and that ogling his broad shoulders and flat stomach was inappropriate—even if he was desperately curious where that scar ended.

"Here," he said as he stepped forward, "let me help." Noah knelt at the foot of the bed and swatted Julien's hand away from the wound to get a better look at it. The monster's teeth had fastened all the way around Julien's thigh, leaving deep gashes on the top and bottom of his leg. The hunter gave a slight flinch when Noah touched the skin, and he quickly apologized. "Well, let's try some modern medicine first," he said, setting his herbs on the floor.

Noah fished in the first aid kit and retrieved a bottle of saline, and he held the hand towel Julien had brought under his leg to catch the excess as he squirted the clear solution across the wound. The hunter hissed but stayed still while Noah cleaned the cuts. Noah couldn't quite reach the open skin at the back of Julien's leg, so he had him stand up so that he could tend to them properly.

Julien seemed even taller with Noah kneeling at his feet. The younger man's mind strayed as his hand touched the inside of Julien's thigh to steady him, but he bit his cheek and focused on anything but the firm muscle under his palm. He would have liked to have been in this position for a very different reason—he could imagine the way Julien's stomach would feel under his hand and the way his breath would hitch as the younger man slid his boxers down his hips—but it wasn't the time to think about things like that, and the right time might never come. He was just torturing himself. He finished up quickly and allowed Julien to sit down again, then took up his mortar and pestle and emptied the bags of herbs into the bowl. Noah could feel Julien's eyes on him as he ground the herbs into a paste, but he refused to look up in case the other man could somehow read his mind.

"What is that? It smells like candy."

"That's the peppermint. It's to help you rest. Also some arrowroot, eucalyptus, wormwood—"

"Wormwood? Isn't that what's in absinthe? It's poisonous."

"It fights infection. It's only poisonous to eat a lot of it; it's fine."

Julien seemed wary, but he gave a short grunt of agreement. Noah sprayed a bit of the saline into his bowl and mixed it with the ground herbs, then set the pestle aside and scooted on his knees to get slightly closer to Julien. "This might sting," he warned, and he scooped some of the mixture up onto his fingers and smoothed it over the open wounds, murmuring a quiet incantation as he pressed his hand to the skin. He looked up when Julien hissed and offered him a soft smile. "Don't be such a baby," he teased.

"How do you keep track of what all of these plants do?" Julien asked in an attempt to keep his mind off of the burning feeling in his thigh.

Noah shrugged. "It's part of the witch job description, isn't it? 'Must know how to make magic with weeds.' It's second nature by now. Maybe we can sense it; I don't know."

Julien leaned back on his hands while Noah smeared the paste into the cuts on the back of his leg, his stomach visibly tensing at the stinging pain. Noah held in his sigh, doing his best to push away thoughts of other ways he could make the hunter gasp. He had to force himself to keep his eyes on his work rather than sneak glances and imagine what lay beneath the thin cotton fabric, just begging to be touched and kissed. Noah bit his tongue; he could feel heat pooling in his stomach already, and the last thing he needed was to get an erection while wearing yoga pants.

"It's not so bad, actually," Julien rumbled softly, sending a shiver down the witch's spine. "It's a good sort of a hurt."

"Glad you approve," Noah said with a small smile. He set down his mortar, wiped his hands, and took a roll of bandages from the first aid kit. He kept his eyes on his task as he wrapped the gauze around Julien's thigh, carefully covering every bit of his injury. He probably wrapped more than was necessary—anything to distract him from the slow movement of the hunter's stomach as he breathed. When he finished, he tore off a bit of tape and sealed the end of the gauze, letting his hand linger against Julien's leg for just a moment.

Julien hadn't been paying much attention to him while he worked, but now he looked down at Noah with a faint, grateful smile. "Thank you. Much better than I would have done."

"We can't have you getting infected," Noah agreed. Julien didn't seem to mind the younger man's hand where it was, but Noah couldn't tell if it was because he was comfortable or distracted by his injury. Despite his better judgment, Noah inched across his thigh, his fingertips just barely brushing the skin underneath the hem of Julien's boxer shorts. He watched the hunter for any sign of panic, but as soon as Julien's gaze dropped down to his hand, he retreated, quickly getting to his feet and gathering up his mortar and pestle to be washed. Dangerous. He shouldn't get carried away.

"Anyway, I brought you some food, and what are we going to do about the giant dead body in your living room?" Noah escaped the bedroom with a silent, resigned sigh, and he rushed to the kitchen to rinse his bowl.

Julien got to his feet, testing his weight on his leg before taking a few limping steps to the bedroom door. "That's a problem," he muttered.

"What do you think it was, anyway?" Noah called from the kitchen, happy to make conversation. "Not too many options if it's a shapeshifting dog."

"I know I've heard of something like this," Julien answered as he looked down at the beast's still jaws. "The iron killed it, and one of its eyes was red. Just the one."

"One red eye," Noah muttered, pondering as he wiped the inside of his bowl clean of herbal remnants.

Julien hummed an agreement. "And it spoke to me. I don't know in what language."

Noah paused, and he turned off the water as he looked across the room at the hunter. "Can you remember anything it said?"

"I was a bit distracted," Julien admitted. He tried to give an approximation of the threatening things the animal had said, mostly butchering them, but Noah held up a hand to stop him.

"Cneasaí?" he repeated. Julien nodded, and the younger man frowned as he set his clean mortar and pestle on the counter. "That's Gaelic, but it means a healer. That doesn't make any sense."

"You speak Gaelic?"

Noah shook his head. "Only a few words. I've been…looking some stuff up, you know, since you said you were tracking a gean cánach." He didn't share quite how many hours he had spent poring over books and websites looking for anything that might have helped his favored hunter, taking notes and gathering ingredients just in case. He dried his hands on the stomach of his shirt and moved forward to inspect the dog's body. "I think this might be a barghest. A cú dorchadas."

Julien snapped his fingers. "Barghest. That's the name. What did you call it?"

"Cú dorchadas. The same thing, but the Irish version." He crouched by the dog and put a hand on the thick fur of its flank. "Think this has anything to do with your fairy friend?"

Julien frowned. "It's pretty coincidental otherwise. The thing was clearly looking for me. The fairy must have sent it."

"But what does a healer have to do with it?" Noah muttered. "A gean cánach doesn't heal anything, and it obviously wasn't coming to you to be healed. Curioser and curioser," he hummed.

The sound of crinkling plastic distracted him, and he looked up to see Julien digging through the bag of take out. Still hardly listening. They ate their cheap noodle bowls together in the demolished living room, both of them staring at the enormous corpse and neither of them knowing what to do with it.

"So, you ever consider a different line of work maybe?" Noah asked, smiling sidelong at him. "One with less risk of bodily harm? There's a gym just around the block from my studio. Or, you know, a Starbucks. Whatever you're into. We could commute together."

Julien didn't seem to be listening. He just stared at the animal's body with a pensive frown, absently forking noodles into his mouth. Too focused to notice, as usual. Noah paused.

"You know, come to think of it, how do you make any money at all? Do people pay you to do this?"

Julien looked up as though mildly irritated at the interruption, but his voice was gentle as always. "I sell things."

"What kind of things?"

The hunter almost looked a little embarrassed. "Not everything I kill is just a monster," he said. "Some of them—vampires, some werewolves, and sometimes witches," he added under his breath, momentarily avoiding Noah's gaze, "they live somewhere. They have apartments, or houses—some of the vampires especially have really nice places. So, after they're gone...it's not like they have a next of kin, really, hm? So I take what I think I can sell, and I sell it."

Noah's mouth had fallen slightly open sometime during Julien's explanation. "You rob their houses?"

"Mais en pas trop," Julien objected, though Noah had no idea what he was saying. He had learned to use context clues to decipher the hunter's Quebecois; in most cases, it wasn't worth asking him to translate. "It isn't like robbery," he explained. "They're dead."

The witch shook his head. "Well just so you know, I don't have anything worth pawning, so don't get any ideas."

Julien frowned at him, looking slightly offended. "You're in no danger from me, Noah."

He looked down into his bowl to hide the small smile on his face. "I know." He felt silly, but the simple reassurance gave the witch a warm calm in his stomach. "Mind if I take some things?" Noah asked after a long silence. "Not every day you get hold of a dead barghest."

"What will you do with it?"

"Dunno. Could come in handy, though. You never know. Don't worry; I'll practice witchcraft responsibly."

Julien frowned at him a moment, but then he shrugged. "Help yourself."

Noah swallowed down the last of his soup and threw away the bowl, then left to gather tools from his apartment. He returned with a few empty containers, some pliers, and a pair of scissors, and he set about taking what he wanted from the animal's corpse.

He cut a large handful of the black fur and tucked it into one of the bags, then used the pliers to pry off claws and pull teeth while Julien slurped noodles in the corner. He filled a few vials with the thick, black blood and twisted the caps on tightly. When he was satisfied with his collection, he put the new containers with his mortar and pestle and looked back at the hunter.

"So what do you want to do with it?"

"We have to get it out of here. You can make us invisible so that we can carry it out."

"Oh, make us invisible, right—why didn't I think of that? Oh, right, it's because invisibility is super hard and I can't do it."

"What, really?"

Noah sighed at him. "Yes, really."

"Hm. The old-fashioned way, then."

"What way is that?"

Julien paused to swallow a mouthful of noodles. "We cut it up and throw it in the dumpster. Preferably lots of different dumpsters."

Noah looked down at the beast with a frown. "Oh."

"You just pulled half its teeth out; don't get squeamish on me now, mon râleur."

"It's fine; I love coming back from an hour and a half in a hot room full of sweaty trophy wives so that I can cut up a giant dog body and hide it in random dumpsters. This is what I always wanted to do with my life."

Julien set down his empty bowl and got to his feet, hiding his wince as he stood on his injured leg. "You don't have to help."

Noah smiled and shook his head. "Come on. But you're ponying up

44

the quarters for my next laundromat trip. This black crap doesn't look like it comes out easy."

Julien chuckled. "I'll put on some pants."

6

As it turned out, a barghest corpse fit neatly into six large black garbage bags. Both men were covered head to foot in black gore by the time they arrived at this realization thanks to a surprisingly enthusiastic artery in the creature's neck, but the job was done regardless. Julien let Noah rinse himself off in his shower, which he took as an opportunity to linger under mildly hot water and smell the hunter's shampoo. Sometimes he could get just a hint of it when he stood beside Julien outside, both of them leaned against the railing to smoke, but he never got to lean close and breathe it in like he wanted to. Even if Julien had been remotely aware of his affections, it would still be a creepy thing to do.

Noah snapped the bottle shut and returned to washing the oily blood off of his skin, watching it spiral down the drain at his feet. His clothes would probably need to be thrown out, which was annoying—thrift shops only carried limited amounts of yoga-appropriate clothing, and he definitely couldn't afford to buy them anywhere else. He turned off the water and shook the excess from his hair. Julien had a single ratty towel hanging over the edge of the counter, and Noah wrapped it around his hips before he poked his head out of the bathroom door.

"Here," Julien said, anticipating his question. He gestured to a pair of pants and a shirt on the bed without looking at him, too focused on tying up the last garbage bag to pay the witch any attention. Noah was glad for once for Julien's distraction; he wasn't positive how he would react to the hunter's eyes on him while he was mostly naked, but he was reasonably sure it would be embarrassing.

He snatched up the clothes and retreated into the bathroom. He let out a soft snort as he held up the pants; the waistband came easily up to his middle. He would have to roll up the bottoms. They were a bit baggy around his hips, but wearable. Noah paused with the worn t-shirt in his hands, rolling the soft fabric in his fingers for a moment. He could smell Julien on it before he even put it on—cigarettes and salt and mint shampoo. He resisted the urge to bury his face in it and just slipped it over his head, lifting his arms experimentally to confirm the large size. Julien was much broader than he was, and the shirt hung awkwardly on his shoulders, but in the back of his mind, he wondered if he would be able to claim it was lost when the time came to return it.

Julien had satisfied himself with changing clothes and washing his face in the kitchen sink, so he still smelled faintly of barghest ichor when Noah emerged from the bathroom.

"Are you ready?" the hunter asked. When he looked up, Noah caught the brief look of amusement on his face at the sight of his companion in the ill-fitting clothes. "Don't trip on those."

"Because it's my fault you're some kind of mountain man."

Julien smiled at him and lifted one heavy bag over his shoulder, hiding his wince as he put weight on his injured leg. "Sure you can manage these? I don't think I ever noticed before quite how little you are."

"Fuck off," Noah laughed as he scooped up one of the bags. "I can do a one-arm handstand in full lotus; I'm pretty sure I can take out the garbage. Ass."

"I don't know what that means, but I'll act impressed if you think it's appropriate."

Noah stared him in the eye and snatched up a second bag, hefting it over his shoulder with an unpleasant squelching sound. "Just tell me what dumpsters you want these in—ass."

Julien chuckled and picked up another bag before limping his way to the door. The trip down the stairs was slow, but Noah didn't comment, only let him take his time until they got to the street. He waited while the hunter lit a cigarette, heaving both heavy bags over his shoulder to keep a hand free as they walked. None of the bags could go in the dumpsters for their building, of course, but they were lucky to live in a run-down neighborhood littered with cheap hotels, grimy bars, and alleyways covered in graffiti, so dumpsters full of horrible refuse were quite common. Nothing they could add would seem out of place among the used needles and broken glass. Julien tossed his first bag into a bin behind a nearby liquor store, and Noah's load was lightened a block away at a restaurant.

A man with a shopping cart full of junk eyeballed them as they passed by, so Julien flipped him a toonie from his pocket and gave him a pointed look as they turned the corner. He dropped his bag in the next dumpster and paused to press a hand against the wound in his thigh.

"Why don't you go back?" Noah suggested. "I'll come back for the last two bags. You shouldn't be walking on that."

"I'm fine," he insisted. "Let's keep moving."

Noah gave a small sigh as he watched Julien walk ahead of him, trying not to show his limp. Tough guys. Why did he always go for the dumb tough guys? He trotted to catch up and walked briskly ahead, tossing his last bag into a bin and turning back to face the hunter. He made a spinning gesture with one finger to urge Julien to turn around, and they walked together back toward the apartment building, following a different route than the one that had brought them.

"So you think the fairy sent that thing after you? How could he do that?"

"It's a killer, Noah," Julien said simply, and the witch shook his head.

"No, I mean actually how. A barghest is a serious spirit; they aren't at the command of any one fairy—or fairies in general as far as I know—and they definitely don't make house calls. So how did he get it to go after you? Maybe it owed him a favor? How do you even do a favor for a barghest?"

"Does it matter how?" Julien grunted. "It didn't work."

"Well, it worked pretty well on your leg." The hunter snorted. "And anyway," Noah went on, "information always matters. Knowing is half the battle, as they say."

"Who says?"

"What? G.I. Joe says."

"Isn't that a cartoon?"

"What are you—of course it's a cartoon! You never watched G.I. Joe?"

"No."

"What did you do while you ate your cereal on Saturday mornings when you were a kid?"

"Target practice," the hunter answered without looking at him, and he started up the stairs at their apartment building. Noah hesitated, watching him climb the steps. Julien never talked about his family much, but the witch had suspected for a while that the other man's life hadn't been what anyone would call normal. He'd clearly been on this road for a long time, but Noah hadn't realized quite how long. Noah had caught Julien reading a worn paperback a couple of times, but there wasn't even a television in his apartment. How did he function with nothing in his life but fighting and putting body parts in dumpsters?

He followed Julien up the steps and tried to grab both remaining garbage bags, but the hunter stared him down until he released one with a resigned sigh.

"When you're still limping tomorrow, I don't want to hear any shit," Noah said. Julien ignored him. They carried the bags to separate dumpsters and threw them away, taking a trip around the block before starting back toward their building.

At Julien's apartment, Noah gathered up his dirty clothes and his collection of barghest parts and lingered awkwardly near the door. Julien never seemed to mind him being around, but he never exactly invited him to stay, either. Noah waited while Julien settled himself on the tattered sofa, but all the hunter said was, "Don't worry about the clothes. Get them back to me whenever. And I'll owe you for the laundromat."

"Nah, I was just joking about that," Noah said softly. He shifted his weight and knew he should be leaving. He wanted Julien to tell him to wait, to move over on the couch and offer him a place. He wanted to curl up beside him and lay his head on the larger man's shoulder, maybe even feel Julien's thumb brushing the back of his arm as they sat together. Julien would lean over and kiss his hair but pretend not to be paying attention when Noah looked up at him.

The witch shook his head. That was never going to happen. Even if, by some miracle, Noah ever got the courage to tell Julien how he felt, it would never be like that. The hunter was too tense, too focused, too...straight. At least Noah seemed to have a consistent type.

"You need something?" Julien asked, startling him out of his thoughts. He was kicking him out.

"No," he answered quickly. "I'll see you later. I'll...make some more of that poultice, for your leg."

"Merci, Noah. You were a great help tonight."

His stomach fluttered at the hunter's slight smile, but he tried to crush the feeling. "No problem," he said, waving off the other man's gratitude as he opened the apartment door. "Later, Julien."

The other man gave a small grunt of recognition as Noah slipped out of the apartment. The witch hurried down the hall in case anyone caught him outside with an armful of bloody clothes and body parts, but he made it to his door without incident.

Noah's apartment was sparse and dingy, but at least he managed to avoid the lingering scent of mildew that permeated the building with the judicious use of incense and oils. He dropped his armful of clothes on the sofa and set his bags and vials on the coffee table, then set about lighting the charcoal for his incense burner.

Alone in his home, he could burn the small black disk in the palm of his hand without worrying about outsiders seeing him conjure flames out of nothing. He whispered soft incantations to himself as he dropped the disk into the settled sand at the bottom of his incense bowl, protecting his fingers from burning, and he chose a vial of resin from the nearby rack. As the smoke started to rise and fill the room with the thick scent of sandalwood and cloves, Noah changed into a fresh set of his own clothes, though he held Julien's shirt in his lap for an inappropriate amount of time. He was hopeless. The hunter was beyond his reach and he knew it, so why couldn't the butterflies in his stomach get the memo from his brain?

Noah had a bad history of falling for the wrong people. When he was fifteen, it had been Abby Greenwood, who, as it turned out, had entirely the wrong physical makeup for them to be compatible. That had been an awkward weekend. Later in high school, after he'd managed to sort out what the problem was, it had been Josh Parker, who was sweet and handsome and turned Noah's legs to jelly with his kiss, but who had moved across the country before the end of the school year. Then there was Travis. The witch's chest still tightened picturing his face. They had met one day while Noah was covering a friend's yoga class at a nearby gym. Travis was tall and muscular, with a hard jaw and piercing blue eyes, and he was adventurous and commanding and all the things a man's man was supposed to be. He had been a forceful, exhausting lover who frequently left Noah lying helpless on the bed long after he had gone home. He was friendly and charming, and it should have been perfect.

It was perfect, at first, when it was just the two of them. The problems had come when Noah had run into him in public for the first time. He had seen Travis across the street with some friends and gone over to greet him but had been stopped short by the larger man's hand painfully tight on his arm. He pretended not to know him; he said they were acquaintances and brushed him aside with insulting jokes when Noah had tried to question him. Noah had thought it was his way of saying it was over between them, that it had just been a brief interlude, but Travis had still shown up at his door later that night and pressed Noah against the wall with his body. Travis told him that he couldn't be affectionate in public. He said that he wasn't Noah's "boyfriend," saying the word with distaste. He wasn't some faggot, he said. They were just having fun. When Noah had objected, Travis hit him. He should have kicked him out of the apartment right then and never seen him again, he knew. But the other man had seemed remorseful, told Noah he hadn't meant it, that he'd been pushed to it, and Noah gave in.

Once the first blow had been struck, it was so easy for it to become normal.

They stayed together—if it could be called that—for three years. They never went out together, never stayed at Travis's apartment, and when they did see each other outside of Noah's apartment, Travis treated him like a stranger. Whenever Noah tried to show some kind of affection outside of the bedroom, Travis snapped at him or told him to lay off. When they argued—and they argued about everything— Travis shouted. He told Noah frequently how useless he was, how stupid and irritating, and still Noah had stayed. He shoved Noah and hit him so often that now he bore the scar through his right eyebrow where the piercing had been dislodged during one of their fights about nothing.

Noah had only broken free when he showed up to work with a black eye, and his boss had demanded that he skip his class that day and come home with her. She had put him up and spent the next two weeks bolstering his courage with kind words and promises of support whenever he needed it. Because of her, Noah had blocked Travis's number in his cell phone, and the next time the other man had shown up at his door, Noah had threatened to call the police. That had been over two years ago, and he hadn't seen Travis since.

He hadn't ventured back into dating since, either, and he didn't seem to be off to a good start with Julien. The hunter was clearly dangerous, but Julien had never shown even the slightest hint of violence toward him. He had a violent job, but he didn't seem like a violent person. In his own quiet way, he was almost sweet, and more than once he had kept Noah from harm when they had worked together on one of the hunter's cases. Noah smiled in the quiet room, remembering Julien's hand on his chest, pushing him backwards and out of the reach of the frenzied werewolf so that he could face it himself. When it was dead, Julien had offered Noah his hand to help him up and asked him if he was all right. That had been the moment that cemented his feelings, he thought. Julien had been so gentle, with a soft, worried wrinkle in his brow and a frown on his thin lips. Only concerned with the witch's safety despite the deep gash in his arm.

Noah sighed and clutched Julien's shirt in his lap. None of that mattered anyway. He could never tell Julien what he felt. It would make things too awkward, too strained between them, he could tell. Julien wouldn't feel the same way. At best, he would tell him they should be friends and then disappear one day, on to the next hunt. Noah wouldn't make the mistake again of putting his heart and his privates ahead of his brain. He wanted the hunter to stay close to him, and he would put that in danger by confessing. So he wouldn't. It would be better this way.

7

Trent lingered in his bedroom in the morning, not wanting to venture into the living room and be forced to interact with Ciaran. He would just stay in his room until it was time to go to class in the afternoon, and then he would leave without having to listen to any more of that taunting Irish brogue.

He stood under the shower for longer than was necessary, letting the hot water run over the back of his neck until he heard his phone chime on the counter nearby. With a reluctant sigh, he turned off the water and stepped out of the shower, rubbing a towel over his head as he picked up his phone. He flicked open the text from Hannah.

Let me in already.

Trent paused. Let her in? He dried off in a hurry and pulled on the first pair of jeans he could reach. He was only beginning to button his shirt when he reached the living room.

He paused on his way to the door and glanced into the guest room. Ciaran lay curled up under the blanket, a very small-looking lump in the center of the overly large bed. He didn't seem to show any signs of moving, so Trent quietly closed the door and stepped down the hall to look through the peep hole in the front door. Hannah stood outside, looking down at the phone in her hand.

Trent unlocked the door and pulled it open, still fighting the buttons on his shirt with his free hand. When Hannah looked up at him, her eyes went first to the bare chest at his collar, then she looked into his face with a slight flush on her cheeks.

"Uh, did I wake you? I've been knocking."

"What are you doing here?"

The girl paused. "Yesterday, I asked if you would help me study for this Econ exam." She lowered her voice. "I said I'd come by today before class so you would have an excuse not to talk to your company, remember?"

Trent only frowned at her. "What are you talking about?"

She stared at him for a moment, and then a look of realization came over her face, and she sighed. "I get it. You were doing that thing you do where you act like you're listening, but really you're just agreeing with whatever I say until I stop talking. I should have known." She shook her head with a small laugh. "Look, I'm here already. Do you want to study or not? I want to see your place."

He hesitated, glancing over his shoulder toward the guest room door. He couldn't even guess whether or not Ciaran would show himself to a stranger. He might come out and make a fuss, but it seemed equally likely that the fairy would stay hidden away in his room until the coast was clear. He had hidden from Trent at first, after all. At worst, Trent would have to explain to Hannah what a strange, pointy-eared man was doing in his apartment, but at best, he would get some peace and quiet while they studied.

"Fine." Trent opened the door completely and stepped back to let the girl inside. She slipped past him, holding the straps of her backpack, and turned a full circle in his living room.

"Holy crap," she muttered as he shut the door. "You could fit my entire apartment in here." She moved to the windows and looked out the tall French doors. "You've got a balcony? Nice."

"Yeah, it's great," he agreed in passing, and he stepped across the room to shut his bedroom door despite how she leaned to get a glimpse of it.

"So," she said, looking a little awkward as she stood near his leather sofa. "Where's your guest?"

55

"Sleeping." He gestured to the guest room door.

"So who is it? Extended family or something?"

"No." He moved toward the office and paused. "Just...put your stuff wherever."

He took his laptop and textbook from the desk and shut the door behind him. Hannah had taken a tentative seat on the sofa, her backpack in her lap, and she shifted uncomfortably as Trent sat down beside her. He opened his laptop and looked over at her. "What do you want to read over?" She only watched him without answering for a moment, but that was all it took for him to say, "What?"

"I don't know," she chuckled, looking down at her bag as she unzipped it to retrieve her notebook. "I'm just...in your apartment, sitting on your couch, and you look like you just got out of the shower. You're not even wearing shoes. It's more casual than I ever expected to see you."

"You're the one who showed up here first thing in the morning."

"I was under the impression you had agreed to that, remember? Anyway, it's fine. Weird, but fine. I can pretend we're even friends, maybe." She set her notebook on the coffee table and put her bag on the floor by her feet. "I've never seen that necklace before," she remarked casually, pretending she hadn't been eyeing his open collar.

Trent glanced down at himself with a frown, then shifted the jade pendant so it was better hidden beneath his shirt. "It's just a good luck thing. It was my grandmother's."

Hannah smiled briefly at him before looking back down at her notebook. "That's sweet."

He only grunted in response as he flipped open the textbook and turned to the latest chapter.

Ciaran had barely shut his eyes the previous night before being woken up by a sharp pain in his heart, and he had rushed to the window and thrown it open, straining his ears to listen through the wind rushing between the tall buildings.

"Maddy," he whispered, feeling the creature's loss in his chest. "I did this. Tá brón orm, a leanbh. So sorry." The cú dorchadas had been close to his family for generations, and had always seemed to have a soft spot for Ciaran himself. He had thought the beast would be an easy solution to his hunter problem, but it seemed he had underestimated the man's abilities. It was a mistake he'd made twice now, first by assuming the human couldn't see him when he went back to Vivian's house to retrieve a shirt he had left behind. He had already suffered for that oversight, and now poor Maddy had suffered for his pride.

He still didn't know how the hunter was able to see through his glamour, but the how didn't matter as much as the fact that he could. The man would clearly need to be handled personally, and Ciaran intended to end their chase as soon as the wound in his stomach stopped aching. If he laid low for another couple of days, he could be on his way. Then he would be able to be gone for good, free to move on and leave Trent the apartment to himself again. Somehow, that thought stung him, and he found himself wishing for a less speedy recovery.

It had been difficult to get back to sleep.

Ciaran stirred underneath the blanket, curling up into a tighter ball and pulling the warmth closer around his chin. His stomach was rumbling. He sat up in bed and checked the bruise on his stomach, gently prodding it with one finger. Better, but sore. He still felt slow and slightly feverish, but he was improving.

He paused when he heard voices through the bedroom door. He slipped out of bed and put his ear to the door, scooping up his abandoned jeans on the way. Someone else was in the apartment. A womanly someone else, at that.

The fairy slipped through the door without opening it and stepped silently past the dining table to peek at his host. A young woman was on the sofa beside him, sharing a textbook. She was cute in a girl-next-door sort of way, with her strawberry blonde hair tied up in a messy bun. Ciaran watched them for a minute or two, listening to them discuss the contents of the book in front of them. It was boring stuff. He was about to help himself to the pantry and go back to bed when he saw her smile. Trent reached across her to point out a formula written on her notebook, and Ciaran caught the slight blush in her cheeks as Trent's chest pressed into her shoulder. Not such an innocent study date after all.

Ciaran realized that he was frowning, and he didn't at all like the sudden tightness in his chest. It wasn't anything to him what Trent did with this girl—he hardly knew anything about the boy, and he didn't intend to get so involved that he should care if he was sleeping with a classmate. Still, the anxious feeling crept into his stomach, though he refused to name it jealousy.

Before he really knew what he was doing, he opened the guest bedroom door and shut it noisily again, feigning a yawn and a slow, sleepy stretch. The couple on the sofa looked up at the sound, one with curiosity and one with frustration. Ciaran allowed both of them to see him as he showed himself to the girl—as himself, minus the suspicious injury on his stomach and the pointed ears that marked him as something other than human—which seemed to relax Trent a bit, but the younger man still frowned as Ciaran approached.

"Oh good, you're awake," Trent said without any attempt at even mock enthusiasm. "Put a shirt on."

Hannah smiled at him as she shifted on the couch. "So you're the house guest," she said. "I'm Hannah, Trent's friend."

"I didn't know he had any," the fairy grinned, but he didn't offer the girl his hand. The last thing he needed was some classmate of Trent's getting any of his toxin on her. It usually only passed through a kiss or some other fluid exchange, but he had accidentally infected people before and wasn't anxious to do it again. "Ciaran. Lovely to meet you, Hannah."

"Oh wow, you're Irish," she said, then she laughed. "As you know, I'm sure. Sorry. Trent, why do you have a, uh...half-naked Irishman staying with you?" She looked back at Ciaran. "Are you a friend of the family?"

"Put a shirt on," Trent ordered again, but the fairy ignored him.

"Oh, Trent and I go way back," Ciaran chuckled. "Bosom mates, aren't we?"

"Sure."

"And look at this; he hasn't offered you a thing to eat or drink, has he? Such a bad host. Can I get you something, love?"

"Oh, I mean, some water would be good, but I can—"

"Not at all," Ciaran insisted. "Your servant, love." He gave the girl a winning smile and padded into the kitchen to fill a glass of water for her. As he leaned over the back of the sofa to put the glass on the table, he braced himself on Trent's shoulder, letting his chest press against the younger man's back and push him forward. Trent growled at him, but Ciaran could feel the boy's muscles tense underneath him as he set down the glass. He lingered half bent over the couch for a moment, his arm draped around Trent's shoulder.

"So, what are you two studying?" he asked, seemingly oblivious to Hannah's open-mouthed stare.

"We're studying get the hell off of me," Trent snapped, but he froze when Ciaran's thumb tenderly brushed his cheek.

"So cold," the fairy murmured against his ear. Trent got to his feet in a rush, jerking himself free of Ciaran's arm and scowling at him.

"We're studying," he said firmly. He paused, noticing Hannah's bewildered stare. "Will you just—be quiet. We don't have that much more time before class."

Ciaran held up his hands and mimed locking his mouth shut. "Not a peep. I won't interrupt. I'll just watch you two be studious." He ambled back into the kitchen, leaving Trent to clear his throat and settle back on the couch.

Trent ignored Hannah's questioning look, instead pulling the textbook into his lap to skip ahead a few pages. The girl glanced over her shoulder into the kitchen, but Ciaran had disappeared into the pantry. By the time she opened her mouth, Trent was already talking about what was likely to be on the exam, so she let her question go and inched closer to him to get a better look at the open page.

Ciaran took up a place across the sofa from them when he returned, a glass of milk in one hand and a gooey sticky bun in the other. He was staunchly ignored when he offered Trent a bite, so he only settled with his legs curled up underneath him and quietly watched them discuss microeconomics. He caught Trent looking at him once or twice when he licked a bit of sugary glaze from his fingers, but a sly smile instantly returned the younger man's focus to the book in front of him. He certainly didn't seem all that interested in the fairer sex.

Eventually, Trent excused himself to get dressed properly before they had to leave for class, but he gave Ciaran a warning look before shutting himself in his bedroom.

Hannah packed up her backpack and then sat stiffly on the sofa, peeking over at Ciaran with questions clearly threatening to burst from inside her.

"So," Ciaran began in her place, "you and Trent have a lot of classes together?"

"Yeah," she answered promptly, seeming slightly startled at being addressed. "We knew each other before, in high school, but we're in the same major, so we still see each other a lot."

"Ah, old friends, is it? That's sweet. You don't strike me as the finance and banking sort," he mused. "I wonder what it is that drew you to it." He smiled at her sudden, shameful blush.

"Stop talking to her," Trent's voice came distantly from behind the bedroom door. He opened the door before he was ready, one hand behind his back as he straightened his tucked-in shirt. He grabbed his messenger bag from the floor and looked down at Hannah as he closed his laptop and scooped it up. "Are you ready?"

"Oh, uh, yeah," she said. She hopped up from the couch and settled her backpack on her shoulders.

Trent strapped his messenger bag across his chest and slipped his laptop into its sleeve. "Then come on." He urged her ahead of him toward the front door, but he paused in the entrance when he felt a light grip at the back of his sleeve.

"Give us just a tick, please, love," Ciaran called with a smiling wave to Hannah. "Very nice to meet you."

"Yeah, you too," the girl answered with less certainty. "I'll wait for you in the lobby, Trent."

With a slow sigh through his nose, Trent turned to face the intruding fairy as soon as Hannah was out of sight. "You couldn't just stay in your room?"

"She fancies you," Ciaran said instead of answering. He gestured out the front door with his chin. "You know that, don't you?"

"What? Hannah? Why?"

Ciaran laughed. "Hell if I know, lad, but I know the way a young girl looks at a boy she likes." He didn't add how seeing the look had turned his stomach.

"So what?"

"Just wondering if you'd noticed."

"I don't care. I'm going now. Don't fuck the place up while I'm gone." Trent pulled his sleeve from the fairy's grip and stepped out of the apartment, not looking back before shutting the door. Hannah was waiting for him when he got out of the elevator, and Trent realized with mild horror that they would have to make the entire commute to campus together. He watched the street for the man who had stopped him that morning as he approached his building, but there was no sign of him. He supposed it was a slim hope to imagine he had given up, but at least he wasn't lingering now. Hannah was looking up at him with a small smile; they didn't even make it to the bus stop before she started talking to him. Maybe once they were on the bus he could put his ear buds in and ignore her.

"So, your house guest," she began, "he's a…friend of yours?"

"More like a pain in the ass," Trent grumbled.

"It's just, you guys seemed…you know, close."

"Close?" Trent echoed with a hint of disgust. He stood at the bus stop a fair distance from the people already waiting, and she stopped beside him.

"Well I mean, he was all leaning on you and touching your face—"

"He's just annoying," Trent cut in. "He does it because he knows it pisses me off."

"So then, you're not…?" She shook her head when he looked down at her with a ticked eyebrow. "No, of course not. Stupid, right? It would have come up by now if you were gay, I hope. And he wasn't even staying in your room, was he? And anyway, he's so much older than you; it would be weird. What is he, in his thirties? A little creepy to be flirting with a college student, even if he is just teasing."

Trent frowned. He didn't want to acknowledge that he had been too distracted by the green of Ciaran's eyes and the wicked twist of his thin lips when he smiled to take much notice of how old he appeared to be. He could look like anything anyway, probably; who knew how old he actually was? Aside from that, Trent's firm position in the closet was the very last thing he wanted to talk about with Hannah.

"But still," Hannah went on, "you clearly like him, no matter what you say."

"What? How does that even remotely follow?"

"Well, with people you don't care about, you're…you know, rude. But it's a different kind of rude. Like you don't even care enough to be actively rude to them. Like not listening when they're talking to you, even when they're trying to invite themselves over to your apartment," she finished with a slightly sad smile.

"You'd rather I was actively rude to you?"

She chuckled. "At least he gets a reaction out of you. I've never seen you so worked up." She smiled up at him as the bus squeaked to a stop in front of them. "But your place is really nice. I'm glad I got to see it. Maybe," she started, fidgeting with the straps of her backpack, "maybe next time you can give me more of a tour."

"A tour?" Trent climbed up onto the bus ahead of her and made his way to a pair of empty seats, letting her take the spot by the window. He didn't like sitting so close. Her arm brushed against his as she shifted her backpack into her lap, but there weren't any more empty seats to move away from her.

"Yeah, you know…after you don't have company anymore." Trent glanced down as he felt her inch slightly closer to him, her thigh lightly pressing into his. "I didn't get to see all the rooms," she added, and she peeked up at him with a faint redness in her cheeks.

"What other rooms would you need to see?" he asked warily. This wasn't happening.

"You're going to make me come out and say it, aren't you?" she chuckled, pushing an escaped lock of hair behind her ear. "I mean I didn't get to see…you know, your room. But maybe next time, we could be alone."

Trent's heart almost stopped cold in his chest. This wasn't happening. "I don't think that's going to happen," he said bluntly. "I didn't even mean to invite you over this time," he reminded her, and he turned his attention to the opposite window of the bus to avoid looking at her.

"Oh," he heard her say in a weak voice. "Right."

They rode in silence the rest of the way to campus, and she walked a few steps behind him until they reached their classroom door. She took her seat next to him as normal, but they didn't speak again until she wished him a hasty goodbye the moment the lecture was finished.

8

Trent shut the door to his apartment with a slight sigh as he saw Ciaran still on the couch, a pile of candy wrappers and dirty plates on the coffee table in front of him. He had put on a shirt at last, and his illusion was long gone; the man that lounged on the sofa had regained his pointed ears.

The fairy looked up as he heard the door. "Welcome back," he said with a grin that showed sharp eye teeth. "Did you see your lady friend home safely?"

"I didn't see her home at all," Trent answered. He dropped his bag on the sofa and sat down a polite distance away from Ciaran, and for a few moments they only sat watching *Trailer Park Boys*. "But you were right," Trent admitted after a moment.

Ciaran snorted out a laugh and sat up straighter on the cushions. "She make a move on you, did she?" He felt an unpleasant tug in his chest, but he attempted to sound cavalier. "Or did you make a move, perhaps?"

"She said next time she came over she wanted to see my room."

"Ah, the shy approach. Meant to draw your mind to all the things you might do to a timid young girl alone in your bedroom, no doubt.

And you said?"

"I blew her off," Trent shrugged, and Ciaran's shoulders suddenly felt less tense. He didn't know why exactly he didn't like the idea of Trent and the girl being alone in a bedroom, or why it was any of his business at all, but he smiled faintly just the same.

"It's just as well," the fairy shrugged as he got to his feet. "She hardly seemed your type, after all; I wouldn't take you for the sort that chases shrinking violets. No doubt you're wanting to focus on your studies in any case, hm?"

"What do you know about my type?" Trent scoffed, but he wouldn't meet Ciaran's gaze. He could still feel the fairy's weight against his back, his soft breath warm on his ear.

"I suspect I know the sort of thing you like, a chara," Ciaran teased. He stretched his arms over his head, a smirk curling his lips as he caught Trent's eyes move to the low waistband of his jeans. "I'm going to have a shower. No peeking," he added with a sly smile, and Trent clicked his tongue at him.

Ciaran invited himself to Trent's bathroom rather than the guest room, but Trent only protested until the fairy was standing in his bedroom unbuttoning his jeans, after which the younger man scowled and shut the door in a rush. This bathroom was nicer than the guest one, and the shower was a glass standalone beside a luxurious bathtub, rather than the unsatisfying two-in-one Ciaran had used thus far. He abandoned his clothes in the doorway and turned on the water, letting it run cool against his skin until it warmed up. He had felt an irritating anxiety in the pit of his stomach ever since Trent had left the apartment with the girl. He didn't know why he had teased him about her; Trent had clearly had his own life before Ciaran showed up in it, so he shouldn't have been surprised even if the girl had turned out to be his girlfriend.

Despite knowing all of these things, the memory of the hard muscle of Trent's back as he leaned against him lingered at the back of his mind, and he could still smell the citrus body wash on the other man's skin. Ciaran was used to going a long time between lovers—he tended to fluctuate between the mild guilt he felt whenever he got a woman caught up in his magic and the demands of his libido. He could avoid poisoning his partner by choosing a man, but that option came with inevitable disappointment as soon as he told them the truth. If they weren't asking him for favors, they were telling him how the whole thing was 'too big' for them, how they couldn't deal with him not being human. Only a handful of them through the years had known the full truth about him. It was easier not to get that far.

More often than not, it came down to greed. Even if they pretended to be his friend, even if they slept together, even if everything seemed fine—it was always so that they could ask him some favor. The women he'd known at least had the excuse of his toxin, but the men were worse. They feigned friendship or even love, and in the end all they wanted was for him to give them his pot of gold or grant them their three wishes—too ignorant to even know the difference between a gean cánach and a leprechaun.

Trent would do the same if he let him. The boy was clearly attracted to him, whether he was ready to admit it or not; it would only be a matter of time before he spoke up. It was fine to tease him—Ciaran got a special thrill out of seeing that scowling face whenever he got too close—but much better to keep things simple.

Ciaran tilted his head back to let the water run down his neck and chest, his fingertips idling over his stomach as he touched the tender mark there. It needed to stay simple. Any feelings Ciaran might have had about Trent's potential relationships or lack thereof could be put down to attraction and passing curiosity. The boy was good-looking, no argument, and the way his mouth turned down into that growling glower made it next to impossible not to want to kiss him. A man like that—brooding and bad-tempered and snide—Ciaran could hardly be blamed for wanting to fuck that look off of his face, to see him panting and open-mouthed.

He felt a tingling heat pool in his stomach and a familiar twitch in his groin, and he gave a soft chuckle with his bottom lip caught in his teeth. He could picture the look Trent would give him if he knew how the fairy thought about him. Flushed and angry, with that crease in his brow, telling him for the tenth time to get out of the apartment and still not really meaning it. Ciaran had seen the way Trent looked at him when he got too close—uncertain, holding back. He was curious at the very least. What would Trent do if Ciaran told him what he wanted?

Ciaran's hand drifted down his stomach, and he hissed a sharp intake of breath as he slipped his fingers around his insistent erection. Trent would shout at him, irritated, but a little embarrassed, perhaps. Ciaran would kiss him, unbutton his shirt and leave it on the floor at the foot of the bed, and the younger man's protests would grow softer. He would ask him if it was his first time and promise to be gentle, and Trent would snap something rude at him that would be cut off with a kiss. Trent would give in the moment Ciaran touched him.

The fairy leaned one hand against the cool tile wall of the shower to steady his weight, and his eyes slid shut as he stroked himself and imagined it was Trent. He could picture him face down on the bed, all frustration and hesitation gone, his hands fisted in the blankets as Ciaran took him, drawing helpless, mewling moans from him in between gasping breaths.

Ciaran let out a soft, strained groan of his own as he moved his hand faster, picturing Trent's flushed face and imagining his desperate pleas for release. He would tease him, bring him to the brink again and again, denying him until he begged with a dry, breathless voice. Then, finally, he would touch him again, his forehead against the younger man's back as he pushed into him over and over, both of them climaxing and falling into a sweaty heap in the disheveled blankets.

Ciaran grit his teeth and held in his quiet grunt as he finished on the shower floor, staying still for a few long, steadying breaths. When he opened his eyes, he slowly straightened again, letting his breath out in a slow sigh. He told himself it could still be simple. Sex could be simple. Maybe all he needed was to get Trent out of his system and move on.

It would be fun to try, at any rate.

He finished rinsing off and turned off the water, snatching Trent's towel from the nearby bar as he stepped beyond the glass door. It smelled like him. Once he was dry, he left the towel in a pile on the floor and slipped back into his jeans with a bit of a bounce. He picked up his shirt and frowned at the crusted black blood stain on the torso, then left it on the floor with the towel and opened the door to Trent's closet. It was a walk-in so large that it had a turn in it, lined with blue jeans, khakis, and dress pants organized from black to blue to grey. He must have had well over a dozen shirts to match, as well as blazers, vests, cardigans, and two or three expensive overcoats along the back wall.

"Must be nice," Ciaran chuckled, and he pulled a simple V-neck shirt from a stack and slipped it over his head. It was a bit large for him, so the sleeves looked too long, but he wasn't picky.

When he opened the door to the bedroom, Trent was sitting on the sofa with a black controller in his hands, slouched against the back cushion and actually looking fairly relaxed. An empty plate was on the table in front of him; he must have eaten dinner while Ciaran was in the shower. His eyes were on the television screen, but he briefly glanced up when Ciaran moved to sit next to him. "Is that my shirt?"

"Aye; were you using it? Seemed like you had a few spares."

"Just don't get anything on it."

Ciaran settled beside him on the sofa, watching the game on the television. The front end of a gun bobbed along the bottom of the screen while people with red names above their heads passed to and fro. The gun occasionally lifted to fill the screen with a crosshairs, firing in time with a quick movement of Trent's hands. Voices sounded from the television speakers, two or three different men shouting at each other.

"What's this then?" Ciaran asked, gesturing between the controller and the television.

"*Call of Duty*," Trent answered without looking at him. "Just a war game. It's mindless."

Ciaran sat quietly in the dim room for a few minutes, watching. "So you just...run around and shoot people, and they shoot you, but then you come back to life so that you can shoot more people?"

"Pretty much," Trent murmured, and as he fired a shot that hit another player in the head, the television erupted into swear words and shouting.

Ciaran pointed at the screen. "That's other real-live people, then? You're all playing together?"

"Never seen an Xbox before?"

"Never been much for video games, myself. Do you know these people?"

Trent shrugged one shoulder. "They're just randoms."

"But he's talking to you, isn't he? Can he hear us?"

"Not without the headset. There's no point in talking to these people; all they do is bitch. I don't bother."

Ciaran hummed a vague agreement, but when Trent fired off another shot from his sniper rifle, the stream of cursing that came from the television's speakers made the fairy frown. "You're going to let him talk to you like that? Didn't he just call you a fag?"

"So what? I don't even know that guy. He's just pissed that I shot him."

"Where's this headset, then? I'll have a chat with the lad."

"What? No. I don't need you defending my honor from preteens on Xbox Live."

"You don't ever want to give them a bit of their own back? Come on. Have some fun."

Trent hesitated, but then he gave a short sigh and gestured to the cabinet under the television. "In there."

Ciaran hopped up to fetch the headset, and Trent allowed him to plug it in to the bottom of his controller. The fairy settled the headset over his ear and fiddled with the microphone while Trent played, and he sat close to the other man to better see what he was doing. He pointed out players running by underneath Trent's sniping spot and laughed when they dropped. Then the screen jerked, and they were treated to a quick replay of Trent's death at the hands of another player who had snuck up behind him.

"Ah, gobshite," Ciaran swore, grunting in annoyance and gesturing at the television.

"How's that you fucking sniping faggot?" the other man's voice sounded into Ciaran's ear.

"Ná bí ag caint cacamais!" Ciaran cut in. "You talk shite to me boy and I'll put the fucking smile on the other side of your face, you hear me?"

"What the fuck?" the voice answered with a laugh.

"Go on then," Ciaran said, nudging Trent with his elbow. The younger man was staring at him. Trent shook his head to clear it and carried on once he had respawned. He only half-listened to the banter going on while he played, but the colorful language coming out of the fairy's mouth was hard to ignore.

Ciaran groaned the next time Trent died by the same player. "Ach, ya aiteann ya," he laughed. "Come out in fucking front instead of sneaking around, you fucking cocktrough ya."

Trent got shot in the head for his trouble, and he let a faint smile touch his lips as he looked at the man next to him. "What's an aiteann?"

"Not for your delicate ears, a chara," Ciaran grinned.

Trent chuckled, and he listened to Ciaran insult teenagers in a sometimes incomprehensible mix of English and Irish for another three rounds. The fairy seemed mildly disappointed when Trent turned off the game, his headset still attached to Trent's controller by the thin wire.

"You're pretty excitable," Trent muttered as he held his hand out for the headset. "Get it all out of your system now?"

"Aye, mostly," Ciaran answered with a smile, and he slipped the headset off and returned it to Trent's waiting hand. He didn't let go of it right away, making Trent pause and look up at him at the resistance. "But I think there's one more thing I'd like."

"You can get your own food. It's late."

"Not quite what I had in mind." Ciaran leaned close to Trent, causing him to move back in an attempt to keep the same distance between them. "So, the girl. Your friend who fancies you. You didn't want to keep that option open, let off some steam with her?" Ciaran shifted to rest his elbow on Trent's shoulder, their faces drawing closer. "You seem a bit wound up."

Trent frowned at him, his stomach tightening at the fairy's touch. "I'm not interested in—letting off steam with her."

"No? Perhaps she's not your type," Ciaran chuckled. He tilted his head with a sly smile. "Something else you want, maybe?"

"Get off of me," Trent growled.

"Ask nicely, now," the fairy murmured, finally releasing the headset to let his hand slide over the other man's thigh.

"I said get off!' Trent snapped, and he shoved Ciaran forcefully away from him and got to his feet. Ciaran fell back against the couch cushions, but even in the dim light he could see the rapid movement of Trent's chest and the redness on his face. "Don't touch me again, do you understand? I'm...I'm going to bed. So just shut up and leave me alone." Without waiting for an answer, Trent turned and shut himself in his bedroom, leaving Ciaran on the sofa with a patient smile on his face.

Trent stood just inside his bedroom door, eyes shut tight as he caught his breath. Too close. Far too close. He had let his guard down, sitting on the couch beside Ciaran like it was normal to have him there. He had felt comfortable having him there.

He shook his head and changed into a pair of sleep pants, scowling at himself in the bathroom mirror as he brushed his teeth. It didn't matter that Ciaran's smile made his chest tense up, or that he wanted to touch a kiss to every single freckle on the fairy's cheekbones every time he got close. Soon Ciaran would be recovered and out of his life, and there was no point making things difficult for himself in the meantime.

He spit out his toothpaste and rinsed his mouth, then dropped his glasses on the night stand with a careless clatter and crawled into bed. He could still see Ciaran's green eyes, wickedly close, and he could still feel his touch on his thigh. A little more, and he would have—no. Trent hid his face in the pillow and let out a frustrated grunt, trying to ignore the aching tension growing in him. For just a moment, he toyed with the waistband of his pants, but then he bit his cheek and stuffed both hands under his pillow to keep them from straying. No more. If he gave in to that, he wouldn't be able to think of anything else the next time he saw Ciaran, and that would only make things harder. He could ride this out. He had to.

9

Trent was determined to pretend the previous evening hadn't happened. He ate his breakfast and sat in the office with his laptop before he had to leave for class, skimming the news while Ciaran made noise in the kitchen. When it was time for him to leave, Trent packed up his bag and pulled the strap over his shoulder, then headed for the front door without even looking at the fairy.

"Oi, you're off again?" Ciaran called to him, and he stopped. "Where to?"

"Class."

Ciaran stepped over to him with a mouth full of raisin muffin. "Hold on a tick. I want to come along."

Trent frowned. "What? Isn't the whole point of this stupid arrangement that you need somewhere to hide?"

"Aye, but I'm feeling a bit better, and I'll go mad if I sit another day in the house doing nothing."

"If you're feeling better, why don't you just leave? You don't have to follow me around. I would rather you didn't follow me around."

"You aren't going to be rid of me that easily," Ciaran grinned. "I still need a little more time. But not much, I suspect," he mused, his gaze drifting down to the tight fist Trent had made around his bag's strap.

"And what about the hunter that's after you? You aren't afraid of him anymore?"

The fairy scoffed. "I was never afraid of him. Anyway, you've been out, right? And you haven't seen him. It'll be fine. He's probably off chasing something far more troublesome than little old me."

"I can't wait for you. I'm going to be late."

"Here, here; I'm ready," Ciaran insisted, shoving the last bite of muffin into his mouth and trotting into Trent's bedroom. He reappeared before Trent had time to gripe at him, wearing a dark blue hoodie that didn't belong to him. He pulled the hood up, hiding his face reasonably well since the sweater was a bit big on him. "See? Incognito."

"You're an idiot. He knows you're with me."

"On with you," Ciaran sighed, waving Trent ahead of him toward the door. He paused to pull on his worn canvas shoes, then followed the other man out the door and down the hall.

"You can't just come into my class," Trent pointed out. "Even if you could, I don't want you bothering me while I'm trying to take notes. You'll disrupt everyone," he finished as they exited the elevator into the lobby, and he caught the curious eye of the doorman on his way by.

"Everything all right, Mr. Fa?" the guard asked, glancing past him into the empty elevator as though looking for someone.

Trent frowned at him in confusion. "I'm fine." He pushed the lobby door open and stepped down onto the street with Ciaran on his heels.

"You'll get strange looks talking to yourself like that," the fairy teased.

"What? He couldn't see you?"

"Not being seen is a fairy's natural state, a chara. I let you see me, but that's a special circumstance."

"Lucky me," Trent snorted. "What about the hunter? He clearly saw you."

"I haven't quite figured that out," he admitted, standing so close beside Trent at the bus stop that their elbows touched. "There are a

Tess Barnett

few things one can do to see fairies, of course, but they're rather specialized. Holding a four leaf clover, wearing your coat inside out—silly things like that. He didn't seem like a very silly sort. Maybe it was a one-time thing, and now he's lost me again. You'd think he would keep a better eye on your building."

Trent opened his mouth to answer and realized he would appear to be talking to himself again, so he said nothing. Ciaran got on the bus behind him—without paying, of course—and stood next to him in the crowded isle, both of them holding on to the same railing. Trent kept his gaze straight ahead as the other passengers pressed Ciaran's body against his, refusing to look down even when a bump in the road caused the fairy to brace himself with a hand on Trent's chest. Ciaran's hand lingered far longer than was necessary, and Trent risked a glance down at his face in an attempt to scowl him into good behavior.

"Don't mind me," Ciaran murmured with a slow smile, his fingers curling into the younger man's shirt. "You're used to public transit by now, aren't you? It can get a bit cramped." He let his hand slip down to brush Trent's stomach, feeling the tightness there.

"Stop," Trent said under his breath. Ciaran couldn't be sure if it was an order or a plea.

"Oh, that's right," Ciaran chuckled. "You said not to touch you again. My mistake." He moved his hand from the other man and tucked it into the front pocket of his borrowed hoodie, instead letting the motion of the moving bus shift them together periodically.

By the time they stepped off of the bus, Trent's jaw felt so tight that he wasn't sure he'd be able to open it again. He walked across campus without waiting for Ciaran, taking such long strides that the other man had to trot to keep up with him. At the door to his classroom, he gave the fairy what he hoped was a suitably threatening look, and then he opened the door and stalked to his usual seat without looking back.

Ciaran took the seat beside him, slouching in the desk and stretching his legs while Trent pulled out his laptop and settled in for the lecture.

"Oi," Ciaran called, leaning over the desk toward Trent. "What class is this, anyway?" Trent ignored him. "How long are we going to be here?"

Trent snapped a warning look over at him, but still said nothing. After the long bus ride with the fairy continually bumping against him, he had very little patience left. He didn't know why Ciaran suddenly had problems keeping his hands to himself, but at least he had seemed to remember Trent's order not to touch him. How seriously he was taking the request seemed to be another matter. He heard Ciaran hum at him but refused to look. He didn't want to see him sitting in class like this was normal. He couldn't let Ciaran get any more involved in his life than he already was.

Trent did his best to pay attention to the lecture even while Ciaran lounged next to him huffing out bored sighs. He wanted to tell the fairy to leave if he was so uninterested, but enough people had walked by without questioning him that the rest of the class clearly had no idea he was there.

It wasn't until the class was half over that Trent realized Ciaran's sighs didn't seem to come from boredom anymore. He chanced a look over at the fairy beside him and almost choked. Ciaran was looking directly at him, his face flushed and one hand moving purposefully over the front of his straining jeans. Trent looked away from him instantly, but the fairy's rumbling laugh sent a shiver up his spine.

"You see, I know how to listen," Ciaran murmured, his breath hitching slightly as his back arched away from the seat. "You said not to touch you."

Trent turned his head, prepared to give the fairy a look that begged for mercy, but the sight of Ciaran's tongue wetting his lips as he gripped himself through the denim washed away any hope of coherent thought. He watched without considering how he must have looked to the people around him as Ciaran's free hand slipped up underneath Trent's hoodie, unable to keep from imagining the fairy's rough fingers running over his nipple. Trent shifted in his seat in an attempt to hide his body's reaction to the sight in front of him, but Ciaran's playful smirk as he bit his lip only made his stomach tense.

"You just let me know when you'd like me to touch you instead, a chara," the fairy teased, and Trent finally turned his eyes away and stared pointedly at his laptop screen. He couldn't block out Ciaran's quiet grunts and moans, and he was fairly certain that his imagination was far filthier than anything the fairy was actually doing, but he refused to look just the same.

At the end of class, he packed up his bag as quickly as he could and hurried out of the classroom, holding his messenger bag strategically in front of his hips. He didn't look back until he felt a hand on his arm.

"Oi, what's the idea running off?" Ciaran laughed. Trent jerked his arm away from him.

"Why are you doing this?" he hissed, knowing his voice sounded less confident than he wanted. "What do you want from me?"

"I'm just teasing," the fairy said. "I didn't know you'd be so bound up you couldn't even have a bit of fun."

"This isn't fun," Trent insisted, and he turned and continued walking back toward the bus stop with Ciaran right behind him.

"Oh, don't be pouty," Ciaran chuckled. He didn't want to admit how hard it was to control himself around the other man. He just needed to have him and be done with it, he was sure. Every time Trent resisted, getting angry at him and telling him to stop with a flushed face and an obvious erection, it just frustrated Ciaran more. Why hold back if it was clear what he wanted? He let out a sigh. "Come on," he said as he jogged to catch up to him. "I'll make it up to you."

"I don't want you to make it up to me. I want you to go away."

"I owe you for your hospitality," Ciaran prodded, hoping to get Trent to finally admit what he wanted. If not sex, something— anything in return. Every day that went by without the younger man asking for recompense made him more anxious. "Let's get something to eat at least. I'll pay."

"You don't have any real money," Trent grumbled.

"Then you pay. Lord knows you can afford it. But let's go regardless. You'd only be going home and sitting around, right?"

Trent stopped walking so quickly that the fairy ran into his back. He turned and looked down at Ciaran with an untrusting scowl. "If we go, you won't do anything. No touching. No teasing. Promise me."

Ciaran sighed. "I promise. I'll be real friendly-like."

Trent hesitated, watching him for any sign of trickery. When Ciaran only smiled at him, he snorted and gave in. "Fine. We can get some food. But you'd better let people see you, because I'm not sitting there looking like I'm by myself while you chatter at me."

"Sure, sure," Ciaran agreed, and they walked together without speaking for a few steps. "So, where can we get some frozen yogurt around here?"

"Frozen—I thought you said you wanted food?"

"It is food! It won't kill you to eat something other than rice and vegetables."

Trent glowered at him for a long moment, then turned and started down a different pathway. "Menchie's," he muttered.

"What?"

"Menchie's. Frozen Yogurt. It isn't far."

"What a pushover," Ciaran laughed, and Trent huffed at him.

"I should have let the Quebecois upstairs and let him take you away."

"Is that what he was? Huh." Ciaran followed along beside him, his hands tucked into the front pocket of his hoodie. "I thought he was speaking French, but I suppose it did sound a bit shit."

Trent let out a reluctant chuckle through his nose, and when they reached the frozen yogurt shop, he let himself inside without holding the door behind him. Ciaran grabbed it before it could close and followed him in. People milled around inside, waiting in line or filling their cups of frozen yogurt, and the few tables inside were full.

Ciaran stood on tiptoe to look past Trent's shoulder at the offered flavors, impatiently bouncing on his feet. Trent sighed and ignored him while he filled his small cup of lemon and mango yogurt. When he stood at the register to pay, he turned to Ciaran to tell him to hurry up and stopped short at the sight of the fairy's bowl. It was almost overflowing with yogurt of every color, though chocolate seemed to be the overwhelming favorite. Trent felt sick just looking at it, but Ciaran set the bowl down on the scale with a pleasant smile, as though half a pound of mismatched frozen yogurt was a perfectly normal thing to have for lunch. How could one person be so attractive and so nauseating in such a short span of time?

Trent paid anyway, and he pushed his way through the crowd and back out the front door, eager to get away from the press of people. They found a spot on a bench across the walkway and sat down to eat.

Ciaran made a show of sitting as far from Trent as possible to prove he was keeping his promise.

"Is this far enough?" he said. "I could stand."

"Is it so hard to understand that I don't want you hanging all over me, or…" He trailed off, not able to look the fairy in the face without picturing him licking his lips. "Don't you have any shame, doing that in a room full of people?"

Ciaran shrugged. "They couldn't see me."

"I could see you!"

"Yes, but it was for you, so that's different."

"For—ugh," he sighed. "Forget it. Eat your disgusting yogurt."

"What, you've never had chocolate watermelon cheesecake cookies and cream before?"

"Do all fairies eat like you, or are you just especially revolting?"

Ciaran stirred his yogurt into one brownish mass of incongruent flavors and swallowed a large spoonful. "Everyone has their favorites."

Trent frowned down at his bowl a moment before glancing back at Ciaran. "So is any of the typical stuff true? About fairies, I mean. Little winged naked women who live in gardens."

Ciaran's brow furrowed slightly as he looked over at him. "Curious all of a sudden, are you? Looking to catch yourself a pixie?"

"You just don't make any sense. And if fairies are real, what else is real?"

"Quite a lot," Ciaran chuckled. "But I'm not an expert. I'm not even an expert on fairies. Fairly sure I've never seen any naked winged women, though."

"So do they all do weird poison sex magic, or is that just you?"

Ciaran sighed. "I'm not the only sort what does this kind of thing, you know. The leannán sídhe do it just as well to men as I do to women, and I've not heard tell of any of them switching teams for safety's sake, so I think I deserve a bit of credit, right?"

"The what? Is that like a banshee?"

"Sure, except I that isn't what I said. A ban sídhe is a messenger, a leannán sídhe is sort of a…life vampire."

"And here I was thinking there was only the kind of fairy that made messes in kitchens and irritated me," Trent muttered.

"We're a diverse bunch." Ciaran took another bite of his yogurt and paused with his spoon in his mouth to press a hand against his bruise. He waved away Trent's furrowed brow and carried on. "And a bit of a secret—fairy is your word. It's Latin. Amongst ourselves, we're the aes sídhe. Ays-shee-thuh," he said again, slowly, before Trent could mangle the pronunciation.

Trent chuckled softly. "I'm going to just keep calling you Ciaran, if you don't mind."

"Not at all. It's a grand name, if I do say so."

They sat together and watched people pass by as they ate their frozen treats, neither of them feeling the need to speak any more. Trent finished his small portion quickly, but Ciaran savored each disgusting spoonful, scraping the bottom of the paper bowl to make sure he didn't miss any melted drippings. When they were finished, Trent looked over at the fairy beside him.

"So, if you 'switched teams,' why is that hunter after you?"

"Well," Ciaran began with a shrug, "I'm weaning myself, aren't I? I won't pretend I don't have an appetite." He grinned across the bench at him.

"Yeah, I could tell." Trent stood and took Ciaran's empty bowl from him to throw it in a nearby bin. "I'm going home. If you're coming, let's go." He started back toward his bus stop without waiting to see if the fairy followed him or not. There wasn't anything special about Trent, then. No real reason why Ciaran had been flirting with him other than that he was nearby. He could have guessed that Ciaran was promiscuous—and probably not particularly picky—but he still didn't like the hollow feeling in his chest.

10

Julien stood far enough away from the apartment building to avoid being seen, a half-smoked cigarette in his fingers. The boy protecting the fairy had left both days he had been watching the building, but not at the same time. He must be in college. Yesterday he had left with a girl; Julien had followed them as far as the bus stop, but she had seemed too enamored with the boy at her side to have been touched by the fairy's toxin. Today, he was going to get inside the apartment while the owner was out. Hopefully the creature would still be too weak to put up much of a fight.

He looked up as the lobby door opened, taking a satisfied drag from his cigarette as he saw the boy step out, but then he paused. A figure in a hooded sweater followed right behind him, and for just a moment, Julien got a look at his face. The fairy. So much for him being weak—he was taking a risk going outdoors knowing that Julien was on his trail. It had only been three days since he'd been injured; there was no way he was recovered by now.

Julien put a hand under his coat to touch the grip of the iron knife at the back of his belt, but he only watched the pair walk down the street away from him. He couldn't attack the creature in the middle of the street in broad daylight, and even if he could, something about the way the two walked together stayed his hand. The fairy wasn't running; this was an outing. They would be back. Did that mean the apartment was empty?

He pulled his cell phone from his pocket and scrolled down his very short list of contacts until he reached the name he wanted. He touched the screen and lifted the phone to his ear, waiting through a disgraceful number of rings before a tired voice answered the phone.

"Noah?" Julien asked, barely understanding the muffled greeting. "Were you still asleep?"

"Of course I was," Noah grumbled. "What's going on, Julien?"

"How soon can you be in Yaletown?"

"Yaletown? I dunno; twenty, thirty minutes." He let out a long yawn and started to speak before he was quite finished. "Is this about your dangerous fairy?"

"Ouais. Will you come?"

"What for?"

"The fairy just left with the one protecting him. I need to get in the apartment while they're out. You must know how to set some sort of trap."

"For a freaking fairy? Why must I know that?"

"Because you spend too much time reading about monsters not to know. You know everything. S'il vous plait, mon râleur." A few beats of silence went by, and then Julien heard a groan of frustration, and he smiled.

"Okay, maybe I know something. Give me half an hour."

"You are perfect." Julien rattled off the address of the building, urged Noah to hurry, and hung up the phone to finish his cigarette.

Julien paced and smoked while he waited, and soon he saw his friend turn the corner and approach. His current jeans had holes in them at the knees and across the left thigh, and the bottom hems were all but worn away from scuffing on the street behind his Converse high tops. He had a torn and faded canvas bag strapped across his chest, the flap fluttering half open with each step he took. Noah raised a hand to greet him as he drew closer, pushing his hair out of his eyes. He had changed the twin piercings in his ear from studs to small silver hoops, Julien noticed.

"Your fairy boy found a swank benefactor," Noah said, shielding his eyes as he leaned back to look toward the top of the tall building. He chuckled, the matching hoops at the corners of his mouth moving with his smile. "How's the leg?"

Julien grunted, shifting his weight on his feet. Thanks to Noah's homemade poultice, the wounds in his thigh had closed up almost overnight. He barely noticed it now. "It's fine. Did you bring what you needed?"

Noah shrugged one shoulder, scratching at his chin. "Usually this stuff takes time, you know? He's gean cánach. That's kind of big mojo to begin with. There's supposed to only be one, or one at a time, or something. And you said you got him in the stomach with an iron blade a couple days ago, and now he's up and walking around?"

"Is that unusual? It wasn't a killing blow." Julien had little experience with fairies. He usually hunted quarry that was more directly dangerous—like lamia, vampires, or shapeshifters. The magical aspect of it was a little beyond his depth, which was partly why Noah had been such a valuable resource.

"Iron is supposed to be deadly to fairies, even in what we'd think of as small amounts. You saw how easily the barghest went down. You sure you're right about what he is?"

"It makes the women it's been with stop eating and get so depressed that they die after it leaves them, it's been using glamours to try to get away from me, and the iron definitely slowed it down. What else could it be?"

Noah gave a hum of agreement and ran a hand through his hair. "Well, I've got what I've got. Let's see if it works."

He walked with Julien to the front entrance, allowing the larger man to reach past him to open the door. When the doorman greeted them, Noah leaned over the desk to smile at him. "Morning," he began, tilting his head to better see the man's nametag, "Brian. Nice to meet you." He offered his hand, and as soon as he had a hold on the other man, he pressed the pad of his index finger to the pulse on the guard's inner wrist. He could feel the man's heartbeat in his own chest, thudding and slow. "Who's the boy who just left a while ago? Young, Chinese?"

"Mr. Fa?" the guard answered promptly, seeming to look past Noah rather than at him.

"Fa. Great. So helpful, Brian. My friend and I are going upstairs now," he said easily, "and we might be a while. You're going to let us up, and you aren't going to tell anyone that we were here, are you, Brian?"

"No," he said.

"Good. And you aren't going to say anything when we leave, are you? You'll just let us walk by."

"Yes."

"Of course you will. You're a peach, Brian." Noah released the doorman's hand and glanced back at Julien, tilting his head to urge him to follow. As they stepped onto the elevator, he noticed the older man glowering down at him.

"You're pushing it," Julien muttered.

"You wanted up, didn't you? We don't know how long they'll be gone." He waved a hand dismissively. "I didn't hurt him. He won't even remember us."

"Hm," Julien grunted. He took the small compass from his coat pocket and clicked it open. "I don't know what floor he lives on. Just push the top floor and we'll see where I get the best reading."

"Could have just asked the guard that, but you're the boss." Noah pressed the button for the twentieth floor and waited while the elevator slowly rose, watching his frowning companion out of the corner of his eye. Julien was always so serious.

"Stop," Julien said suddenly, touching the younger man's arm to get his attention, and Noah reached out just in time to slap the button for the next floor. "This is it."

They stepped out of the elevator and paused in the hallway, glancing around at the different doors. Julien's compass was lit bright green, but they were too close to get a more precise reading. "Something is interfering with the signal," he muttered.

"Let me." Noah moved toward the closest door and gently laid his hand on it. He leaned close, almost letting his cheek brush the wood, and then he shook his head. "Not here." He checked the next door with the same result, but at the third door, he felt the silent thrum in his skin that told him magic was nearby. It was a strange sensation, though—there was something in the apartment that seemed to stifle the magic. Had the fairy really chosen here to hide out? He lightly tapped the door with one knuckle as he looked back at Julien. "Here."

"Step back," the larger man muttered, and he knelt in front of the door. "And keep watch."

Noah waited, enjoying the look of deep concentration on Julien's face while he used his lock pick set to unlock the door, something Noah could have done in an instant. He knew the hunter was wary of magic, and he supposed be didn't blame him. He had apparently devoted his life to hunting supernatural baddies, and it must have been easy to see Noah as a ticking bomb. At least he never treated him like one.

The door clicked open, and the two men stepped into the apartment. Julien shut the door behind them while Noah inspected the mirror in the hall. That was meant to ward off spirits. The fairy apparently didn't count.

"This'll be what was blocking the signal," he said, lightly tapping the glass with one knuckle on his way by. "Very swank," he confirmed as he moved into the living room, running his hand along the back of the sofa to feel the leather. "You said a kid lives here? By himself?"

Julien stuck his head into the guest room and found it rumpled but empty. "Seems that way," he said. "So what do you have?"

Noah flipped open the top of his much-abused bag and retrieved a slim, rectangular box, popping the top open and setting it on the nearby kitchen island. "I don't have any practice dealing with fairies, especially ones that take iron gut shots and walk away, so I'm kind of winging it here, you know that, right?"

"Je sais. You didn't have to come at all, Noah. I appreciate it."

The witch hesitated a moment, then let out a quick scoff and returned his attention to the case on the counter. "Yeah, well, I wasn't doing anything anyway." He picked the incense out of the box and started a quick fire in his palm to light it, shaking his hand to snuff the flame before Julien could give him a dirty look. "There's rowan in this, and some myrrh, some sagebrush. Supposed to be bad for spirit-y fae types, and fairies hate rowan especially. I made it once you said you were tracking a fairy, in case it turned out to be useful. Good thing, I guess. So we'll let this burn, and I'll see about putting a circle on the floor to trap it. If that's possible," he added under his breath.

Noah carried the burning incense throughout the house, letting the smoke touch every doorway, while Julien watched him with folded arms. He neglected to mention to the hunter how time-consuming making incense was—how long he had spent with bits of wood in a hand crank coffee grinder and sticky resin and herbs in his molcajete, carefully measuring and mixing the powder with gum arabic, leaving it to dry for weeks. He had been glad to do it, and he doubted Julien would appreciate the nuance in his meaning even if he had told him.

When he had circled the apartment, he handed the incense sticks to Julien. "Just let that burn." He knelt down on the floor near the entrance and ran a hand over the cold tile, then turned to dig in his bag for the Angry Birds pencil bag full of chalk and charcoal.

"Totally winging it, just reminding you," he called as he began to draw the circle on the floor, sketching the outside and starting carefully on the symbols around the inner edge. He hummed to himself as he drew under Julien's patient gaze, periodically pausing to sit back on his heels and peer down at the forming circle. "Ugh. What was it. Airches. No—broth? Brath. Brathlang. Wait. Shit. Is it B or H that the line goes on the right side? Fuck, Irish is stupid." He bent back over the circle with a small huff and scooted around it on his knees as he finished the inscription, then carefully stood to take the pouch of salt from his bag. He poured a handful into his palm and drizzled a line around the outer edge of the circle, then brushed his hands together to sprinkle the excess across the center.

"You're sure about all this?" Julien asked, still dutifully holding the sticks of incense.

"Not in the slightest," Noah laughed, earning himself a mild glare. "Hey, you're the one who called and woke me up, called me pet names and begged me to come work magic for you. Do you want magic or don't you?"

"I need the creature still so that I can kill it before it causes more trouble," Julien admitted. "If you think this will trap it, then do it."

"Well I mean, I *think* it will," Noah shrugged, and he positioned himself at the top of the circle. He held out his hands and shut his eyes, muttering a soft incantation that Julien couldn't quite hear. The hunter watched with a wary eye as the chalk markings began to glow a dull blue. When the witch knelt to touch his palm to the floor to activate the circle, a shockwave blew him backward, and Julien dropped the incense in his scramble to keep Noah from hitting the floor.

Julien knelt on the floor with one arm behind the smaller man's shoulders, lightly tapping his cheek in an attempt to rouse him. "Noah, aweille," Julien commanded, and he bent down to check that the witch was still breathing. He cupped Noah's cheek to keep his head upright, and the younger man gave a short grunt before opening his eyes. "Ah, Dieu merci," the hunter sighed.

Noah looked up at Julien with a loud ringing in his ears, and he blinked a few times before he realized quite how closely he was being cradled. Julien's eyes really were the most pleasant muted hazel. He didn't move for a few moments, purposely lingering to burn the scene into his memory.

"Es-tu correct?" Julien asked, though his voice was muffled by the tinny sound in Noah's ears. "Sit up." He helped Noah balance himself and stood to frown across at the darkened circle while the witch sat cross-legged on the floor.

"Why did it backfire?" Noah muttered to himself, wiggling his finger in his ear to try to work out the noise. "There shouldn't have been anything that—" He paused. "Julien, the guy who lives here, is he the fairy's *friend* friend? Or, you know, is he making him put him up, or what?"

Julien made a noncommittal noise as he bent to scoop the sticks of incense up from the floor. "The boy knows what it is. I gave him the opportunity to turn the fairy over to me, and he refused. Beyond that, I don't know."

Noah pushed himself up and stepped over to the circle, smudging the charred mark with the toe of his shoe. "That's old magic," he muttered with a pensive frown.

"What's old magic?"

"If this is the fairy's home, I can't put down anything to hurt him."

"But this isn't its home. I've been tracking it for months and never saw it here before this."

Noah shook his head. "It's magic, and fairy magic at that, so of course it's a technicality. When you stay with someone, you're accepting their hospitality. This kid took him in and from the looks of things fed him, so right now, this is his home. He must have done something to consecrate the apartment. Shit," he cursed. "I should have thought of that."

Julien swore under his breath. "Let's get out of here. I'll think of something else."

Noah gestured at the marking on the floor. "You want to leave that? They'll know we were here."

Julien pondered a moment, but then shook his head. "No. Better if he thinks I've stopped coming after him."

The two men got down on the floor to scrub the tile floor clean, and Noah stuffed the stained hand towel into his bag rather than leave it for the occupants to find. The witch gave a quick glance around to make sure he hadn't left anything behind, and they shut the door behind them on their way out.

"What are you going to do instead?" he asked, looking up at the taller man as they waited for the elevator. Julien frowned and folded his arms without answering, and Noah gave a small sigh. "Just don't do anything stupid."

11

Back at the apartment, Trent sat on the sofa with a textbook open in his lap while Ciaran lounged beside him and watched a soap opera on the television. The fairy had complained for a solid half hour after they got home about a strange smell in the apartment, but he had finally settled down after they opened the balcony doors and let in some fresh air. They managed to pass the afternoon without sniping at each other, and even while Trent cooked dinner, he only gave the fairy a small sigh as he sat at the kitchen island with a large slice of cake and a glass of milk.

Ciaran opened his mouth to speak, but he stopped when Trent's cell phone buzzed on the counter nearby. He heard the younger man sigh as he checked the cracked screen, but he flicked his thumb to answer it anyway.

Trent put the phone to his ear and sighed, "Wei?" Ciaran listened with curiosity as the other man spoke rapid Cantonese into the phone, not understanding a word. It was a lilting sort of a language that was pleasant to listen to, but Trent spoke it with a tight jaw and a furrowed brow. Whoever he was talking to, it wasn't a pleasant conversation. When he hung up the phone, he sighed and dropped it onto the table, leaning his elbows on the counter beside Ciaran.

Without a word, he took the fork from him, lifted a bite of cake to his mouth, and handed it back.

"My father is going to be in town tomorrow."

"Is that bad, then?"

"It's a pain. Mostly because you're here. I don't suppose you'll be out of here by then?"

"Not likely, lad."

"But you're invisible. Or you were. You can just be invisible."

Ciaran took another bite of cake and washed it down with the last of the milk. "What's the problem with your father? He don't let you have guests?"

Trent's expression hardened slightly, and he pushed away from the counter to put some distance between them. He couldn't avoid talking about it anymore, he supposed. "Male guests," he said flatly.

Ciaran gave a wicked grin, and he let his fork drop to the plate with a small clink as he turned to face the younger man. "Now why should he mind if you have male guests, eh?" Trent only scowled at him. "I'm asking. I don't understand," he said, putting on his most innocent face.

"Because he doesn't want me to have sex with them," Trent answered, refusing to play Ciaran's game. "Because I'm gay and he doesn't like it."

"You don't say," Ciaran mused, earning himself a scowl. "That does put a bit of a damper on a relationship," he added in an attempt to be more sympathetic. "So you've been keeping secrets, then?"

"What secrets? I just said he knows."

"Yes, yes, but secret lovers, of course."

Trent hesitated. He didn't want to say that he hadn't been with anyone since he'd been discovered that day over a year ago. It wasn't out of guilt. He could have easily brought someone back to the apartment with him and kicked them out afterward; his parents always gave him enough notice for that at least. He just didn't see the point when the only outcome would be a lecture and his father's refusal to acknowledge any relationship he might have. He wasn't stupid enough to pretend he could get by without his parents' financial support. It was easier to be alone.

"Sure," he said instead of telling the truth. "Lots of secret lovers."

Ciaran hummed a skeptical agreement. "Well, don't you worry. You've been a good sport; I won't make more trouble for you."

His shoulders seemed to relax ever so slightly. "I appreciate it." He wasn't sure why he felt grateful toward this person who had invaded his home, and he would be surprised if Ciaran even remotely kept his word about not causing more trouble, but he wasn't going to argue.

The fairy sat quietly while Trent cooked a substantially healthier meal for himself than anything Ciaran had eaten that day, and they sat together on the couch watching an old kung fu movie. It would have been almost pleasant, if Ciaran hadn't kept asking him if the translation was correct despite Trent's repeated assurances that he could not read lips and hadn't yet memorized the original script.

"How do you expect to know what's going on if you won't shut up and watch it?" Trent snapped after the seventh interruption.

"Ach, what do I need to pay attention for? These are all the same. Prodigal student comes back from abroad, the master's in trouble or killed or some such, and the student avenges him. It's not exactly Chaucer."

"More fart jokes in Chaucer," Trent muttered. "Isn't there one about literally kissing some woman's ass in the dark?"

Ciaran snorted out a laugh. "And he knows it's her arse because he feels her 'beard?' Aye, that's the one."

"Classic literature."

They sat quietly for a while, watching the poorly-dubbed movie while Ciaran snacked on chocolate. The fairy eventually grew drowsy, lulled by a full stomach and a dim room, and he let his head rest on Trent's shoulder as his eyes drifted closed. Trent sat still, his stomach tightening from the slight weight of the other man's body against his. Ciaran shifted to make himself comfortable, his messy hair falling over his eyes, and Trent watched him with a furrowed brow.

He reached up to brush the fairy's hair from his face, but it only fell back into place as soon as he removed his hand. His fingertips lightly touched Ciaran's jaw, and for just a moment, he let the pad of his thumb brush the other man's bottom lip. Too close. The touch caused a stirring in him that he usually tried very hard to ignore, but he couldn't let this man sway him now. Not after he'd resisted for so long. He wouldn't give in just to be this fairy's latest conquest.

Trent pushed to his feet and clicked off the television, letting Ciaran slip to the side and jerk awake.

"Movie's over," he said as he dropped the remote back onto the coffee table. "Don't trash the kitchen." He shut himself in his bedroom before the fairy could respond. His father would be there tomorrow. He felt an unpleasant weight in his gut as he set his glasses on the night stand and crawled into bed.

Trent cleaned up the kitchen as soon as he woke up, since Ciaran had failed to keep the kitchen tidy for even a single night. As soon as he was finished, he walked into the guest bedroom and shook him by the shoulder.

"Get up," he said when the fairy opened his eyes. "I have to clean these sheets."

"I didn't bleed on them much," Ciaran protested, but Trent only clicked his tongue and jerked his head to urge him out of the way. The fairy obliged, though he took his time getting out of the bed and periodically paused to groan and hold his stomach.

"Go stuff your face some more," Trent grumbled. "You'll feel better."

"I haven't any more food."

Trent stopped with the sheets halfway off the bed and turned to look at him. "You what?"

"It's gone. You didn't get very much."

"Are you kidding me? You should be in a diabetic coma after eating so much sugar in a day. I'm not buying anything else."

"Oh, come on. After I was going to do you a favor."

"Please don't. Whatever favor you thought up, I'm sure I don't want it. What happened to leaving me alone? Staying out of my way?" He gathered up the sheets and pushed by Ciaran in a bit of a huff on his way to the laundry room. He could hear the fairy padding along barefoot behind him. "My father is going to be here tonight," he called over his shoulder, in case the other man had forgotten. "It's almost twenty hours travel time from Hong Kong to Vancouver, so he's going to be tired. When he's tired, he's cranky. If the place is a mess, he'll be cranky. If the room isn't set up the way he likes it, he'll be cranky. If I haven't lit the incense on the altar before he gets here, he'll be cranky."

Ciaran leaned against the doorway of the laundry room to watch Trent bend over and load the machine. "So you're saying he's going to be cranky."

"He's going to be cranky," the younger man echoed, slamming the washer door and turning to face him. "When he's cranky, he tells me everything that's wrong with me. He tells me all the ways I have and continue to let him down. He stays out of my life three hundred and sixty days out of the year and then thinks he can tell me when he doesn't like my clothes. He's going to say I'm getting fat, and then tell me to eat more when we go to dinner. He's going to ask me about my *problem*. So you'll understand if buying you more damn cake isn't exactly high on my list of priorities."

Ciaran watched him with lifted eyebrows, not speaking. Trent seemed to remember himself, and he sighed, running a hand over his short hair.

"Forget it," he said. "It's not your problem. What the hell do you know? You probably don't even have parents. You just sprung up from under a daffodil somewhere."

"Oi, I've got parents," Ciaran protested as Trent moved past him again.

"Well when Tinker Bell starts giving you shit about who you're fucking, get back to me," he snapped.

Ciaran frowned, crossing his arms over his chest. "That's a bit rude."

"You're welcome to leave."

"You are a nasty sort, do you know that?" the fairy chuckled. "What if I could solve your problem? Your father, not the liking-to-sleep-with-blokes bit."

Trent hesitated, an uncertain frown on his lips. "What does that mean?"

"It means I'll get him off your back. For good, if you like." He waited, watching the crease deepen in the younger man's brow. He might not even mind granting this one. It would be the least of the favors Trent could ask.

"I don't want anything you can give me," he said.

Ciaran let his hands drop to his sides. "You understand what I'm saying, lad? It isn't as though I'll hurt him; it's magic. You'll never have another opportunity like this."

"I can solve my problems without any of your fairy bullshit. I can't just have you change his mind."

"Would that be something you wanted, then? If I could change your mind?"

Trent stopped with one hand on the cabinet door, ready to take out the trash, and he slowly straightened with his eyes on the floor. If he could magically be attracted to women, would he? It would make everything so much easier. He could find a girlfriend easily enough, a pretty companion to keep his father happy. Get married, have a couple of kids, be content—but never happy. He looked up at Ciaran's waiting face and shook his head. He wanted more than that, even if he would never get it. Even if he could become attracted to women, he would always know what he'd done, how he'd given in. How could he live with himself after that?

Just..." He sighed. "Just stay away from us tonight. He'll only be here for a couple of days, and if you're still here after that, we can...figure that out. But just leave us alone."

Ciaran let out a slight scoff and slumped back against the door frame. "Have it your way," he muttered. He didn't like it one bit. If not this, what was Trent waiting to ask for? He hoped if he put Ciaran up for long enough, he'd be able to ask some grand favor, certainly. No one did things without expecting something in return—especially when the person giving the potential favor could do magic. Whatever kindness Trent had shown him thus far had been out of a sense of obligation at the very least, if not outright manipulation.

Trent left him in the kitchen and set about cleaning up the rest of the apartment before he had to leave for class. He threatened Ciaran with bodily harm should he mess anything up, but as he was walking out the door, he hastily agreed to bring home some more appropriate food for his finicky guest.

Ciaran did his best to behave himself. It was difficult with nothing to eat but stale cookies from the back of the pantry and nothing on television but a show about who was or wasn't the father of some woman's baby, but he tried. His gut still ached, and he felt lightheaded from fever, so it was a little easier not to get into too much trouble. The iron he could sense inside the large armoire near the window didn't make him feel any more at ease, either. He wanted to know what was in there, but not enough to open the doors and risk properly exposing himself.

He dozed on the couch for a while, but it wasn't very comfortable. He stood on the balcony and watched people go by on the sidewalk until his stomach pained him too much, and then he ran a hot bath in the massive tub in Trent's bathroom. The hot water felt good on his pounding wound as he stretched in the deep tub. He reached for the vanity and took Trent's shaving mirror from its place by the sink, using it to inspect his face in the steamy room. His skin still looked a bit pale, but the infection seemed to be improving. He was honestly lucky not to be dead. He'd forgotten how painful iron poisoning could be. If that hunter had another chance at him, he'd know to do more than break the skin.

Ciaran put the thought out of his mind. The man doubtless hadn't given up on catching him, but for all he knew, Ciaran was long gone. Even if he thought he was still in the building, he had no reason to think he would purposely put himself in a place with so many anti-magic artifacts. It was pointless to fret about it. He inspected his teeth in the mirror, running his tongue over slightly pointed canines. Finding what he saw less than satisfactory, he stepped out of the tub to help himself to Trent's toothbrush, sloshing water onto the floor as he went. He brushed his teeth and scrubbed behind his pointed ears, then dunked his head under the water and scrubbed his hair clean with Trent's shampoo.

The front door opened and shut with a distant click, and Ciaran heard his host's voice in the kitchen. The bathroom door handle turned, but Trent barely took half a step inside before he heard the slosh of water and realized what he would be walking in on.

"Da here yet?" Ciaran called as he pushed himself out of the tub, flicking the plug open on his way.

"Not yet. I see you managed not to make too much of a mess."

"I told you I wouldn't make more trouble."

"Just stay in here, will you? Or at least in the bedroom. It's easier this way."

"I'll make it easy on you, lad, don't worry."

"I don't like how you're not just agreeing to stay in the bedroom."

Ciaran wrapped a towel around his hips and pushed the door open, urging Trent out of the way. "It'll be fine. You just finish getting ready for your father."

"See, that's still being pretty evasive."

The fairy grinned as Trent's gaze purposely avoided his naked torso. "You manage yourself. Don't worry about me."

Trent gave a short, resigned sigh and shut the bedroom door on his way out, hoping that the nagging feeling in his stomach was unwarranted. He opened the doors to the armoire and dusted the icons inside to give the illusion that the altar had done more than sit neglected since his father's last visit. He gave a quick bow out of habit before lighting the incense, then set about putting the sheets back on the guest bed. Ciaran would have to sleep on the sofa again, but at least he wasn't actively bleeding anymore.

He had just shut the door to the guest bedroom when the doorbell rang. Trent took a final look around the apartment, and he quickly pushed a muffin cup into the garbage before walking to the front door. With a low, steadying sigh, he opened the door to his father's staring face.

The visit began just like every other. Trent shook his father's hand and waited patiently while he put his luggage in the guest room, then they exchanged pleasantries while standing near the bedroom door. Any minute, his father would suggest going out to eat dinner, where the real questions would begin.

Instead, a loud thunk sounded from Trent's bedroom, and he briefly shut his eyes, his whole body tensing. All he had asked was that Ciaran keep quiet, and he hadn't even managed to do that.

"Is there someone here?" his father asked, looking between Trent's face and the door with a suspicious frown.

"No. There isn't anyone," he lied, and the moment the words were out of his mouth, the bedroom door opened, and Ciaran appeared in the doorway. He had dressed himself in the same dirty jeans he had been wearing for two days and one of Trent's shirts, which was noticeably long on him.

"Gracious, pardon me," he said with a smile as he approached.

Trent didn't consider himself a violent person, but in that moment, he could have wrung the fairy's neck. One request—one simple request that would make this visit bearable—and Ciaran couldn't handle it.

"Trent," his father said, his tone one of pleasant surprise rather than the expected outrage, "why didn't you tell me you had a guest?"

"Fu chan, this isn't what—"

"Isn't what it looks like?" Ciaran finished for him, and he slunk up beside him and hooked their arms with a sly grin.

Trent's jaw tightened as Ciaran's side pressed into his, but his heart stopped when he spotted their reflection in the glass of the balcony door. Instead of the scruffy fairy that had been sleeping in his apartment for days, the person on his arm appeared to be a tall, slender woman, with red hair that fell in soft curls around her face. She seemed to be wearing a long, dark green skirt and a cream-colored blouse that bared her delicate shoulders. Trent looked from the reflection back to the man at his side, unable to make his mouth form any coherent words.

"So sorry to surprise you, sir," Ciaran said, smiling pleasantly at Trent's father. He disengaged his arm to offer his hand to the older man. "Cara Hickey; I've heard a lot about you."

Trent could only stare while his father shook the fairy's hand, clearly seeing the reflection in the glass as the truth.

"Daniel Fa," his father answered politely. "I am sorry I can't say the same," he added with a pointed glance in Trent's direction.

"Trent was hoping to introduce us properly," Ciaran answered for him, "but I'm afraid I was a bit slow getting out of the house before you arrived."

Trent's father looked at him with a furrowed brow. "You were going to leave this woman shut in your bedroom until you could sneak her away from me? Why would you do such a thing?"

"I was—" he started uncertainly, but Ciaran cut him off.

"He's just a bit shy," the fairy teased, slipping his fingers into the other man's and giving them a small squeeze. He leaned closer to Mr. Fa and added in a stage whisper, "I think he thinks I'll embarrass him."

The older man gave a faint smile. "Regardless, I'm pleased beyond measure to meet you. My son and I were about to have dinner; will you join us?"

"Oh, I'd love to!" Ciaran said immediately despite Trent's warning grip on his hand.

"Excellent. Please give me a moment; it has been a very long flight." Mr. Fa excused himself into the guest bathroom, and the minute the door was closed, Trent wheeled on his fairy guest.

"What the hell are you thinking?" he hissed. "Why are you doing this?"

"I'm solving your problem," Ciaran shrugged. "If he thinks you like girls, he won't bother you about it anymore. You can call him later about our tearful breakup."

"And why would you leave the house again? You're not well," Trent said before he realized that sounded suspiciously like concern. "And it's no help to me if that hunter person shows up and starts trouble."

"Oh, come on. It's only for a couple of hours, right? I'll risk it. Besides," he said, reaching up to slip an arm around Trent's neck and bring his lips very near to the corner of his mouth, "it's going to be such fun putting on this show."

The bathroom door opened before Trent could react, and Ciaran purposely lingered long enough to pretend they'd been caught by accident. He pulled away with a demure giggle, leaving Trent attempting to rein in his scowl. The fairy held his hand while they rode down in the elevator, and Trent was forced to admit to himself that despite his frustration, that part wasn't so bad.

They took his father's car to the same restaurant they always went to when he was in town, and Trent had to repeatedly remove Ciaran's hand from his knee in the back seat. When he leaned over to hiss at him to stop, Ciaran only laughed and kissed his cheek, playfully pushing against his chest and telling him to keep his hands to himself. Trent growled to force the warmth of Ciaran's palm against his chest from his thoughts, and he paused at the sight of his father's small smile in the rear view mirror. He actually seemed pleased.

"I told you," Ciaran whispered into his ear, and he grit his teeth to avoid showing the slight shudder that ran down his spine. This was too much. A terrible idea. He was lying to his father—a lie he had no hope of maintaining once Ciaran was gone from his life, and one he shouldn't have to tell, besides. More than that, he was unable to escape the heat of Ciaran's body beside him and the memory of warm breath on his ear. He tried to convince himself he wasn't lying when he said it hadn't been too long.

At the usual restaurant, they took their seat at Mr. Fa's usual table and ordered their usual meals. The only difference was that now, there was a fairy sat in the seat beside Trent who his father thought was a woman, and who refused to be deterred from touching him. Trent eventually settled for holding Ciaran's hand on the table, if only to keep it from wandering.

"So this is quite a secret you have been keeping, son," Mr. Fa said, sipping his small cup of tea. "An important secret," he added with a pointed frown. Even now, he didn't want to speak aloud what he was really thinking, in case this pretty girl didn't know Trent's shameful secret.

Trent did his best to hide his sneer as he answered, "Should I have mentioned it over the phone?"

Mr. Fa shifted in his seat, directing a polite smile at Ciaran before looking back at his son. "I am just pleased that you found someone so…appropriate."

Trent's grip on Ciaran's hand tightened, and the fairy actually felt slightly guilty. He didn't have any frame of reference for being shamed for his sexual choices, but he didn't imagine it was a pleasant feeling.

"He's been lovely," Ciaran cut in with a smile, leaning over to nudge him with his shoulder. He moved his free hand up to rest on Trent's forearm. "Nothing about him in the world I'd change."

Trent paused, and he looked over at him with a slightly softer expression.

"Well, be glad you don't see him through a father's eyes," Mr. Fa chuckled, completely reversing his son's momentary calm. Ciaran put a steadying hand on Trent's knee, laughing politely at Mr. Fa's attempted joke.

"So, how did you two meet?" Mr. Fa asked, and Ciaran felt Trent's hand tighten around his.

"Oh, there isn't much of a story there," the fairy answered, rescuing Trent from his momentary panic. "We met on Grindr—I mean Tinder. Tinder is the one, isn't it?" He looked to Trent with an innocent smile, ignoring the glare that threatened to burn through him. "It's online dating," he explained when Mr. Fa looked puzzled. "I saw this one's pretty face and just had to get to know him better." Trent grit his teeth as Ciaran reached up to give his cheek a tender stroke.

"Ah, I don't know about all this online dating," Mr. Fa said. "But if it works for my son, what can I say?"

"He's been a perfect gentleman," Ciaran smiled.

"I should hope so," Mr. Fa said, and he gave a polite smile. "Are you in school, Ms. Hickey?"

"Me? Oh, of course. I'm studying history. Ancient Greece, specifically. You know, their social acceptance of the erastes and the eromenos—"

Trent squeezed his hand so tightly he thought it might pop off. "That isn't dinner conversation," he said through a tight jaw.

"Oh, well I don't want to jabber on," Ciaran said with a girlish smile, and Trent relaxed ever so slightly beside him. "I hope to be a teacher someday," he went on, glancing sidelong at Trent and lightly stroking his thumb over the other man's knuckles.

"A teacher is a good job," Mr. Fa agreed. "The world will always need good teachers."

He asked Trent about his classes, which was much too boring a conversation for Ciaran to pay attention to. He picked at the food when it was placed in front of them, but it was all vegetables and oil and flesh—nothing substantial.

"Is it not to your liking, Ms. Hickey?" Mr. Fa asked after a few minutes of Ciaran pushing his broccoli around his plate. "Are you not hungry?"

"She eats all day long," Trent muttered without looking up from his plate. "She's getting fat."

"Aiya, what a thing to say," his father scolded.

Ciaran lifted an eyebrow as he turned to look at the man beside him, giving a small laugh as his fingers dug pointedly into Trent's knee under the table. "My love does like to tease," he said, and he slid his hand up the other man's thigh, his palm brushing the front of his trousers and causing a barely audible growl.

Trent purposely kept his gaze from Ciaran's face to avoid snapping at him, but he couldn't help the heat the pooled in his stomach at the light touch. He asked his father about work and pretended to listen while Ciaran's fingers grazed his inner thigh through his pant leg. The touch drove him to distraction, but he didn't dare reach under the table to stop him.

His father droned on about meetings and market changes, interest and price fluctuations, but Trent's entire being was focused on the slow movement of Ciaran's hand on his leg. Every time he thought he could return to reality, he felt the heat of the other man's palm brush over him, until he was forced to draw his chair closer to the table to make certain his growing erection was hidden by the tablecloth. It put him slightly out of reach of Ciaran's wandering hand, which was both a relief and a torture.

At the end of the meal, Mr. Fa excused himself to the restroom, and Trent let out a breath he felt he'd been holding for a lifetime as he finally turned to face Ciaran.

"What is wrong with you?" he asked in a hoarse voice, an unwelcome heat in his face. "What are you doing?"

"Just a bit of fun," the fairy smirked, bringing Trent's hand to his lips to brush a light kiss over his knuckles.

"Stop it," he hissed, shaking his hand free of the other man's grip. "This isn't a game. This is my life."

Ciaran leaned an elbow on the table to move in close to him, a sly smile on his lips. Trent almost shoved him away, but he wasn't willing to cause a scene in the middle of the restaurant.

"I'll make you a deal," the fairy murmured, reaching up to finger the open collar of Trent's dress shirt. "If you tell me just once without stumbling that you want me to stop..." He trailed off, and he touched the faintest of kisses to the corner of the other man's mouth. "Then I'll stop," he whispered against Trent's cheek.

Trent bit the inside of his cheek so hard that it almost bled, but it was only the sound of his father returning to the table that broke the helplessness he felt with Ciaran's lips so close to his.

"I hope you don't mind if I cut this short," Mr. Fa said with a good-natured clearing of his throat. He smiled faintly at Ciaran's carefully fabricated giggle. "I have had a long day. Trent, would you like to see

Ms. Hickey home safely?"

"Oh, there's no need for that," Ciaran answered in his place. "I'm quite near to here, actually."

Trent did a bit of last minute adjustment before he got to his feet along with them, hoping he wasn't as obvious as he felt. The three of them left the restaurant and returned to the car, where Trent and Ciaran were forced to fake a goodbye. The fairy thanked Mr. Fa politely for the meal and said how pleased he had been to meet him while Trent stood to the side, clenching his fists.

"And good night to you," Ciaran said, standing on tiptoe to wrap his arms around Trent's neck. Trent hesitated, awkward and frustrated, but he returned the embrace for the sake of appearance, one hand settling on the small of the other man's back. Ciaran pressed close to him far more tightly than was necessary, and Trent's fingers dug into his skin as the other man's hips rolled against his in the subtlest of movements.

"I am going to murder you," he whispered into Ciaran's ear as the fairy kissed his cheek.

Trent got into the front seat of his father's car while Ciaran slipped into the back—somehow without Mr. Fa noticing. Trent could feel the fairy's teasing fingertips on the back of his neck as they drove, but he was startled away from the sensation by his father's voice.

"So, Ms. Hickey," Mr. Fa began, glancing briefly away from the road to look at his son. "You and she are...serious?"

"No," Trent said immediately. "We're just...seeing each other."

His father tutted. "Seeing each other. Is this 'hooking up?' She is serious enough to be in your bedroom." When Trent didn't answer, Mr. Fa shifted uncomfortably in the driver's seat, and he cleared his throat. "Does this mean that your...problem is not a problem?"

Trent set his jaw and took a single breath before answering. "I don't have a problem," he said honestly. He knew how his father would take it.

A few moments of silence passed. "Then, you've decided that you're not...that you actually aren't attracted to—"

"I don't want to talk about it, ba ba," he snapped, looking out the window rather than at his father's face. "You're just happy I've got a girlfriend, right?"

Mr. Fa let out a silent sigh. "Yes. She seems very nice. I'm glad you've made this decision, son."

"Sure."

It should have felt good to finally hear his father think highly of some aspect of his life, but it was a lie. A lie that he was reminded of every time Ciaran's fingers brushed the skin of his neck or slipped under the collar of his shirt, impossible to ignore.

Inside the apartment, Trent bid his father good night, forced to stand still while Ciaran lurked unseen behind him, the fairy's chest against his back and one hand lightly clawed into his stomach just above his belt. The guest bedroom door shut, and Trent turned on the man behind him, snatching him up by the wrist and gripping his jaw to cover his mouth and keep him from speaking.

"Go," he growled, jerking Ciaran ahead of him toward the master bedroom.

12

Trent shut the bedroom door while Ciaran stumbled ahead of him with a laugh.

"You don't have to be angry," the fairy teased as Trent stalked toward him. "It was just a bit of fun."

"Shut up," he whispered, fisting one hand in the other man's shirt and pushing him backward until he hit the nearby dresser.

"Easy now, lad, I'm still injured," Ciaran chuckled, and Trent put a finger to the fairy's lips with a hard scowl.

"Shut. Up." He pressed the other man into the dresser with the weight of his body, his hand moving to grip his jaw as his thumb roughly brushed the fairy's bottom lip. He leaned in to him, tilting Ciaran's chin up as he drew close, but he skipped his mouth entirely and instead fastened his teeth on the tender skin of his neck. Ciaran's small sound of surprise and approval was all he needed. This was what the fairy had wanted all along, after all. Just a conquest. Just another lover. Trent could use him just as easily, he told himself. He slid his hand between them, deftly unbuttoning the fairy's jeans and slipping his hand inside. He couldn't hold in his own soft groan as he felt Ciaran pulse against his palm, and he squeezed the silky skin until the other man was bucking into his grip.

Trent bit hard kisses down Ciaran's neck as he stroked him, but when the fairy's whimpers got too loud, he pushed his thumb into his mouth, shuddering at the gentle scrape of teeth and the heat of the other man's tongue. He shut his eyes as he ground his hips into Ciaran's, his breath quickening into light pants. He had lied. It had been too long. He looked up when he felt Ciaran's hands on the sides of his face, and he held him fast by one side of his neck while the other man slid his glasses down his nose and discarded them on the far end of the dresser.

"You're not half pent up, are you? We could have done this ages ago," Ciaran taunted, lightly scratching his fingernails down Trent's cheek.

"If you don't shut up," Trent growled, letting the threat die off as he pulled away. He tugged the other man's shirt up, his heavy amulet thumping back against his chest, and tossed it away. He turned him around and shoved him toward the bed so hard that he tumbled backward, then hooked his fingers into the fairy's jeans and jerked them down his thighs. Ciaran obliged him by propping himself up on one elbow, his free hand setting to the task Trent had abandoned. He stroked himself slowly, looking up into the other man's eyes like a challenge.

Trent's heart pounded uncomfortably against his ribs, but he focused on his shirt buttons, only managing to undo three before giving up and pulling the shirt up over his head. He tugged on his belt to loosen it, but he hesitated just a moment as he stood at the edge of the bed, Ciaran shamelessly touching himself right in front of his eyes. He didn't want to seem bumbling, especially after Ciaran had so effortlessly aroused him, but he wasn't sure at all how to ask the other man to touch him again. He was certain it would come out as begging, and that was the one remaining line he refused to cross.

Instead, he removed his pants as quickly as he could and crawled over the top of the other man, tightening his fingers around Ciaran's own and matching his pace. The fairy let his head fall back with a soft, growling laugh, and Trent knelt over him to put a hand across his mouth.

"My father thinks I'm alone in here," he whispered against Ciaran's cheek as a warning, following him lower as he dropped down from his elbow. He meant to add a threat, but his breath caught in his throat as he felt the other man's fingers slip around his aching erection. He let his forehead fall helplessly against Ciaran's shoulder as he struggled to support himself, and both men kept time with each other, stroking and squeezing and panting together.

Ciaran's breath was hot against his ear, but when the fairy turned toward him in an attempt to catch his mouth in a kiss, Trent pulled away, unwilling to make the connection. It would have been too much. Too close.

Ciaran let out a groan of mock frustration and fisted his free hand in the hair at the back of Trent's head, his tongue tracing a teasing line along the other man's upper lip. Trent shuddered against him but still refused him a kiss, instead pressing their hips together until he was unsure exactly whose hand was touching who. Ciaran ground up against him despite the injury on his stomach, but when his brazen moans grew loud, Trent fastened his hand over the fairy's mouth and kept it there, letting the other man groan into his palm. He grit his teeth to avoid making noise himself, eventually forced to bite down on Ciaran's shoulder to muffle his growls, and he kept his hand over the fairy's mouth as he let the full weight of his body rest against his lean torso.

Their hands worked together, both of them stroking themselves and the other all at once until Trent let out a telltale whimper, and Ciaran tightened his grip and quickened his pace, panting against Trent's clutching hand. The younger man's hips jerked, and he hid his moan in Ciaran's shoulder as he finished, spilling hot liquid onto the fairy's stomach. Ciaran rolled his hips against Trent's lingering erection, his back arching away from the bed, and he bit his lip, his breath held in his chest as he came. His head fell back to the bed as both men gave a final shuddering jerk, their seed mixing between them from the press of their bellies.

Ciaran was eventually forced to return to reality as the wound in his stomach began to throb, and he shoved Trent off to lie beside him instead. The younger man hadn't yet opened his eyes, his chest rising and falling with slow, uncertain breaths. Ciaran wanted to tease him, but he only curled up nearby Trent and shut his eyes, listening to him breathe. When he was clearly asleep, Ciaran slipped out of the bed to clean himself up. He stood in the bathroom doorway and watched Trent in silence for a while until he noticed the quiet smile that had formed on his lips and shook his head. This had been frustration and lust, nothing more. Very fun frustration and lust, but empty nonetheless. Just a pleasant diversion. It wouldn't do for him to forget that.

With a short sigh, Ciaran crawled back into bed and wrapped himself in the blanket, then tossed what he could over Trent's sleeping body and shut his eyes.

Trent opened his eyes to Ciaran's sleeping face, and a swell of panic grew in his chest as he sat up. He tugged the blanket up around his hips and folded his arms, gripping his jaw with one hand to cover his mouth as he looked down at the man in his bed. It had gone too far—he had *let it* go too far. He had let a sly smile and a freckled nose tempt him, and now there was a fairy asleep next to him who would doubtless have certain expectations about them now that this door had been opened. He could just imagine trying to get anything done now with Ciaran's hands on him, those sharp teeth nipping at his ear or his shoulder, lithe body pressing into him in the office—Trent shook his head.

"No," he said aloud, more to himself than his sleeping companion. He threw the blanket off and shut himself in the attached bathroom, turning the shower on as hot as he could make it. He touched the dried fluid on his stomach and frowned, eager to rinse it away. The room was too large to steam up properly, but the glass door of the shower turned opaque as he scrubbed himself under the scalding water.

This couldn't go any farther than it had. After breakfast, his father would leave for the day to take whatever meeting he had come to Vancouver to have, and Trent would tell Ciaran plainly that last night had been a mistake. It had been. He had no room in his life for drama, he told himself. He was alone, and he liked it that way. No one bothered him. He lived however he liked, and he wasn't responsible to anyone outside of making sure he passed his classes. Without sex and relationships, he had no problems. There was no stress, no drama, and no possibility of having to ever again see the look on Jason's face when Trent had told him they couldn't be together anymore.

He heard the bathroom door click open, and he saw Ciaran approach through the clouded glass. Trent purposely ignored him until he heard the ceramic thunk of the toilet lid being lifted.

"What are you doing?" he asked over the sound of the shower. "No. Get out."

"What?" Ciaran said, already in position to relieve himself. "You want me to go in your dad's bathroom?" He chuckled. "After last night, I thought we were at this level."

"No. We'll never be at this level. Go away and wait until I'm done."

"It's too late; this is happening. I can't stop it now."

Trent sighed as he heard the unmistakable trickle into the water, doing his best to ignore it as he ran his hands through his wet hair. The water was too hot for Ciaran's flush to make much of a difference, and Trent let out a short breath of relief as he heard the other man's footsteps again. Then the shower door slid open, letting in a rush of cool air, and he was faced with the sight of Ciaran's naked body through the escaping steam, his hair delightfully mussed.

"No," Trent said immediately, retreating until his back touched the cool tile wall. "Get out."

Ciaran only smiled at him, lingering in the doorway and drumming his fingers on his flat stomach.

"Get out," Trent said again. "Just go somewhere and be quiet until my father leaves."

"It was cold in that bed after you left," Ciaran murmured, stepping inside and letting out a soft, happy hum as the hot water touched his shoulder and chest. "Not much for pillow talk, are you?"

"I don't want to do any kind of talking with you," he snapped, conscious of the volume of his voice. He dropped to a harsh whisper to add, "I just want you to get out."

"So rude," the fairy chuckled, his gaze dropping to Trent's hips with a slow smirk that made the other man's stomach tighten. "You're sure? And here I woke up thinking how much I wanted to taste you."

Trent shook his head in an attempt to avoid seeing Ciaran lick his lips, but the image was burned into his brain.

"How about we give it a go, and when you've had enough, you tell me to stop?" Ciaran took a step forward, letting his fingertips brush down Trent's bare chest to his stomach. He smiled at the other man's shudder and paused with his fingers buried in the nest of black curls at Trent's hips, waiting for a protest. Ciaran moved close to him, leaning up as though to kiss him but settling for nipping at the other man's jaw when he turned his head away. "Now's the time, friend," he whispered against the wet skin of Trent's neck, but he heard only the other man's soft hitch of breath as he wrapped his fingers around his rising erection.

Trent let his head fall back against the tile wall, his hands in tight fists at his sides. He needed to say no. He needed to shout, to push Ciaran away, to ignore him and get dressed and pretend none of this had ever happened. But when the other man pressed a warm kiss to his chest, he couldn't help the sigh that slipped out of him, and as Ciaran dropped to his knees, Trent found himself with one hand tangled in the fairy's messy locks.

Ciaran hummed his approval as he took Trent into his mouth, his tongue running eagerly over the rapidly hardening flesh. Trent gasped and tightened his fingers in the fairy's hair, urging him deeper and finding no resistance as he touched the back of Ciaran's throat.

"Fuck," he swore. He felt heat beyond the warmth of the shower rise in his face when Ciaran looked up at him, green eyes clear and tinged with mischievous promise. The other man's mouth was hot and overwhelming as he groaned around him, and Trent bit his lip to hold in his moans as he saw Ciaran's hand move down to tend to his own aching arousal. The fairy kept a quick pace, his hand matching the rhythm of his mouth, and he groaned as Trent guided him with a hand in his hair.

Trent swore again, gasping and desperate, until his grip tightened and he panted out, "Stop. I'm—I'm going to—"

Ciaran only hummed an agreement, shifting closer on his knees and taking every inch Trent had to offer into his mouth. When Trent let out a gasping groan and emptied himself into the fairy's mouth, Ciaran swallowed it down without spilling a drop, though he did make a bit of a mess when he spilled his own climax onto the shower floor a few moments later.

He leaned in to press a kiss to Trent's hip, a teasing chuckle in his throat as the other man shivered, and he got to his feet under the cooling shower. For a moment, neither of them moved except to catch their breath, each watching the other for some sort of sign or hint of what to do next, each waiting for the other to speak.

Trent jumped at the sudden, sharp rapping on his bedroom door, and he barely heard his father's voice over the sound of the shower, "Trent? Are you still asleep?"

With a soft curse, Trent ushered Ciaran out of his way, wrapping a towel around his waist as he strode quickly out of the room. He opened the bedroom door just enough to see his father's face.

"I'm sorry, fu chan," he said automatically. "I was just getting out. I'll be just another minute."

Mr. Fa clicked his tongue and glanced at the clock, but he nodded and allowed Trent to shut the door again.

"Just getting off, more like," Ciaran chuckled from the bathroom door, still completely naked and dripping onto the tile floor.

"Shut up," Trent hissed, glancing over his shoulder at the door. He stepped over to Ciaran only to keep his voice low. "You need to stop this. I'm going to talk to my father, and you are going to stay in here and not make a single. Fucking. Sound."

"Yes, sir," Ciaran smirked, giving a mock salute as Trent turned from him.

He didn't have time to argue. Trent dried off as best he could and dressed himself, pointedly ignoring the fact that the fairy was watching him. He left without looking at him again, and he shut the door behind him and went to greet his father.

"I have a meeting at ten," Mr. Fa said, tugging lightly on the sleeves under his suit jacket. "I will be out after lunch, but my flight doesn't leave until quite late tonight, so I expect you will be available for dinner?"

"Yes, fu chan."

"You could bring Ms. Hickey."

"She's…busy tonight."

"Ah. That's a shame. A nice girl," he added with a small nod. "Good for you."

"Yeah, she's…great."

Mr. Fa glanced at his watch. "I need to be going. I will call when I'm finished, and we can meet for dinner."

"Yes, fu chan." Trent walked his father to the front door and leaned his forehead against it once it was closed.

"I'm busy tonight, am I?" Ciaran asked behind him, startling him. Trent was glad to see that the fairy had at least dressed himself when he turned around, even if he was wearing Trent's same hastily-removed button-down from the previous night. "If you want to go out, I promise I won't paw at you," he teased, a sly smile on his face as he moved toward the other man and hooked one finger into his belt loop. "I'll save it for when we get back."

"Stop it," Trent said, swatting Ciaran's hand away from him and brushing by him on his way to the kitchen.

"You know, you keep saying stop, but you never actually seem like that's what you want." Ciaran hopped up to sit on the kitchen island, watching Trent fill a glass of water from the tap. He drank the whole thing, then took a slow breath and moved to face the fairy on his countertop. Ciaran grinned and reached out to tug on Trent's collar, but he gripped him by the wrists and threw his hands away.

"Don't you get it?" Trent spat. "I don't want this. I didn't ask you for your help. I told you *not* to help. I have a life that I plan to get back to the minute you're out of this house, and that can't come soon enough."

Ciaran frowned at him, unexpectedly stung by the other man's words. "It's just a bit of fun," he countered, immediately wishing he hadn't. He wouldn't plead for this man's affection. He had hoped that with this, it would be enough, and he would stop feeling that pounding in his chest when Trent was nearby. But that hadn't happened. Even now, he wanted to reach up and touch the other man's face and ask him why. "And anyway, a mhac," he tried again, slipping down from the counter to look Trent in the face, "don't forget that you started this. I may have done some teasing, but I'm not the one pushing folk down onto beds and such. You ought not have begun something you wanted to say later you didn't like."

"I started—" Trent stopped himself and let out a short sigh through his nose. "It was a mistake," he said. "That's it. A stupid mistake, and it won't happen again."

"Then why don't you tell me what it is you really want?"

"What are you talking about?"

"Don't be daft. You let me stay here, you buy me food, you keep me from that hunter—you want something in return." He didn't mean to sound so bitter. What could Trent want from him, if it wasn't sex? He had thought they were on the same page—but using each other was only victimless if they both agreed.

Trent ran a hand through his damp hair and shook his head. "What I want is for you to be gone."

"You have to want something," Ciaran insisted. "Some repayment. I can do magic, or have you forgotten?"

"What is it you think I need that you could possibly give me? I said no. Now just…leave me alone. Please," he added as an afterthought, and he walked past Ciaran and shut himself in the office.

Ciaran stood in the kitchen, scowling as he folded his arms across his chest. Trent was lying. He would ask; they all asked. And Ciaran was going to be right there waiting when he did, even if it was just to tell him "no."

13

The apartment seemed a little too quiet without Trent's grousing. Ciaran went in and out of the pantry half a dozen times, each time expecting to find something appetizing and each time coming up short. He opened and closed the refrigerator, hoping that the milk or cream would reappear, but he refused to knock on Trent's office door and ask for it.

There wasn't anything interesting on television, so Ciaran had resigned himself to a nap when he spotted the telescope on the small balcony nearby. He clicked open the French doors and poked his head outside, hesitating as though he expected the hunter to pounce on him nineteen floors up. When nothing happened, he stepped out, leaving the door open behind him and bending over to look through the eyepiece of the telescope. Since it was daylight, there wasn't much to see except blue until he tilted the lens down toward the street.

A woman walked by with a small dog on a leash, faltering in her too-high high heels and doing her best to play off the stumble with grace. Two men passed each other with a small nod of acknowledgment, but one of them turned and took a few steps backwards to watch the other just a little bit longer.

Ciaran straightened to look down over the balcony, trying to spot the people he saw through the lens, but it was harder to make them out from so high. He briefly considered spitting over the side and trying to catch sight of the unfortunate person below through the telescope, but the sound of the office door opening inside caught his attention.

He didn't want to look at Trent. He didn't want to see that scowl on his face or that lonely defeat in his eyes when he talked about his father. The fairy huffed and slumped down with his elbows on the balcony railing, frowning down at the distant street. What did he care if Trent got along with his father? Who the hell was he? He happened to live in an apartment where Ciaran's trail would be masked, that was all. And his hair was just as soft as Ciaran had imagined, and he made the hottest little growling noise when he was about to come. And he had looked so grateful just to hear someone say they wouldn't change him.

Ciaran sighed with his chin on his arms, his cheeks puffing as he let out the breath. This was problematic. He hadn't anticipated developing any actual feelings during this little adventure, especially for someone who seemed the absolute least likely person to return them. Not that he wanted him to. As soon as Trent asked for his favor, he would be gone, and that would be the end of it.

Trent stood at the balcony door, watching Ciaran pout with a slight frown. He hesitated to speak first after the things he had said, but he felt an uncomfortable pit in his stomach at the sight of the fairy's hunched shoulders.

"What are you doing out there?" he asked, sounding more accusing than he meant to.

"Spitting on pedestrians."

"What?" Trent stepped out to stand beside him, peering over the railing.

"I haven't really. Why, do you want to?"

"I'll pass."

A few moments of tense silence passed between them, and Trent gripped the balcony rail with both hands so that he didn't fidget. He didn't know what to say. He wouldn't apologize. Ciaran had gone too far by interfering with his father, and what had happened afterward—

he had to push it out of his mind. They couldn't continue this way.

Before he could muster up the courage to speak, Ciaran said, "Ach, look at this article here," as he leaned over to the telescope and put his eye to it.

"This what? Are you spying on people?"

"You'll miss it," Ciaran said instead of answering, and he waved Trent over and urged him toward the telescope.

Trent looked through the eyepiece while Ciaran steadied it, and he saw a woman on the street, her dark hair wild and loose, circling and shouting at a man who seemed to be doing his best to ignore her.

"What do you reckon they're talking about, eh? She's right rollickin ain't she?"

"She's what?"

"She's pissed off," Ciaran laughed.

The woman on the street threw up her hands when the man finally acknowledged her, and she paced in front of him, ranting silently through the lens of the telescope.

"She seems to be," Trent agreed.

"Let's have a look," Ciaran said, lightly pushing Trent out of the way with a hand on his chest as he bent back to the eyepiece. It was a thoughtless, easy gesture out of place with the argument they had had less than an hour beforehand. "Who was she?" he said, laughing and mimicking a woman's voice. "You tell me who that slag was!"

"She probably didn't say 'slag,'" Trent scoffed, leaning over the balcony to get a better look.

"She wasn't anybody," Ciaran went on, lowering his voice to play the male part of the imaginary drama. "I told you, nothing happened!"

Trent chuckled despite himself, watching Ciaran's smile as he adjusted the telescope to follow the couple down the street.

"I can't believe you would do this!" Ciaran argued with himself, falsetto. "After what I gave up for you!"

"Nobody told you to quit your job at the factory," Trent joined in, and the fairy laughed beside him as the woman on the street shoved her partner in the shoulder.

"You're the one who said you didn't like me coming home smelling like mustard!"

"Who ever heard of a mustard factory, anyway?" Trent snorted.

"I quit to take care of you and our illegitimate children!" Ciaran said. "I cook and I clean all day, and this is how you repay me!"

Trent felt himself smile, and he leaned over to look through the telescope as Ciaran straightened. The man on the street had his arms folded, refusing to be goaded into shouting by the clearly distraught woman. "Well, if you ever cooked anything other than mustard toast—"

"Now my grandmother's mustard toast isn't good enough for you!" Ciaran snapped, so perfectly in time with the woman's exasperated gesture that Trent couldn't contain his laughter. He stood back from the telescope and found Ciaran smiling faintly at him, causing an uncertain tightness in his stomach.

The silence was quickly becoming awkward, so Trent started, "Look, I—about this morning."

"You want to have this conversation?" Ciaran said softly, tilting his head to look up into the other man's dark eyes.

"No, I don't," Trent admitted, forcing himself to look the fairy in the face instead of staring at the floor. "But not having it doesn't make this situation any better."

"You going to tell me what it is you want, then?"

"I don't want any more of your fairy bullshit than I've already got," Trent sighed. "That isn't—that's not what I meant."

"You don't want to be on your own?" Ciaran prodded, taking a step closer to him. "Away from your father, free to do as you please?"

"I already do as I please," he countered, knowing it must have sounded hollow.

"All those secret lovers of yours, you mean."

"I don't have—" Trent pressed his lips together and took a quick breath before answering. "However many lovers I have or don't have is my decision," he said. "My father doesn't have anything to do with it."

"Ah, tripe," Ciaran scoffed. "Tell me you're afraid if you're afraid, but don't tell lies."

"I'm not—" Trent gave a small huff and pushed by to escape from the suffocating corner of the balcony. "This isn't what I wanted to talk about."

"Then what is it you want to talk about?" Ciaran lifted his hands and let them slap back to his sides. "I haven't the energy to bicker anymore. You've done me a favor, and I'll stay until it's repaid. That's it. How long that takes is up to you. In the meantime, if you want to be hands-off, I'm not about to force you." He was proud of himself for sounding so cavalier when all he really wanted was to bite Trent's frowning lip and push him down onto the sofa.

Trent shook his head, hesitating at the balcony door. "I was...unfair. I did start this, kind of. And I...enjoyed it." He looked away from Ciaran to keep him from seeing the slight flush on his face. "But I can't do it anymore. I can't be...lovers with you, or whatever, but I don't want—" He stopped, not quite able to make his mouth form the words he really wanted to say. *I don't want you to go.* "I don't want to argue," he said instead.

"Fine," Ciaran agreed, feeling a bit deflated but hoping he was hiding it well. Rejection wasn't something he was accustomed to, and hearing it from someone he was actually a bit fond of—he could admit it to himself, if not out loud—was more difficult than he would have expected. "You just let me know when you want that favor, then." Trent had used him to let out his frustration, and that was all. They weren't friends, they weren't lovers, and as soon as Ciaran was well and he could refuse Trent his favor, he could be on his way with no more than a fare thee well.

Trent shifted on his feet for a moment. "Fine," he echoed. His mouth felt dry. "I wanted to say I...appreciate what you tried to do. It won't work long-term, and it was a really terrible idea that's only going to make things harder on me—" He stopped himself and tried again. "But I know you were trying to help."

"It's your life," Ciaran shrugged. "If you want to pretend for his sake, at least now you've got a starting point. I mean, it's all going to be downhill for you after losing a pretty little thing like me, but I'm sure you can do decently for yourself."

Trent sighed through his nose and sat down on the sofa, leaning his elbows on his knees. He looked up as Ciaran approached him, but the fairy didn't get too close, choosing to linger in the doorway to the balcony.

"I don't want to pretend," Trent said in a low voice. "But I can't do what he wants. So I don't...do anything." He shook his head.

"You mean to tell me you haven't had scads of secret lovers?" Ciaran laughed. "I never would have guessed."

"Fuck you," Trent grumbled, and Ciaran kept himself from accepting the invitation only with Herculean effort. "It's just…easier." His brow furrowed slightly as he looked up at the man standing in front of him—the man who frustrated him, and made him laugh, and who he wanted desperately to touch again. "Wouldn't it be easier for you if you stopped sleeping with women? You wouldn't have had that hunter after you in the first place, right?"

"Aye, but some things aren't worth giving up," Ciaran chuckled. "Perhaps someday I'll find something better." He stopped at the soft, uncertain look in Trent's eyes. Too far. Too close to admitting that every woman and every man he had been with through the years had invariably broken his heart. He had a good image with the younger man as it was. Carefree, independent, and mostly unconcerned with the huge nuisance he was being. He didn't want to ruin that by talking like a heartsick child. "I'm having fun torturing you just now, in any case," he added, hoping it was enough.

"You said you have parents?" Trent asked, apparently sufficiently fooled by Ciaran's pretended indifference. Or maybe he just wanted to change the subject, too. "As in, real ones?"

"Of course, real ones. What do you think you were touching last night, if I'm not meant to have children the proper way?" Trent scowled at him, so he held up his hands. "Fine. Yes, I have real parents. And fathers are a shit whoever you are." He tilted his head. "Why not just pass for straight, if it bothers him so much? I'm sure there are plenty of women in just your situation who wouldn't mind a superficial marriage. Then you could have as many secret lovers as you liked, and your father would be none the wiser."

"I've thought about it," Trent murmured. "But I…shouldn't have to. And I won't. I couldn't live that lie, and I wouldn't ask anyone to live it with me. I'd rather be alone. As long as I can, anyway." He looked up at Ciaran and shook his head, attempting to change the subject. "Why is your father a shit? He doesn't like how many people you kill with your fairy sex magic?"

Ciaran gave a single sniff, watching Trent with a flat expression. "You done?"

"Well what else do I call it?"

"You don't have to call it anything!" He sighed and moved to sit next to him on the sofa. "Anyway, my father's a bit of a special case. We had some familial strife some time ago."

"What kind of familial strife?"

"Well, the sort where he killed one of my brothers, for one."

"Your father did?" Trent said, visibly taken aback. "His own son? Why?"

"You wouldn't know how it is with my kind," Ciaran answered with a dry chuckle. "It isn't all toadstools and butterflies and dancing. There's a fair bit of war, too—at least there was in the old days. My people can be cruel, and these days, things as they are, it's better I stay away."

"These days?"

Ciaran waved a hand dismissively. "Politics and ancient history."

Trent tilted his head slightly as he looked over at him. "How ancient? How old are you really?"

"Ach, what does that matter? You haven't missed my birthday."

"How old?" Trent pressed, shifting on the cushion to face him.

"You see, it isn't quite so simple as when you're talking about calendars and things—"

"Ciaran," he sighed, and the fairy paused at hearing his name so familiarly on the other man's lips.

"Well, if you must know, I suppose it's been..." He puffed out a sigh. "What, not even four."

"Four? Four what? Four years? Decades?"

"Millennia?"

Trent stared at him. "Four millennia."

"Not so long at all, when you consider the age of some other things," Ciaran shrugged.

"Rocks. Rocks are older than that. You're saying it's fine that you're sitting in my house right now, claiming to be four thousand years old, because rocks are older than you."

"Well it's a bit silly when you say it like that. How long did you think fairies lived for?"

"I never thought about fairies at all until you showed up." He managed to avoid admitting that now he thought about them too much.

"Then you should hardly be surprised to find your assumptions incorrect, should you?"

"You don't seem four thousand years old."

"And what is a four thousand year old person like, if I might ask?"

"I would have guessed less watching trashy television."

Ciaran scoffed. "Well, you'd be wrong, wouldn't you?"

Trent smiled faintly despite himself, and for a moment, the silence that passed between them was calm. Ciaran was close enough that their knees touched, and that simplest of touches was enough to make Trent's heart beat uncomfortably fast. He didn't like it at all. He wanted to leave, and he wanted to stay. He wanted Ciaran to touch him, to push him down on the sofa and feel his tanned skin. He wanted to kiss him and let his father see it happen. The way Ciaran was smiling at him now, he didn't care if his father saw it or not, as long as he got to taste the fairy's lips. But that was a fantasy, and a dangerous one. When he didn't think about it, it was so easy to be around Ciaran. It felt like being alone—comforting and relaxed and simple. Wasn't that what it was supposed to be like? Maybe. But it wasn't supposed to be with a fairy, certainly, and in Trent's case, it couldn't be with another man.

"Something on your mind, a mhuirnín?" Ciaran murmured, nudging Trent with his shoulder. He gave a sly smile at the frown on the younger man's face. "You know, it doesn't have to be so serious."

"What are you talking about?"

Ciaran let his hand rest on Trent's thigh, a grin pulling at his lips as he felt the instant tension in the other man. No matter what he said, he didn't have the willpower to keep away from him when he looked so serious. "You'll be kicking me out as soon as I'm well, right?" He slipped his hand up to tug lightly on Trent's belt. "You can go back to denying yourself whatever you like. But while I'm here," he purred, lifting himself onto the younger man's lap in one smooth motion. He leaned close and nipped at Trent's ear. "It can be just a bit of fun."

Trent fastened his hands onto Ciaran's waist without thinking, not sure if he meant to pull him close or shove him away. The fairy felt too light in his lap, but the press of his hips was firm enough, and his fingers in Trent's hair made the breath leave his lungs too quickly. "I thought you said you'd be fine with hands-off," he said through gritted teeth.

"Aye, but what a waste," Ciaran chuckled. As long as they understood each other, neither of them would get hurt. As long as he didn't expect too much, didn't hope for too much. There was no point to denying what he wanted, especially since Trent clearly wanted it too. Whatever favor he would inevitably ask for, this was what he wanted now. And it was a favor the fairy didn't mind granting. If they were using each other, neither of them could call it unfair. Ciaran could pretend that was as far as it went.

"I told you I can't do this," Trent said, but his voice was hoarse and slightly weak. He shuddered when Ciaran's lips found the hollow of his throat, brushing the skin-warmed chain around his neck.

"You seem able to me," Ciaran smirked, lifting his hips and sliding a hand between them to touch him. Trent's breath caught in his chest. He was already painfully hard, despite his objections, and Ciaran let out a soft chuckle as he stroked the firm flesh through his trousers. He leaned up to whisper in the other man's ear, pausing to give his earlobe a teasing lick. "Why don't you tell me what you want me to do?"

Trent's fingers dug into Ciaran's hips, and he let his eyes close for just a moment as the fairy's lips brushed his neck, then his jaw. "Fuck," he sighed, unable to keep his hips from twitching up into the other man's hand. "I can't—I don't want this."

Ciaran sighed, removing his hand and settling back onto Trent's lap with a frown. He let his arms rest on the other man's shoulders, fingers lightly touching the hair at the back of his head. "You're a mess," he muttered. "If you don't want it because you don't want it, fine. But if you don't want it because your father disapproves—that's just sad. You won't pretend to be straight for him, but you'll be celibate? Come on."

"It's none of your business," Trent growled.

"You're right." Ciaran rolled his hips against the younger man's, drawing a sudden, trembling moan from him. "Just because I want you sweaty and begging, it doesn't mean you have to agree." He smiled and nipped at Trent's chin, barely missing his parted lips. "Maybe you'd prefer I did the begging?" He kissed his throat at his open collar. "Moan and plead for you to touch me, desperate to have you inside me?"

"I don't—" Trent could barely find the breath to answer. He tried once more, but his brain was empty of objections. He did want this. He wanted him. Tomorrow didn't matter; the future didn't matter. He was here now. With a frustrated groan, Trent pulled Ciaran tightly against him, burying his face in the fairy's neck. He kissed everywhere he could reach, eager to taste the other man's skin, and he slid his hands under his shirt to feel the lithe muscles in his back.

Ciaran gave a low, rumbling chuckle as he nipped at Trent's ear, working quickly on his belt buckle. He unfastened his own jeans, pausing to let Trent lift his shirt over his head, and he groaned out a laugh as he was tugged forward, Trent's tongue running impatiently over his nipple. He ground their hips together, thoroughly pleased by the moan it drew from the other man and the sharp bite he gave in return. Ciaran slipped Trent's glasses from his face and dropped them onto the coffee table behind him with a soft clatter. He pushed Trent's pants out of the way as best he could without breaking their embrace, and the younger man shuddered beneath him when his hand found his erection.

"Let me up," Ciaran whispered against Trent's temple, but he only grunted in response.

"No." Trent lifted the fairy in his lap just enough to pull him closer, and he slid his hand down Ciaran's back and below the waistband of his loosened jeans. His heart thudded painfully in his chest as he closed his mouth over the other man's nipple, his hand moving down Ciaran's backside until he could press his middle finger against the ring of muscle there. He tested it with a slow pressure at first, groaning as Ciaran's hands tightened on his shoulders. When he only heard the fairy's soft panting instead of disapproval, he pressed harder, and both men let out low sounds of satisfaction as Trent's fingertip slipped beyond the barrier.

Ciaran pushed back against Trent's touch with an eager moan, his head falling back as he fisted his hands in the younger man's shirt. Trent pushed into him without hesitation now, teeth grazing Ciaran's nipple as he slid in and out, occasionally brushing the tender spot deep inside him. Ciaran managed to free one of his hands from its grip, and he reached down to return his attention to his task, panting and stroking Trent in time with the rhythm he set.

"Fuck's sake," the fairy gasped, his free hand gripping the side of Trent's neck as though he was afraid to fall. He moaned and shivered with every intrusion, his forehead falling against Trent's as he looked up at him and their breath mingling in the scant distance between their lips.

Trent could almost taste the sweetness he knew he could find on Ciaran's lips, and he ached at the sight of the fairy's tightly knit brow and panting mouth. He leaned closer to him, feeling the heat of Ciaran's breath on his lips as his nose brushed the other man's cheek, but at the barest touch of their lips, Trent's stomach tightened. He pulled away, removing himself from Ciaran's embrace too quickly and dropping the other man to the floor in an undignified heap.

Ciaran hissed as he hit the tile floor, sitting up with a slight wince as Trent stood and quickly refastened his trousers and belt.

"What just happened?" Ciaran asked, not yet bothering to try to hide his obvious erection.

Trent wouldn't look at him. His heartbeat was deafening in his ears. Without answering, he stalked across the room to the kitchen sink, rinsing his burning face and scrubbing too hard at his hands. It couldn't be just fun, and he couldn't lie to himself and say that it could. He shut his eyes as he leaned his elbows on the edge of the sink, letting the water run. He had almost—it was too close. Too much. He couldn't do this and then forget.

Ciaran got to his feet and buttoned his jeans, watching Trent without approaching him. "What happened?" he asked again.

"I can't," Trent whispered, too softly for the other man to hear. He turned off the tap and pushed away from the sink, wiping a drip of water from his chin. "I made a mistake," he said out loud.

"Seemed to be going quite well to me," Ciaran chuckled, and Trent sighed through his nose and kept his gaze on the floor.

"I can't...do this. It's not—I know that I should say I don't care what my parents say. I've heard all of the inspiring propaganda. I've been told that it gets better. I know that I can't...I can't change this. About myself. But I can't help this—this weight," he said, not knowing how to explain it any better. He put a hand to his stomach where the pit always settled, where it weighed heavily now, and he shook his head. "It's none of your business. It's not your problem. But I just...can't."

Ciaran frowned, taking a few steps toward him. When Trent shrank away, Ciaran reached out and put his hands on either side of the younger man's face, forcing him to look at him. "There is *nothing* wrong with you," he said firmly, clicking his tongue and lightly slapping Trent's cheek when he tried to pull away. "Listen." He looked into the taller man's dark eyes, letting his thumb brush over his jaw. "Nothing."

For a moment, neither of them spoke. They stood in the kitchen while Trent's heart slowed to a less painful rhythm, and Ciaran kept gentle hands on his face until he seemed to relax. Trent reluctantly pulled away and took a few steps back, trying not to seem like he was purposely putting distance between them.

"I should...go and get you something you can eat," he said. He hurried over to pick up his glasses, then turned and scooped his wallet and cell phone up from the kitchen island on his way to the door without waiting for the fairy to answer him. He slipped out the front door and shut it behind him with an unpleasant churning in his stomach.

He rode the elevator down to the lobby and pushed open the glass door, ready to head down the street toward the grocery store for another day's worth of milk and sweets. He turned the corner and lost sight of his building, then found himself face to face with the man who had brought Ciaran to his door in the first place.

"Afternoon," Julien said, feigning friendliness in the face of Trent's scowl. "You and I need to have a chat."

"I don't have anything to say to you," Trent muttered, but Julien gripped him tightly by the arm as he tried to pass by.

"Not that kind of a chat."

Before Trent could snap out an insult, a sharp pinprick touched the side of his neck, and Julien moved to support his weight as he stumbled, his vision blurred.

"What did you—" Trent managed to get out, but Julien only gently shushed him, and then he slumped into the larger man's grip and slipped out of consciousness.

14

Julien had limited time before the sedative wore off. He didn't like to resort to involving outsiders, but the boy had clearly involved himself by protecting the fairy to begin with. He buckled Trent's sleeping body into the back seat of the car and drove back to his safe house as quickly as he could. He parked near the back entrance of the building to avoid being seen carrying an unconscious teenager into his apartment, but he still had to wait near the corner for the room to clear before hefting Trent over his shoulder and hurrying into the elevator.

He had cleared the living room of everything that wasn't appropriately intimidating, leaving only a heavy metal chair and a dresser laid out with various tools. His sofa had been a casualty of the barghest in any case. Julien wasn't really in the business of kidnapping people, but if that's what it took to get the creature off the street, his conscience would be clear.

He dropped Trent in the chair and cuffed his hands behind his back, looping the chain through the bars on the back of the chair. He only had the one set of handcuffs, so duct tape would have to suffice for the ankles. Julien stood back and looked at his captive, checking for any possibility of easy escape. This boy was a human, he reminded himself—not much chance of catching Julien off guard with some unpredicted ability. He took the wallet and phone from Trent's pockets and set them on the dresser out of reach. Now he only had to wait.

By the time Trent opened his eyes, Julien was in the middle of a piece of toast, but he jumped to his feet and dusted off his hands on his jeans at the younger man's soft grunt.

"Bon matin," Julien said, bending over to look Trent in the face. "Sorry for the, you know...fft." He mimed injecting his own neck. "I had no other choice."

Trent watched him without answering for a moment, his brain not quite caught up with his eyes. He tried to move his arms and found his wrists bound together. "What the hell is this?" he snapped, jerking the chain against the metal chair.

"Ah, don't hurt yourself," Julien chuckled, and he dragged a second chair into the room to sit across from Trent, slouching back in it to light a cigarette. He took a drag before speaking with a lungful of smoke. "I won't be accused later of damaging you on purpose, tsé?" He let Trent see the handgun tucked into his belt while he let out the breath of smoke. "Relax. Julien Fournier. And you are Mr. Fa, ouais? You can make yourself comfortable."

"Are you crazy?" Trent gave one more experimental pull on the handcuffs. "You can't get into my building, so you kidnap me?"

"I can get into your building," he said. "Getting what I want out of it is another thing entirely. Much easier to have the monster come to me, hm?"

"Only one of you has kidnapped anyone that I know of, so who exactly are we calling a monster, here?"

Julien shook his head and rocked his chair on its back legs. "Je veux pas péter ta balloune, Bibou, but that creature you've been protecting is a killer. You have to know that." He took another drag from his cigarette and tilted his head back to exhale the smoke. "The last woman it killed died only three months ago. It moves quickly."

Trent hesitated, an unpleasant weight in his chest. Three months ago, Ciaran had been with some woman, and now he was acting like—Trent frowned at the twisting in his stomach that he refused to admit was jealousy.

Julien let his chair drop back to the floor, and he leaned forward to peer into Trent's avoiding eyes. "What's that face, Bibou?" He stood to move closer to his captive as he took a breath of smoke, pausing to tap the ash into a small ashtray on the dresser. A slow realization came over him, and he bent down again to look Trent in the face. "Wô minute, là. You *like* it. You two have gotten close, hm?" Trent wouldn't look at him.

"Tch," Julien scoffed. "Tabarnak, t'es ben niaiseux! You don't know what you're involved in. I should have seen it, though. It seems to go for the pretty ones." He chuckled.

"Are you done?" Trent snapped. "Or did you just bring me here because you're lonely?"

Julien took Trent's phone from the dresser and held it in front of him. "It's at your apartment, right?" Trent didn't answer, so Julien flicked the phone screen to turn it on and scrolled through the saved contacts as he put out his cigarette. He found one named 'Home' and called it, turning on the speakerphone. He glanced back at Trent. "You think it'll answer the phone?"

"Why the fuck would he?"

The phone rang and rang until the voicemail clicked on, and Julien listened to the simple message while he waited for his turn to speak. "Bonjour, Monsieur la fée," he started cheerfully, circling Trent as he spoke and lingering behind him. "You should pick up the phone if you want to keep your human friend in one piece." He waited a moment and heard nothing. "No? But he misses you so badly. Say hello, Bibou," he said, and he held the phone close to Trent's face and snatched his head back by his hair, drawing a small grunt from the younger man. Julien leaned down until his cheek almost brushed Trent's, and he chuckled. "Ask your lover to come for you," he said. "Or I'll break your hands."

"Fuck you," Trent ground out, but before Julien could respond, the line gave a telltale click, and the robotic woman's voice on the other end told him to press 1 if he wanted to re-record his message. The hunter paused, uncertain, and then he ended the call as he pulled away from his captive.

"It didn't answer," Julien muttered with a frown, purposely

avoiding Trent's glaring eyes. He hadn't anticipated this. Had he overestimated the creature's attachment to the boy? What could he do if the fairy wouldn't come? He couldn't just kill a human teenager for no reason. He would try again, he decided. In a minute. He pressed his lips together to keep his worry from reaching his face, and he slipped Trent's phone into his pocket. "Perhaps he doesn't care what happens to you, hm?" he teased, hoping it hid how troubling the thought was for the hunter as well.

Trent scowled up at him. "That sucks for you," he snapped. "Guess you'll have to let me go."

Julien tutted at him with a small chuckle. "I think not. Your fairy friend probably just needs more convincing."

Back at Trent's apartment, Ciaran sat cross-legged on the sofa with the Xbox headset on, firing wildly across the map and shouting curses into the microphone, the sound of gunfire and explosions completely drowning out the sound of the ringing phone.

Trent slouched back in his provided chair and snorted. "He's not an idiot. He's not going to put himself in danger for me."

"We'll see," Julien murmured, and he leaned against the bedroom doorway to light another cigarette. If he gave it a few minutes, surely the fairy would hear the message, or change its mind, or pick up if he called again. He couldn't kill the boy, but he couldn't exactly just give up and let him loose after this, either. He had kidnapped a teenage boy—who by all appearances seemed to come from a very wealthy family—and tied him up in his apartment. He had threatened him. At this point, Julien was what you would call committed to the plan.

The hunter exhaled smoke as he watched Trent, hoping he hadn't horribly miscalculated. If he was forced to let the boy go, he would surely go straight to the police, and Julien would have no choice but to leave the city. He wasn't ready to leave yet. Not with the fairy still on the loose.

As he reached the end of his cigarette, the cell phone buzzed in his pocket, and Julien did his best to hide his relief as he saw the number marked "Home" show up on the screen.

"Bonjour," he answered pleasantly, and he took one last puff from his cigarette before snuffing it out in the ashtray.

"Who the hell is this?" Ciaran's voice came through the speaker.

"I think you know," Julien said, and he approached Trent with a slight tilt of his head. "And I think you know who I have with me, hm?"

"You think you can ransom him?"

"Ouais, I do," Julien murmured with a faint smile on his lips.

"Just hang up the phone, Ciaran," Trent said loud enough to be heard, and Julien's hand whipped out, his knuckles cracking against the younger man's jaw as he backhanded him. Trent grunted as his head snapped to the side, and he tasted the blood at the corner of his mouth.

"I would so hate for things to get violent," Julien said with mock sincerity.

"Stop it," Ciaran snapped. "He isn't who you want."

"C'est vrai!" Julien took hold of Trent's chin to look down into his glaring face. "I don't care about him at all. But you do."

"I didn't expect you to fight dirty," Ciaran spat. "Aren't you supposed to be the good guy?"

"Pantoute," Julien answered gravely, shaking his head. "I'm not the good guy. I just hunt the things that are worse than me. Today, that means you. You want him safe and sound? I'm happy to trade."

"This is bullshit," Trent called up toward the phone. "He's not going to do anything, Ciaran. You can't hunt people from jail."

Julien laughed. "It's your choice, friend," he said into the phone. He picked a small knife from the collection on the dresser and dug the blade into Trent's arm, earning the desired shout of pain. "Your lover has a lot of blood," he said, wiping the blade of the knife clean on Trent's shirt. "You really should come before he loses it all."

Trent heard Ciaran give a hiss of annoyance through the phone, and then the fairy finally said, "Where?"

"Good choice." Julien gave him the address of the small apartment. "We'll do a fair trade, hm? If you don't start trouble, I'll let your pretty friend go about his business. Nobody wants this to get messy."

"I'll be there." The phone gave a small click as the call ended, and Julien dropped it back onto the dresser along with the knife.

"Now we wait," he said, and he turned his seat around to sit with his arms on the back of the chair. "He isn't going to play fair, you know." He reached into his pocket for his lighter and lit another cigarette.

"Why the hell should he? You're crazy," Trent muttered, trying to keep his throbbing arm still as it dripped blood onto the floor.

"You're sleeping with a murderous fairy, and I'm the crazy one?"

"We're not—" he started, but then he grit his teeth and went silent.

"Ah, unrequited love perhaps?" Julien laughed in a puff of smoke. "The creature has that effect on people. At least you'll be able to move on soon."

Trent didn't answer him. When Julien left the room to watch the street from the window, he tested his legs and hands again, but the handcuff chain only clanked against the metal of the chair and cut painfully into his wrists. If Ciaran didn't come, how long would the hunter keep him here? He hoped Ciaran didn't come. He was recovering, but Trent had still caught him more than once leaning against the counter for balance or taking slow breaths to hide his fatigue. He probably hadn't helped himself by maintaining an illusion for Trent's father all night—if that even mattered. Was magic physically exhausting? Trent knew absolutely nothing about how any of it worked.

He couldn't tell how much time passed before the front door opened. There was no knock, no hesitation—Ciaran stepped into the room as though he belonged there. Julien stood just behind Trent's chair and smiled broadly at his guest.

"So glad you decided to come," he said despite Ciaran's sneer.

"Let him loose," the fairy snapped without preamble.

"Tsk tsk," Julien tutted, shaking his head. "I'm not chasing you again. Let's get this over with, and then I won't need your lovely friend anymore." He let his arm rest on Trent's shoulder, his thumbnail lightly scraping down the bound man's jaw. Trent twisted his head away with a scowl.

"Don't touch him," Ciaran growled. "I didn't come to play games."

"I hope not," Julien answered grimly, and he stepped out from behind Trent's chair, pulling a long knife from its sheath at the back of his belt. "You remember this?" The iron blade glinted in the light as Julien used it to gesture toward the fairy at his door. "I won't miss again."

"Just go, Ciaran," Trent called, jerking once more on his bound hands.

"Too late for that," he said with a faint smile. "He knows how to get me now." He nodded across the room to Julien. "All right then. Let's have it done."

The hunter approached him with a cautious step, watching for any sign of trickery, and at the moment the fairy was within reach, he vanished. He flickered out of sight right in front of Julien's eyes, reappearing behind him and hitting him hard in the jaw as he spun around. The hunter stumbled back a step but immediately recovered, lunging forward with practiced certainty. Ciaran grimaced as the edge of the knife grazed his arm, and he lifted a hand to Julien's face, letting loose a blinding flash of light that sounded with a sharp crack. The hunter grunted and turned his face away too late, colored spots dancing in front of his eyes.

"Not so easy when you don't sneak up on someone, eh friend?" Ciaran taunted, and when Julien charged at him again, he snatched the hunter by the wrist and pushed forward against him, forcing him to double over as his arm twisted backwards. Ciaran pressed against the other man's wrist, prying the knife from his hand and hissing as the iron touched his skin. The knife dropped to the floor with a loud clatter, and Ciaran gave one more shove forward, the bones in Julien's wrist breaking with a sickening crunch hidden by his cry of pain. Ciaran shoved the hunter away from him and let him hit the floor with a thud.

Julien cradled his broken wrist as he got to his feet, but Ciaran didn't give him time to recover. He moved close to him in one long stride and gripped him by the jaw, bending near to his face and softly blowing a cool blue smoke into the other man's lips. Julien could only fight until the vapor reached his lungs, and then he went slack, crumpling to the ground as Ciaran released him.

Ciaran kicked the iron blade away from him with a small grunt of disgust, his breath coming in weak, shallow pants. "Glad for my fairy bullshit now, aren't you?" he said with a glance at Trent that earned him only a small smile. He clutched at the wound on his arm as he walked to the dresser, knocking aside jars and various tools until he found a knife made of steel instead of iron. He held it tight in his hand as he moved to stand over Julien, and he tugged the man onto his back by his shirt.

"What are you doing?" Trent spoke up from his chair, pulling helplessly at his bonds.

"I won't live with a shadow," Ciaran muttered, dropping down on his knees to straddle Julien's unconscious body with a heavy, exhausted thud.

"You're just going to kill him? Just like that?"

"Just like that," Ciaran snarled over his shoulder, sweat beading on his brow and beginning to trail down his ashen face.

"This is exactly who he said you were," Trent said quietly. "A killer. Was he right?"

Ciaran paused, frowning at the look on the younger man's face. Trent didn't know him as well as he thought he did. He didn't know who he was. Not really. Ciaran wasn't sure he wanted him to.

He looked back at Julien, helpless and exposed, certain to come after him again if he left it like this. Certain to put Trent in danger again. The knife felt heavy in his hand as he lifted it, the blade ringing softly as it scraped across Julien's shirt. He stopped with the tip resting over the hunter's heart.

"I thought he was wrong about you," Trent said behind him, the disappointment in his voice like a weight on the fairy's shoulders.

This man had bested him once. He had killed Maddy. He had tried to take Trent from him and might try again—but without him, he never would have known Trent at all. That was worth something. And vengeance wasn't worth what Trent would think of him afterward.

With a frustrated grunt, Ciaran tossed the knife away. He put a hand on Julien's chest to push himself to his feet, and he opened the handcuffs keeping Trent in the chair with a simple touch. As soon as the younger man's hands and feet were free, Ciaran stumbled, and Trent had to rush to catch him before he hit the floor with as much grace as the hunter.

Ciaran weighed next to nothing in his arms, though he slumped against Trent with his eyes shut and his breath slow. Trent shifted the other man to lift him behind the shoulders and knees, pausing with a short sigh as Ciaran's head fell against his shoulder.

Tess Barnett

"You're stupid for coming," Trent murmured, but Ciaran couldn't hear him. He hesitated a moment, watching Julien's motionless body on the floor, and without a second thought, he set Ciaran down in the nearby chair and knelt down beside the hunter. He reached to take the gun from Julien's belt, watching him for any sign of consciousness, but the other man lay still. Trent grabbed his cell phone from the dresser, had a quick look outside, and then fired two shots, burying one bullet in the wall and breaking the window with the next. He wiped the handle of the gun with his shirt, dropped it back by Julien's hand, and gathered Ciaran quickly in his arms again. The fairy stirred but only gave a tired groan, and Trent shushed him as he hastily made his way out of the apartment, leaving the door open behind him. As soon as he was on the street, he called the police to report gunshots inside the building and hurried down the sidewalk in search of a taxi.

15

It was surprisingly easy to get Ciaran back to the apartment without questions, once Trent remembered that passers-by couldn't see him. He probably looked a bit strange walking with his arms cradling air, and the taxi driver gave him an odd look as he hefted nothing into the seat beside him, but it was better than trying to explain the unconscious man whose blood was the wrong color. He let Ciaran rest against him the entire drive home and carried him up his building's steps to the lobby, holding the smaller man against his chest and brushing aside the doorman's probing questions. His injured arm was throbbing painfully by the time he reached his apartment door, but he held the other man tight until he could lay him on his bed.

The cut on Ciaran's upper arm oozed black blood into the sheets, and Trent could already see the infection spreading like cracked glass around the edges of the wound. He put a hand to Ciaran's sweat-covered forehead, feeling his heated skin, and he rushed to fetch a cool, damp cloth from the bathroom. He laid it across Ciaran's brow and set about cleaning the wound as well as he could, wiping the blood from his skin with a gentle touch. He hadn't seemed this bad when he first arrived—but then, the old injury on his stomach hadn't fully healed, and now here he was injured again by the same weapon. What had he said it was, iron? Whatever the hunter had cut him with, it definitely didn't agree with him.

While Ciaran slept, Trent cleaned and bandaged his own wound, which hurt but wasn't nearly as dangerous. Hopefully, whatever the fairy had done to knock the hunter out would stick, and the cops would have an easy time collecting him. Firing the gun had been the easiest way Trent could think of to get the cops after the hunter without actually involving himself and having to try to explain Ciaran. A jail cell would be enough to get him off their backs until— until Ciaran left. Trent finished the thought with a slight frown.

It was never a question whether or not the fairy would leave. He supposed it would be longer now that he was even worse off than before, but he would still leave. As soon as Trent asked him for a favor, he had said.

Trent shook his head and took the cloth from Ciaran's brow, rinsing it in the bathroom sink and replacing it once it was cool again. He watched the fairy take a few uneven breaths, and then he settled beside him on the bed, interlacing their fingers as he shut his eyes on the pretense of being woken up if Ciaran moved.

The sound of the front door closing woke him before Ciaran did. Trent sat up in the bed, hissing a soft curse as he put weight on his arm, and he hurried to the bedroom door just in time to see his father enter the living room. In a panic, he stepped out and slammed the bedroom door behind him, holding the door knob behind his back as though he could hide his secret by hiding the door.

Mr. Fa looked at him curiously, his gaze immediately dropping to the bandage on his forearm. "What happened there?"

"Nothing. It's not serious. I went to the store, and…a bike messenger clipped me. It's fine."

His father tutted at him, walking over to pick up his wrist and inspect the bandage. "You should see a doctor."

"It's really not that bad. I'm fine." He pulled his arm away and moved into the kitchen in an attempt to get his father away from the bedroom door. At least Ciaran was sleeping, and thus at least less likely than usual to make trouble.

"You don't look fine," Mr. Fa said, watching Trent as he filled a glass of water from the tap. "You're a mess. Aiya, were you sleeping at this hour? You need a better schedule."

Trent drained his glass and set it on the counter without turning to look at his father. The day had been too long for him to care what his father thought about how much he slept.

"Well, you should get yourself cleaned up," Mr. Fa went on, not seeming to notice that he was being ignored. "I've made us reservations for dinner."

"I really don't feel like dinner right now, fu chan."

His father clicked his tongue in annoyance. "I thought you said you were fine? Hurry up and get ready. Are you sure Ms. Hickey can't join us?"

"No, she can't," Trent said softly, his hands slowly tightening into fists on the kitchen counter.

"She can't have classes this late. You should take her out more often, even if it is with your father—I'll need to get to know her better."

Trent wanted to shout at him. He wanted to argue, to tell him the truth—about himself, about Ciaran, about everything. He couldn't. But he wanted to.

"Son," Mr. Fa started behind him, and Trent heard his footsteps on the tile floor as the older man approached him. "I know we have had…troubles. But you have a nice place to live, you go to a good university…and now that you have decided to give up this lifestyle—"

"Lifestyle," Trent echoed, finally looking up into his father's face. He almost laughed. "You have…no idea what it's been like for me since that day." He turned to face the older man, his hands clenched tightly at his sides. "Back then, I thought…I thought you would be upset that I brought someone home. I thought that when I told you the truth, it would be a shock, but that you—" He paused, his confidence wavering in the face of his father's stare. "That you would understand."

"Son, there are simply certain things that are not—"

"I know," he cut him off. "Things that aren't suitable for a family like ours. You told me." Trent hesitated, a weight in his chest that he hadn't felt in some time. He had spent so long avoiding this very conversation, dodging questions, changing the subject. But he could remember Ciaran's green eyes looking into his, his soft voice and the warmth of his hands on his face. *There is nothing wrong with you.* "It's not a *lifestyle*, ba ba. I can't just…turn it off. It's who I am."

His father's brow furrowed as he frowned. "But, Ms. Hickey—"

"She isn't real!" Trent snapped, and he let out a frustrated sigh. He couldn't tell the truth, but he couldn't listen to one more relieved comment about his imaginary girlfriend, either. "She's just…a friend. She thought she was helping by pretending to be my girlfriend while you were here."

Mr. Fa stared silently for a moment, mouth slightly open in disbelief, and then his face twisted into a scowl. "You lied to me."

"Isn't that what you want?" Trent growled. "You want me to tell you that I'm straight, and I'm—"

"Now that's enough," his father cut in, taking a step forward and lifting a threatening finger to his son's face. "This has gone too far, Trent. You were young before, and I was willing to overlook some—indiscretions. But you're a man now, and soon you'll have a man's responsibilities."

"I'm doing what you want," Trent answered, exhaustion in his voice. "I go to class, I study, I don't get into trouble. I've always been top of my class. I don't drink, I don't party, I don't stay out all night. What else do you want me to do? I'm doing everything I can—"

"Do you understand that everything you have is because of me?" Mr. Fa gestured around the apartment. "This place and everything in it. Those clothes you're wearing. The tuition for that school you go to. I have given you everything, and all I've asked in return is that you make me proud. Do well in school. Get a respectable job. Have a family. This is what I want for you; do you understand that?"

Trent couldn't contain his scoff. "You're saying I'm ungrateful?"

"I'm saying you have responsibilities to this family!"

Trent's shoulders fell slightly, and he took a step back from his father and shook his head. "Don't worry, fu chan. I've known for a long time that being your son comes with strings."

Mr. Fa cleared his throat as if to distract from his outburst, and he checked his watch. "If you aren't coming to dinner, I'm going to meet some coworkers. I'll get to the airport on my own." He turned and disappeared into the guest bedroom, returning a minute later with his small suitcase. He moved to the front door and paused in the hall, turning to look across the kitchen at his son. "You need to think very carefully about your future, and how much this means to you. The next time we talk, I will expect you to have made a decision."

As Mr. Fa turned the door knob and left the apartment, shutting the door behind him with a soft click, Trent slumped back against the kitchen counter. He supported himself with his hands and stared down at the floor with an empty feeling in his chest. His father was saying that his financial assistance wasn't a certainty. That his love was conditional. Trent knew that—he had known it for a while—but to hear it out loud was a different matter. His choices were to tell the truth and be cast out onto the street, or to live the life his father wanted for him, dead or screaming on the inside.

A quiet creaking from the bedroom pulled him from his thoughts, and he stepped over to the door to find Ciaran sat up on his elbows in the bed with a pensive, frowning look on his face.

"You should be sleeping," Trent said. The fairy only looked up at him with a furrowed brow.

"So that's really how it is, eh? With your da."

"It's not your problem." He sat at the edge of the bed and pushed Ciaran down by his shoulder, testing his forehead with the back of his hand. "You're still feverish. Go back to sleep. I'll go get you some more food."

Ciaran gripped the younger man's hand before he could pull it away, squeezing it tightly and refusing to let go. "I came for you," he said in a low voice. "I bled for you, and I spared that bastard's life for you. So don't tell me what's my problem."

Trent paused, an uncomfortable clenching feeling in his chest. "I don't want your sympathy," he said rather than acknowledging it, and he tried to pull his hand from Ciaran's grasp. "I didn't ask you to do those things—I didn't ask you to come here in the first place."

"As ucht Dé, you are a spiteful thing," the fairy grumbled. "I'm here whether you want me or not."

"I don't want you here!" Trent snapped, his resolve weakening under the other man's patient stare. His throat felt tight from holding in the flood of shouting that threatened to escape him. When he felt

Ciaran's fingers squeeze his, just slightly, he let out his held breath in a sigh and sank forward until his forehead touched the fairy's chest. "I don't want any of this," he said weakly.

Ciaran put a hand to the back of Trent's head, letting him take as many slow, steadying breaths as he needed. When he calmed down, Ciaran let him sit up, but he kept a hand on the side of his face to keep him close. "It's not as bad as all that, you know," he said softly.

"How can I make this choice? I lie, or I…I lose everything."

"Ask me to fix it," the fairy said, and Trent looked down at him without answering. Ciaran's thumb brushed his cheek, threatening to break what little composure he had left. "Ask me to fix it," he whispered.

"I won't," Trent answered, his voice strained. "I won't solve my problem by becoming him. He wants to change me, and I…want to be better than that." He reluctantly removed Ciaran's hand from his face, pulling away from him as he got to his feet. "I'm going to get some food. I'll…I'll be back in a minute." When Ciaran opened his mouth to speak, Trent held up a hand. "Don't. I…need to think about this. About everything."

He left the fairy alone in the bedroom and hurried out of the apartment, fighting the urge to hold his own stomach as he walked out onto the street. He didn't want to admit the real choice he was making. It wasn't between a show wife and a nebulous, potential future love. It wasn't even between a wife and being alone. A week ago, he would have said the answer was easy. He would be alone until he couldn't put his parents off anymore, and then he would give in, find a woman he didn't hate too much, and marry her. Force himself to be with her, have a child or two. He would have been the ideal son, and his parents would have been proud. Even though he had accepted this future for himself, now the thought of it turned his stomach. He wasn't choosing between pretending and living on the street.

He was choosing between pretending and Ciaran.

Trent stopped walking, letting the other people on the sidewalk swerve to avoid him. As much as Ciaran irritated him—he was sarcastic, messy, demanding—he had never felt at ease around someone the way he did with him. People in general were boring, superficial, and only occupied with the pointless minutiae of their own lives. Trent never enjoyed talking to people, and he absolutely despised the mindless chit chat that seemed to be a necessary part of social interaction. But Ciaran sat beside him without speaking, and neither of them felt the need to fill the silence.

Ciaran made him laugh, and he was patient with him when he acted like a petulant child. He wasn't human, and it was absolutely a terrible idea for Trent to get attached to him. He barely knew the first thing about what Ciaran even was, or what it would mean for them to be...*together*. But he'd never felt his heart race just from being near to someone, or wanted so badly to touch them. He'd never seen that soft look in anyone else's eyes, or that faint smile on anyone else's lips. Without Ciaran, he never would have had the courage to stand up to his father as much as he had. Even as socially stunted as he was, Trent could do the math. He loved him. He loved him, and the realization was terrifying.

Trent was brought back to reality by someone bumping into his shoulder as they walked past, and he muttered a quick apology as he resumed his journey toward the grocery store. He walked in a daze, his heart loud and too fast in his ears. Love? Love had never entered into any scenario he'd imagined for his future.

What would he say? Should he say anything? How could he? Ciaran was apparently four thousand years old and definitely well acquainted with relationships of all kinds. What would he possibly say if Trent confessed how he felt? Even the thought of saying something so embarrassing made him queasy. Ciaran would laugh at him, definitely. Even if they did get along, what could someone like Ciaran possibly feel for him outside of a passing interest?

He filled his grocery basket with whole milk, cream, sweet bread, and cakes, cookies, and muffins of all kinds. He paused with his hand on a box of mint cookies and gripped them too tightly, his thoughts seeming to go faster than he could keep up with. He had always thought that finding someone he could stand to live with would be enough of a challenge. Love was a completely foreign word to him. What were you supposed to do when you loved someone? What did you say to them? How did you treat them? Most importantly, what if they didn't feel the same way?

Trent dropped the box of cookies into his basket and made his way to the checkout, barely making eye contact with the clerk as he paid for his groceries. The bags seemed heavier than they should be in his hands as he walked back to his building. At the door to his apartment, he hesitated, his heart thumping in his chest so loudly he was sure other people could hear it. There were two possible outcomes. Either Ciaran felt the same way, and the choice would be easier, or he didn't—and everything would go back to the way it was. Ciaran would get well, he would leave, and Trent would end up doing what his father wanted. With that at stake—he had to know what the fairy's answer would be. He would have to say something. He just needed time to figure out what that something would be.

He opened the door and set his bags on the kitchen counter before peeking into the bedroom. Ciaran was fast asleep, one arm draped over his stomach. Trent let out a sigh of relief. He couldn't talk to him yet. He needed more time. He put the groceries away as quietly as he could, then lingered uncertainly near the bedroom door. He wanted to go in only a little bit more than he wanted to shut the door and never have to look at Ciaran again. It was too big a gamble. The fairy was injured right now, anyway—this was no time to be having serious discussions. He would let him rest.

Trent pulled the bedroom door closed without actually clicking it shut, and he settled on the sofa in the quiet living room, the full weight of the day finally hitting his shoulders. Just that morning, Ciaran had cornered him in the shower—a memory he quickly pushed to the back of his thoughts—and then in the same day, he had been kidnapped and subsequently rescued by fairy bullshit, then told his father that yes, unfortunately, he was still gay. Oh, and he had also realized that he was in love with the fairy currently asleep in his bed. Somehow, that last one still seemed the most problematic.

16

Trent eventually dozed off on the sofa, only waking up when he heard a cabinet door drop shut behind him. It was dark out; he must have been asleep for some time. He turned to face the sound with panic in his chest that was confirmed as he saw Ciaran in the kitchen, searching through the cabinets. The fairy had changed out of his dirty clothes but again decided against a shirt, instead helping himself to a pair of Trent's sleep pants. They were a bit long on him, so that the hems pooled on the floor around his feet, and they hung low enough to show the lines of his lean hips and a hint of the soft hair just below the waistband.

Ciaran looked over at him with an easy smile that made his stomach tighten. "Not quite so panicky now?" His voice still sounded a bit weak.

"I bought food," Trent said instead of an answer, and he stood to walk to the kitchen, taking the long way around the island rather than squeezing by the other man. "But you shouldn't be up. You need to be in bed—sleeping. You need to be sleeping in bed." He couldn't look him in the face. He could feel the burning heat in his own cheeks, and the last thing he wanted was for Ciaran to catch him blushing. How could he be so calm? With a brief sigh, he reminded himself that his revelation had only been one-sided. "So you…go. And I'll bring you something."

"Such service," Ciaran chuckled. He leaned against the counter in an attempt to hide how tired he was, but his chest still ached from the exertion of holding himself upright. "Are you all right now, after all that?"

"I bought lots of food," Trent said again, turning away from him and hiding behind the refrigerator door. He didn't know how the other man could be concerned about him when he was clearly still sick himself. "Lots of things you'll like. So just…go away. Lie down, I mean."

Ciaran hesitated, waiting to see how long Trent would pretend to be looking for something in the fridge, but the younger man was determined not to look at him. "Fine," he said at last, and he slowly pushed away from the counter and made his way back to bed. He heard Trent moving around in the next room for a few minutes, and then he appeared in the doorway with a tall glass of milk and two slices of spiced cake. He still pointedly kept his gaze away from the fairy's face as he approached the bed.

"There's honey in it," Trent said as he pushed the plate and glass toward him, his eyes on the door.

Ciaran took the offered food with a confused frown. The glass was warm. As soon as the items were out of Trent's hands, he took a step back from the bed and awkwardly shoved his hands into his pockets. Ciaran obediently took a sip of the warm milk, sighing at the calming effect the sweet mixture had on his empty stomach.

"You sure you're all right, there?" he asked, trying to catch Trent's avoiding gaze. "You're a bit scattered."

"I'm fine," Trent answered too quickly, almost before Ciaran had finished.

The fairy tilted his head skeptically, and for the first time he noticed the hot flush of color in the other man's cheeks. Trent, looking nervous and shy? This was a treat. A sly smile curled his lips, and he set the glass and plate on the night stand beside him.

"Won't you sit with me a while?" he asked, feigning only slightly more feebleness than he felt.

"I have—studying. Homework. I have homework."

"You know it's the middle of the night, don't you?" Trent did his best to hide his grimace, but he could only look down at the floor. "Come on. Sit." He patted the bed next to him, and Trent hesitated before slowly circling the bed and taking a seat at the very edge, keeping plenty of distance between them.

"Just...eat your food, okay?" Trent grumbled.

"I don't know if I feel up to it," Ciaran sighed, slouching against the headboard. "You might have to feed me."

"Have to—" Trent stopped, biting the inside of his cheek in a vain attempt to curb the heat rising in his face. This was all wrong. He was supposed to have time to think, to work out the right thing to say, not have Ciaran in his bed half naked and asking to be spoon-fed. He didn't at all like the rapid pattern his heartbeat had taken on, and he definitely didn't like the tiny, twitching smile at the corners of the fairy's mouth. He was being teased.

"Unless there's something you'd rather talk about," Ciaran pressed with as much innocence as he could muster. He almost felt bad taunting the younger man, but truth be told, he felt just as much quiet anxiousness in his stomach as he could see on Trent's face. Trent was going to ask him for that favor now, he knew. He'd decided to take Ciaran's offer of changing his father's mind, or even worse—his own, and he was embarrassed to say it. Ciaran kept a smile on his face, but in the back of his mind, he was waiting to be proven right and set free. He didn't think this was a request he could say no to, despite his earlier spitefulness. If Trent asked him now to use magic on him, he would do it, and he would leave, the same as he'd left all the others as soon as he had outlived his usefulness.

He watched Trent with a more serious expression than he intended. "Go on then," he said softly. "What do you want to talk about?"

Trent shifted anxiously on the bed, looking down at his hands. "I wanted more time," he said without looking up. "I don't—how am I supposed to say this?" He shook his head. "No. I need—I need more time."

"Just ask me!" Ciaran snapped, more harshly than he meant. His heart felt heavy as Trent looked at him with an uneasy frown.

"Just...let's have it done," he finished in a softer tone.

"Ask you?" Trent hesitated. "I don't...want to ask you anything. Unless—I guess I do. But I need to tell you more than ask you."

Ciaran paused, his eyes narrowing slightly as he watched the younger man stumble over his words. "Tell me what?"

"I don't know. Maybe nothing. This is stupid. You're stupid," Trent said in a rush.

"You wanted to tell me I'm stupid?"

"No, I—this isn't right."

"I don't think I'm following, Trent."

Trent huffed out a sigh, finally looking up at Ciaran's face. "I think I'm in love with you," he said, his face burning red.

"You—" Ciaran started, but then he didn't know how to finish. All the air had left his lungs. He could only stare, his mind wiped clean of all thoughts except the other man's words on repeat. *I think I'm in love with you.*

"I said it, okay?" Trent got to his feet and took a step toward the door. "So just—get all your laughing done already so I can forget this ever happened."

"Stop," Ciaran called as Trent moved to leave. "Come here." He sat up straighter on the bed and touched the spot beside him. When Trent didn't move, he frowned at him and said again, "Come here."

Trent reluctantly did as he was told, taking his assigned place on the bed with a hesitant glance at the other man.

"I'm not laughing," Ciaran said. "If this is how you've decided to play it, then don't. I know I've teased you a lot, but this—don't do this." He couldn't listen to this again. He was done entertaining lies, and he was done risking himself. "Just tell me what you want."

Trent frowned at him. "I don't understand you," he murmured. "You follow me around, you try to help me with my father...you came to get me from that hunter when you could have just skipped town and not had to deal with any of it. All of that, and all of the teasing and the flirting—was all of it just because you feel like you have to...pay me?"

"I won't be lied to," Ciaran insisted. "Too many—" He stopped himself. With Trent's softly furrowed brow staring at him, he had almost let it all slip.

Trent got to his feet again and turned away from him. "You can't just do everything that you've done and—and be the way that you are, and then—you made me think that—" He sighed, holding his elbows in his hands as though he could keep the weight from settling in his stomach. "I should have known better than to tell you. Stupid," he cursed at himself. "Just...forget I said anything."

Ciaran's heart sank. When Trent took a step, he reached out to grip the back of his sleeve. Trent glanced at him over his shoulder with a pained expression that made Ciaran want to pull him close and never let him go. He hated to think he was the one who had put that look on the younger man's face.

"That isn't...what I meant," the fairy said in a whisper. "I'm sorry." He glanced down at the bed, urging the other man to retake his place there. Trent seemed wary, but he sat, his hands tightly gripping the edges of the mattress. There was no point in keeping it from him now. Trent deserved to know why Ciaran was so untrusting, and Ciaran wanted to tell him. He would tell him anything to wipe that frown off of his face.

"It's been the same with me for a long time," Ciaran began softly. "People...want things from me. They pretend to be my friend, but they know what I am, and they think that by being friendly, they can get what they want. The honest ones come right out and ask without pretending, but others...I've been led on, is what I'm saying, and I'm just—I can't do it again."

"Ciaran," Trent said, disbelief on his face, "I...can't *stand* you. My life has been nothing but trouble and drama and bullshit since you showed up here. You make a mess of the apartment, you bother me while I'm studying, you watch stupid TV shows, your eating habits are absolutely disgusting, you...you have no sense of personal space, you interfere with my family—if I wasn't in love with you, I would have murdered you by now."

Ciaran let a faint smile touch his lips. "Well, when you put it like that."

"You know what I mean." Before he could start again, Ciaran took his face in his hands, leaning in close to press their foreheads together.

"Say that again," the fairy whispered, and he shut his eyes at the feeling of Trent's wavering breath on his lips. "That last bit."

"I would have murdered you?"

Ciaran hissed at him in frustration, but Trent smiled. "I'm in love with you," he answered softly.

"Tá mé i ngrá leat," Ciaran murmured, his fingers curling into the soft hair at the back of Trent's neck. "A ghrá geal."

"Yeah," Trent said after a moment. "I don't...actually know what you're saying."

"I love you," Ciaran clarified, leaning back just enough to look him in the eyes. "I love you."

Trent scoffed and then regretted it when he saw the look on Ciaran's face. "You're serious."

"Weren't you?"

"I—of course I was! You think I'd say something like that just—to anyone?"

Ciaran smiled at him, and Trent felt a calm warmth in his stomach that he hadn't anticipated so soon after such an embarrassing confession. Any thoughts about his father and his future were a thousand miles away. Ciaran was there, in front of him, not laughing at him, but saying that he felt the same. Saying that he trusted him not to hurt him like the others. Anything beyond the next moment didn't seem to matter.

"I'm glad we cleared that up," Ciaran chuckled, letting his thumb brush the younger man's cheek. He leaned close to him until his nose touched his cheek, but he paused as Trent's fingers gripped the blanket uncertainly. He waited, Trent's breath mixing with his own, until the other man moved ever so slightly and closed the gap between them. Ciaran's grip tightened on him as their lips met, and he pulled Trent closer to him, finally nipping at the bottom lip he'd been watching for so long.

Trent couldn't breathe, couldn't think, couldn't do anything but lose himself in the sweet taste of honey on Ciaran's lips. He let his hand move to the fairy's hip as he tried to steady himself, but the hot flesh under his palm only made him more lightheaded. He moved as Ciaran guided him back, kneeling over the other man on the bed and pressing into him desperately as he deepened their kiss. Ciaran's tongue brushed his, drawing a slightly startled groan from him, and Trent pulled back, holding himself up on his hands to catch his breath. Beneath him, Ciaran's face was flushed, his lips parted as he panted for air. Trent would have liked to take credit for the breathless and half-lidded look on the fairy's face, but he knew it was at least partially due to his lingering fever.

"We should...slow down," Trent said, but he didn't move from his position over the other man. He didn't want to forget the sight of Ciaran's hair against the pillow, his gold amulet fallen back and pulling the leather strap tight around his neck. Trent gently tugged the pendant from underneath Ciaran's shoulder and settled it back on his chest. "You need rest."

When Trent moved to leave, Ciaran's fingers fastened tightly into the front of his shirt. "No more running from me," he said softly.

Trent hesitated. He put his hand over Ciaran's and gently pried his fingers away, laying his hand back on the bed as he got to his feet. "You need rest," he said again. He had never considered himself the sort of person who couldn't hold back, but every time Ciaran touched him, he felt a yearning tug in his gut that he'd never known before. He knew that if he kissed the fairy again now, he wouldn't be able to stop, and Ciaran wasn't well. "Eat something, finish your milk, and go back to sleep. I'll...be right here. Just give me a minute."

He went into the bathroom and shut the door behind him, then leaned on the vanity to wash his face. His heart was still racing, and he felt just as feverish as Ciaran looked. He glanced down at himself and attempted to will away the ache that had begun to stir in him. He refused to be that typical—rescued from danger, then confessing love to his rescuer and falling into bed with him the very same day? It was too much. The memory of Ciaran's flushed face and the unsteady rise and fall of his chest would be enough for now. That, and the softly whispered Irish that he could still feel against his lips.

By the time Trent opened the bathroom door again, Ciaran was dead asleep, but the glass of milk on the night stand was empty, and he had left only a few crumbs of spiced cake behind. Trent found himself smiling faintly as he watched the fairy in his bed curl up on his side and draw the blanket up around his chin. He considered leaving him be and sleeping on the sofa or in the guest room, but Ciaran was right. If he was going to be honest—if he was going to admit how he felt—he couldn't keep running. He couldn't keep avoiding him.

Trent unbuttoned his shirt and slipped it from his shoulders, dropping it into the nearby hamper. His pants followed shortly after, but for the sake of his own sanity, he kept his boxer briefs right where they were as he set his glasses on the night stand. He paused at the edge of the bed, feeling awkward in his own bedroom, and then he gave a quick, steeling sigh through his nose and pulled the blanket back to climb into the bed beside Ciaran. Ridiculous to feel so embarrassed after what they'd already done together. But this was different. He lay facing Ciaran's back in the darkness for some time, watching the silhouette of his shoulders rise and fall with each breath. Somehow, lying beside him like this, not even touching, was just as exciting as any passionate touch they'd shared in the last 24 hours.

Ciaran shifted after a while, giving a small grunt of discomfort, and Trent inched closer to him. He hesitated after every incremental movement, doubting himself and trying to calm his pounding heart, until he could feel the heat of the fairy's back against his chest. Then he slipped his arm forward and wrapped it around Ciaran's waist, letting his hand lay near the other man's chest. Trent's stomach tightened as Ciaran's fingers intertwined with his, holding his hand close enough to feel his heartbeat. The fairy fit perfectly into the curve of Trent's body as he settled against him, back to chest, and Trent could smell the faint natural sweetness of the other man's hair. If this was what love felt like, he would give up every cent of his father's money just to make it last a little bit longer.

17

Noah found Julien's apartment door open when he returned home from work, and when he looked inside, his dinner and his yoga bag slipped from his hands and fell to the ground.

"Julien!" he cried out before he could help himself, and he rushed into the apartment and dropped to his knees at the hunter's side. He pushed the other man's blonde hair out of his face and tried to rouse him, but he only laid still on his back. Noah's breath left him at the sight of Julien's broken wrist, the flesh reddened and swollen and his hand twisted to an unnatural angle.

"Jesus, what happened to you?" He was almost afraid to touch him. "I told you not to do anything stupid," he said, and he leaned down to check the hunter for breath. Steady breaths, and no sign of injury that Noah could see aside from his wrist. Was he unconscious or asleep?

Noah perked up at the sound of footsteps on the stairwell outside, and when he spotted the dark blue uniforms in the hallway, he rushed to his feet and shut the door in a panic. He stood with both hands on the door, listening and praying that this was a horrible coincidence, but then he jumped at the loud banging knock a few moments later.

"VPD," a man's voice said clearly through the door.

"Oh God," Noah whispered to himself, silently cursing Julien's relentless stupidity. He had warned him. He had told him.

"We had a report of gunshots," the voice pressed. "We're going to need you to open the door."

Noah clicked open the door just enough to peek out, attempting to put himself between Julien's sprawled body and the officer's line of sight. "Evening," he offered, knowing how shifty he must have looked. Noah didn't even like police on a good day.

"Heard anything suspicious tonight, sir?"

"Uh, nope, just the usual poverty-stricken neighborhood problems here," Noah rattled off too quickly. "Don't know anything about any gunshots, sorry, you gentlemen have a good—"

"How long's that window been broken?" the officer cut him off, putting a hand on the door to keep Noah from closing it. As he leaned to get a better look, Noah instinctively turned around, and then he found himself pushed backwards into the room as the officer forced the door open.

"Hands on your head!" the man snapped, his hand already on his sidearm, while his partner knelt at Julien's side to feel his pulse.

"He's alive," the officer confirmed.

"Of course he's alive! Nobody got shot!" Noah insisted, lacing his fingers behind his head as the officer spotted Julien's gun on the floor. This was bad. This was so bad. They were definitely going to be curious about the amount of guns in the apartment, and they were definitely going to think that Noah had broken Julien's wrist and knocked him out—though how they supposed he had beaten up a man almost twice his size, he couldn't imagine. They were going to ask questions about how they knew each other, and who Julien was, and maybe even talk to neighbors who saw the two of them carrying a number of black garbage bags out of the building the previous night. Oh, this was so bad.

The officer on the floor was already talking into the radio on his shoulder. Noah raised his gaze to the ceiling for a moment, a steam of obscenities running through his head, then he took a deep breath. He dropped his hands from his head, and at his word, a gust of wind tore through the apartment with Noah at its center, sending both men flying backward and crashing into the walls. Noah pulled their guns from their hands without touching them, letting them clatter to the floor at his feet. When the men tried to get up, he forced them down with a word, pinning them to the floor and silencing their shouting voices with a gesture.

"Fuck," he swore, panic setting in now that their eyes were on him in the quiet room. "Just, this isn't what it—fuck!" He trotted into Julien's bedroom and pulled the bedding from the mattress, then gingerly laid the blanket over the top of one of the officers, making sure he still had room to breathe. He covered the other man with Julien's sheet and stood in the center of the room, then lifted his hands and let them fall helplessly to his sides with a heaving sigh. This was so, so bad.

Noah did a quick sweep of the apartment for anything that might have Julien's name on it, then made a renewed effort to wake the hunter up. He shook him, slapped his face, and shouted at him, but got no response. With a huff, he lifted Julien by his uninjured arm and attempted to pull him to the door, the larger man hardly seeming to move.

"Oh, for the love of—you are so fat," he hissed. Noah carefully positioned himself and heaved Julien's torso onto his back, lifting to his feet with a strained grunt. He took slow steps to the front door and poked his head into the hall to check for witnesses, then carried on, Julien's toes dragging along the concrete walkway behind him. "You had better be so grateful," he muttered. "You stupid, stupid—you had better be okay," he finished in a smaller voice.

Noah had nowhere to take him. He just had to get him away. He moved as fast as he could with the hunter's large body on his back, taking quick, labored steps to his own apartment door. This was so stupid. But he didn't have a car, he didn't have any family in town— not that he would have wanted to bring a monster hunter to their door in any case. This was his only option. Noah managed to get his apartment door unlocked and dropped Julien onto the sofa, then darted back to the hall to retrieve his dropped belongings.

As soon as he was shut inside, he raced into his bedroom and snatched his pencil case from his bag, fumbling with the sticks of charcoal as he returned to the door. He started to draw a large circle on the wall around the entrance, but he had to drag a folding metal chair from his kitchen to stand on so that he could finish the top curve above the door. He sketched his chosen symbols around the edge of the circle and at the center, muttering to himself as he racked his brain for the right words. He couldn't make the door invisible, per se, but he could hide it. If he could just remember the words, he could create an illusion on the opposite side of the wall, making it appear flat and concealing the door itself. Someone could still touch it if they knew it was there, but Noah hoped the illusion would be enough to protect them from intruders at least until he could figure out something better.

Noah pressed his palm to the center of the circle, pausing to make sure he had the incantation right in his head, and then he shut his eyes to whisper it. A low pulse flowed from the door under his hand, making him sway on his feet, and he opened his eyes to peer at the circle. It seemed intact, which was a decided improvement over his last attempt.

He turned back to look at Julien, still snoozing on the couch. It must be sleep; at least, Noah hoped it was sleep, since if he was just unconscious, he would almost definitely have some sort of brain damage by now.

The witch gave a small sigh and stacked up what pillows he had under Julien's dangling arm. His fingers were beginning to look quite purple. Maybe it was better if he was asleep until Noah could fix his wrist. If Noah could fix his wrist.

"Fuck," he whispered again, and he gathered up anything he thought might be helpful. All he had was herbs and stones—not even a real magical knowledge of how to set a broken wrist, let alone a practical one.

Noah set down his armful of supplies and pulled a dusty book from its shelf, wiping the cover with the bottom of his shirt as he knelt beside the sofa. With book in hand and a variety of ingredients at his disposal, Noah was at least able to set the bone and wrap it with some herbs and small chunks of agate, which he hoped would be helpful to the process. Now all he had to worry about was the fact that Julien was still, despite all the witch's prodding, fast asleep.

He tried a number of spells that he knew off-hand and some that he had to look up, but nothing would rouse the hunter from what was clearly an enchanted sleep. Had the gean cánach done this? Noah didn't like his chances against fairy magic. Was it even possible to undo a fairy curse, if that's what this was? Was Julien going to waste away, or would he stay healthy and handsome until the spell was broken? Noah imagined him pricking his finger on a spinning wheel.

A faint heat burned Noah's cheeks as that daydream reached its inevitable conclusion. If it was an enchanted sleep, then—Maleficent was a fairy, after all, wasn't she? Now he was taking cues from Disney movies. Noah scooted closer to the edge of the sofa on his knees, looking down at Julien's peaceful face, and he brushed aside a lock of the hunter's dirty blonde hair. He bent down close on the pretense of checking his breath, but he paused very close to the other man's face, his heart thumping rapidly in his chest. He licked his lips, hesitating, and then he let out a groaning laugh and pushed himself to his feet. He paced the living room with his hands in his hair, puffing out his cheeks in a sigh. Ridiculous. Even if there was the slightest chance of that actually working, if he ever was going to kiss Julien—and that was the biggest "if" he could think of—he didn't want it to be while the hunter was unconscious.

Fine. Time to break out the big guns. Noah gave a final huff and let his hands drop, then stepped into his bedroom and opened the dresser drawer. Candles of every color rolled to the front of the drawer, and he picked out every white one he could find. He nudged the drawer closed with his elbow and clicked open the chest of incense on the floor, digging out the scented sticks he needed and kicking the lid closed on his way out. He set up the candles wherever there was flat space and tucked the incense into the frog-shaped holder on his coffee table.

Noah went to the kitchen and took the large box of salt from a cabinet, then poured a wide circle around his sofa and coffee table, enclosing Julien inside the ring. He paused as he set the box back on the counter. Iron. Iron would be helpful.

He went back to the bedroom, tossing aside dirty clothes and empty water bottles as he searched. He finally found the small box he sought and pried it open, revealing a small collection of various bric-a-brac he had collected over the years—including an old railroad spike he had found in an empty lot some time ago. When you're a witch, collecting random interesting bullshit frequently pays off, and this was one of those occasions.

Noah carried the spike to the living room, carefully stepping over the circle of salt on the floor. He set it down gingerly on Julien's slowly breathing chest, and then he set about lighting the candles and incense. He clicked off the lights on his way back to the sofa and sat cross-legged on the floor, taking a deep breath as he settled. It was hard to focus, as anxious as he was, but he shut his eyes and tried.

He wasn't certain how much time went by with the incense filling his nostrils as he whispered to himself in the dim room, but he slowly became aware of the air around him growing hot. He could feel sweat forming on his brow the longer it went on. The cheap wind-up alarm clock in his bedroom ticked so slowly that it sounded like a sledgehammer, each second booming in Noah's ears. Eventually it blended together into a heavy, deafening drone.

The room felt tighter, closer somehow, as though the air itself was closing in on him. His head pounded as he struggled to stay upright, and when he thought he couldn't bear it anymore, something cracked. He felt a sharp pain in his chest and had to catch himself on his hands as he fell forward. He opened his eyes to a dark room full of snuffed candles and cold incense, sweat dripping from his chin as Julien stirred in front of him.

Noah let out a breath of relief as the hunter opened his eyes. "Thank God," he chuckled.

Julien only stared at him in a daze for a few long moments. "Noah?" he croaked, his voice dry and weak.

"Just wait," the witch insisted, and he pulled himself to his feet and rushed to the kitchen to fetch Julien a glass of water. He kneeled on the floor beside him and helped him drink, setting the glass aside once he'd had his fill. "Your wrist is broken, and you were asleep," Noah said softly. "But you're all right now. Except for being stupid," he added as an afterthought.

"The creature," Julien started. "I underestimated it. I thought it would be weaker. It came for the boy—I think he's been affected. He seemed defensive of it. They're...more than friends, I think."

"More than—oh. Oh," Noah said, his eyebrows lifting. "Well that's...something. Isn't a gean cánach supposed to seduce *women?*"

He desperately wanted to ask how Julien felt about the idea of two men being more than friends, but this didn't seem like the time. He would definitely use it as an excuse to ask later.

"I don't know for sure that it's the toxin." Julien shook his head. "If it is, it's too late for him anyway."

"Wait, wait," Noah interrupted. "What do you mean, he came for the boy?"

"I used him to lure the creature here. I thought I would have an advantage."

The witch put a hand to his forehead. "Julien, you kidnapped someone? What is wrong with you?"

"I need to get back there before they try to run," he said, apparently choosing not to address the question.

"You need to not do anything else stupid today," Noah objected. "This thing already broke your wrist. You're lucky he didn't kill you."

Julien sighed. "He may have been weak. I'm sure I cut him with the iron knife. But he was so fast, I—" The hunter swore. "I need to try again before he recovers."

"Tomorrow, okay? At least give it until tomorrow."

Julien frowned at him, but he was already settling back into the couch cushions. "I am...a bit tired."

"Give your wrist a night's rest. I tried to help, but it's still going to take a while to heal. You need to take care of yourself."

Julien sighed. "Fine. ...Thank you, for your help."

"Anytime," Noah smiled. He could bring up the police in the morning. They had probably gotten up by now; he had only intended to keep them pinned for a short time. Who knows what they had told their fellow officers when they got free. There hadn't been anyone coming to break down the door yet, so at least his illusion seemed to be holding.

"Are you hungry? I mean, I dumped my supper on the ground because I came home and you were unconscious on the floor, so I'd have to scrounge something up, but that's doable."

"It cast some spell on me," Julien grumbled. "Some sort of—I'm not sure. There was a kind of smoke. I barely realized what was happening before I was asleep. How long would I have slept if you hadn't helped me?" he asked quietly, and Noah wasn't sure if he was talking to him or not.

"Until you were old and wizened," Noah grinned, hoping to lighten the mood and distract himself from the soft, grateful look in the older man's eyes. He hopped to his feet and moved to the kitchen, searching his cabinets and fridge for anything that wasn't crackers or beer. "You should definitely be grateful."

Julien sat up slowly and watched him over the back of the couch. "I am grateful," he said, a sincere frown on his face.

Noah's smile faltered, and his hand tightened on the refrigerator door. He bit anxiously at one of the piercings in his lip and shook his head. "I'm kidding. It's not...a big deal, you know? Just...being neighborly," he finished in a softer voice. He hid his head in the fridge and took two beers from the door. He held them up for approval and popped the caps off at Julien's nod, handing him one of the bottles and turning back to his empty kitchen.

"Well, I've got some eggs," Noah shrugged. "Or there's enough bread left for some grilled cheese. Pick your poverty dinner poison."

Julien took a long drink of his beer before answering. "Do you know how to cook?"

"I know how to cook *eggs*, Julien," Noah scoffed. "Just shut up. I'll make something."

Julien relaxed on the sofa while the witch made simple omelets, listening to him hum softly as he worked. They ate together, Julien on the couch and Noah on the floor near him, neither of them entirely satisfied by the meal but neither one complaining, either.

"So why do you do what you do?" Noah asked when his beer was almost empty. "You know, kill things. You seem to get hurt a lot, and there clearly isn't any money in it."

"It's the family business," Julien answered with a small shrug. "There are many Fournier men, and this is what we do. I was born for it." So he hadn't been kidding about having target practice as a kid. What kind of family trains up their kids for such dangerous work on purpose? Noah couldn't imagine.

"Well that's...a little depressing, actually," he said after a moment.

"Pourquoi depressing?" The hunter drained his bottle of beer. "There are many monsters in the world, mon râleur, and the more I kill, the better."

"How many of you is a lot?"

"I have six brothers, as does my father before me."

"Holy shit," Noah laughed. "Fertile family, huh?"

"I'm not sure it wasn't on purpose," he mused. "As the seventh son of a seventh son, I'm said to have been blessed. There must be some truth to it, as I've always been able to see through creatures' illusions. Beyond that, I'm not sure it means much."

"Well that's a sort of magic of its own, isn't it?" Noah smiled.

"Perhaps," Julien grumped. "But I won't be lumped in with monsters."

"How do you classify a monster?" Noah watched him with a soft frown. "Does something have to be...you know, bad, or...does anything magic count?"

Julien looked down at the witch without answering for a moment. "It depends on the magic."

"Magic like mine," he pressed, regretting the words almost as soon as they were out of his mouth.

The hunter sighed as he reached down to set his empty bottle on the floor. "You aren't a monster, Noah. I hope you know that. Some witches are dangerous, but...I do not believe you are. You have the potential—all witches do—but you have a good heart." He shifted on the sofa, avoiding the younger man's gaze. "Aside from that, you are...my friend."

The word dropped a hundred pounds of weight on Noah's shoulders. His friend. "You really...think of me that way?" he asked in barely more than a whisper. He didn't want to hear the answer. He didn't want that final confirmation that his feelings were baseless, hopeless.

"Of course," Julien answered carelessly, offering the witch a small smile.

"Of course," Noah echoed, nodding without looking up at him. "But what if—" he started, but he stopped himself, and instead of continuing, he gathered up their plates and empty bottles and carried them to the kitchen.

"You don't have to be afraid of me," Julien insisted, completely misinterpreting the younger man's meaning, as always. "I'm not going to hurt you."

"Yeah," Noah agreed, though a pit had formed in his stomach and a lump in his throat threatened to choke him. He swallowed it down and washed their plates, setting them upside down on a towel on the counter. "It's been a long day," he said when he found his voice again. "You should rest. You can have the bed if you want; I know that couch is a piece of shit."

"This is fine. You've done enough for me, Noah. Thank you."

"Sure. Now get some sleep. Some real sleep," Noah clarified, and Julien offered him a resigned nod as his eyes drifted shut from exhaustion.

The witch sat on the floor beside him, listening to the faint snore that told him the hunter was resting naturally, and he leaned to let his head rest against Julien's shoulder. "Idiot," he muttered, a small sigh escaping his lips.

18

Ciaran woke first in the morning, his hair stuck to his forehead with sweat. He began to grumble out a complaint, but paused when he woke up enough to feel the slow breath against his shoulder. He turned his head to see Trent's sleeping face on the pillow behind him, looking far more serene than he ever did while he was awake. For as brusque as he acted, Trent really was quite insecure. Ciaran would have to tread carefully with him, he knew. He would have to tread carefully with himself, for that matter—it had been more years than he could count since he had gotten far enough to admit to someone that he felt more than lust, and even longer since he had believed anyone else's heartfelt confession. If Trent woke up and decided to ask him for gold or wishes, he would probably give up on relationships altogether.

He was distracted by Trent's fingers tightening on his hip, and he let out a soft chuckle as the younger man pressed against him with undisguised urgency. So much for taking things slow. Ciaran reached behind him to touch Trent's hair, and he rolled his hips against the hard press of the other man's erection. Trent gasped softly behind him, his forehead falling against Ciaran's shoulder.

"Good morning," Ciaran murmured as the other man pressed back against him, hands clutching him tightly and pulling him close. Ciaran twisted in his grip, ignoring the pain in his arm as he put weight on his wound, and he caught Trent's lips in an eager kiss with none of the other man's previous resistance. Trent accepted him with a soft, breathless groan, his fingernails scraping the fairy's back as he clung to him. When Ciaran's hand slipped down between them, Trent jumped, and he broke the kiss without retreating, breath coming in heavy pants.

"Stop," he whispered, which was clearly contrary to his wishes. "Please."

Ciaran pulled away from him with a slight frown, though he was relieved to lie on his back again instead of pressing on his injured arm. Trent's hand held his with a pleading grip. Ciaran reached out for him, running his fingers lightly through the younger man's hair and letting his hand rest on his neck.

"What's the matter?"

"I'm sure that this isn't such a big deal to you," Trent murmured. "The...sex. But I can't just...this is life-changing for me." He glared up at the fairy as soon as he opened his mouth. "Shut up. No dick jokes." He sighed. "I mean, if I do this with you—not just sex, but everything—then my father will kick me out. I won't have anywhere to go. Something like that...it has to be because I've decided, and not because I just got carried away and slept with you. I know that doesn't make sense."

Ciaran smiled at him and tilted his head to catch Trent's eyes. "You are a tender thing," he chuckled, earning himself a spiteful frown. "Fine." He leaned close and pressed a long, lingering kiss to the other man's lips. "We'll go slow."

Trent sat up, keeping the blanket around his hips, and he looked down at the fairy in his bed with a quiet sigh. "I didn't think I'd be so sentimental about it," he muttered.

"Well, you're such a sentimental person," Ciaran quipped, and Trent shoved a pillow over his face.

"I'm having a shower," he said as he stood. "Alone. You stay in bed."

"Slow sucks," Ciaran called behind him as he shut the bathroom door.

Trent knew that if he lingered under the hot water, his mind would wander, so he scrubbed himself as quickly as possible and wrapped the towel around his waist to keep decent until he could step into his closet. It all felt too surreal. He was half convinced that he would wake up soon, and his entire yesterday would be a lie. He only hoped that the police had actually been able to catch his kidnapper—the man hadn't shown up at Trent's door in the middle of the night, so that was something, at least.

Ciaran was watching him from the bed when he emerged from his closet, and Trent could practically feel the fairy's eyes on him as he buttoned his shirt.

"So what happens?" Trent asked, finally looking over at Ciaran as he fastened the last button. "If we're...together. If that's what we're doing. Is that what we're doing? Shut up," he added before the other man could even speak. "Never mind."

"Do you fret this much about everything? Is this just my special peek into your running inner monologue, darling?"

"Don't call me—I don't *fret*," Trent insisted. "I just want to know what to expect." He sighed. "I don't know what *you* expect. From me."

"I expect that you'll fret and fuss for another day or so, and then you'll give in and finally let me ravish you properly."

Trent frowned at him. "I didn't think it was just about sex."

"Of course not," Ciaran laughed, "but we've gotten the difficult bit out of the way, haven't we? Feelings are complicated; sex is simple."

"It isn't simple to me."

"Come a little closer and I'll explain it to you."

"I'm serious!" Trent snapped. He hesitated and bit his cheek. "I haven't ever—" He didn't want to finish the thought. Ciaran would definitely laugh at him. The fairy was—supposedly—four thousand years old; his sexual history would probably be incomprehensible to someone like Trent, whose entire experience consisted of rushed, fevered touches and awkward kissing after school.

Ciaran sat up in the bed with a deadly serious look on his face. "You haven't ever what?"

"Shut up."

"You haven't ever what?"

"Nothing."

"Haven't ever what, Trent?"

"I haven't ever had sex!" he finally snapped, his face burning red.

Ciaran let out a single laugh and then covered his mouth to stifle it. When Trent scowled at him, he said, "No no, that's amazing." He let his hands drop back to his lap and looked across at the younger man with a predatory smile. "That means you're all mine."

Trent's stomach tightened at the fairy's low voice, and he took a small step backward out of instinct. "You said we'd go slow," He reminded him, only slightly wary.

"Oh, I'll go so slow you won't be able to stand it," Ciaran promised.

"I was trying to ask you a serious question."

"Well you can't lead with 'I'm a virgin' and expect me to keep paying attention," Ciaran chuckled.

Trent gave a short huff, feeling a flush in his cheeks as the fairy spoke the word he'd been trying to avoid. "It's not like I've never done anything," he objected in a grumbling voice.

"I'm sure. I was there for our interlude on the couch, remember?" He perked up slightly. "Was that your first blowjob, in the shower?"

"What—no," Trent sighed, and Ciaran seemed slightly deflated by the response. "Look, I'm just trying to ask you—what this means. Aside from sex. I know it's all easy for you, but you aren't the one who's going to have to tell my father that I'm giving up his money and most likely having to quit school and be homeless."

Ciaran's face softened slightly. "You think I won't be standing right beside you when you tell him that?"

Trent paused, the other man's words causing an uncomfortable throb in his chest. "I hadn't...thought about it."

"You aren't alone, Trent." Ciaran pulled himself out of the bed, though it was clearly difficult for him, and he stepped over to the younger man and took both of his hands in his. "That's what this means."

Trent looked down at him and gave a quiet sigh. "You aren't wearing any pants."

Ciaran leaned his head on the other man's chest. "I took them off while you were in the bathroom. It was hot."

Trent smiled at the fairy's soft weight against his chest. "Get back in bed. You're burning up."

"You aren't going anywhere, are you?"

"No. I'm not going anywhere."

Ciaran nodded and let Trent guide him back to the bed, then burrowed under the covers like a child. Trent sat beside him to check the wounds on his arm and stomach. The old injury seemed to have been reinvigorated by the new infection—the bruising looked darker than it had before. The fresh cut had almost sealed, but the spiderweb of black veins was troubling. Trent looked up at Ciaran's drowsy face, slightly flushed and beginning to show dark circles under his eyes.

"Are you...going to be all right?" Trent asked as he pulled the blanket back up over him.

"I'll be fine," Ciaran assured him, though his eyes were already closing. "You just got me a bit worked up with all this virgin talk." He smiled despite Trent's sigh. "I am going to absolutely ruin you," he promised. It was slightly harder to be embarrassed when the words were half-mumbled into a pillow.

"Shut up and go to sleep," Trent said as gently as he could manage. When Ciaran was still, Trent leaned over to check the clock on the night stand. He should have been getting ready to go to class. There wasn't any point anymore, was there? He'd never really cared about banking in the first place—it was just to make his father happy. His father wasn't going to be happy about anything anymore.

Trent stood up from the bed with as little jostling as he could, and he moved into the living room and pulled the door shut behind him to let Ciaran sleep. He looked at his phone, abandoned on the kitchen counter, and he felt a strange churning in his stomach that was somewhere between anxiety and excitement. The worst possible end scenario was that he told his father to screw himself and then it didn't work out with Ciaran—he'd be alone on the street. If that happened, would he go back? Would he apologize to his father on hands and knees, beg his forgiveness, and have a wife after all? He couldn't imagine caring what else happened to him if Ciaran decided he was a mistake.

He shook his head as he leaned his hands on the kitchen island, staring down at his phone. He felt like a coward. It was the right thing to do to stand up to his father, even if Ciaran had never existed. He should stand on principle and be strong. Maybe someday he would make his own YouTube video about how it got better. Maybe it never would get any better. Trent put his elbows on the counter and let his head rest in his hands.

He had already decided. He had seen the warm smile on Ciaran's face and felt it in the pit of his stomach when the fairy softly whispered to him. If he was ever going to take a risk on anything, it had to be this. This had to be worth it.

Trent picked up his phone and unlocked the screen, then scrolled through his contacts to his mother's phone number. He had never spoken to her about that day. When he had tried to explain, she shut him out, practically plugging her ears rather than have to listen to him. His father had informed him repeatedly how much he was upsetting her, but she would never talk about it herself. His infrequent phone calls with her were the usual superficial pleasantries—she asked about his school, if he was making many friends, if he was getting enough to eat and had enough money—but she never asked him about his "problem" the way his father did, as though it was an illness he was having a particularly slow recovery from.

He touched her number and lifted the phone to his ear to listen to the ring. He fully expected to get her voice mail like he did nine out of ten times he called her, but she picked up on the second ring. She worked for HSBC just like his father did and had just as little free time, but it was late evening in Hong Kong now.

"Mou chan," he started, but she cut him off with rapid Cantonese.

"Yunxiang, what is going on? Your father called me; aiya, he was so upset! What did you say to him?"

Trent sighed. His mother always called him by his middle name; what she called his "real" name. She was much more attached to Hong Kong than he and his father were; her English was still spotty and she had protested him staying in Canada for university. She was the reason he had spent every summer as a child back in Hong Kong, until he was old enough to stay home by himself. Whenever he had visited as a teenager, it had been because she prodded at him for weeks on end and claimed that he was losing his culture.

"We had an eventful visit," he answered her in Cantonese. "He didn't tell you what happened?"

"He was so pleased when I spoke to him before. He said you had a girlfriend! But then yesterday he calls and says that it isn't true and that you've been lying to him? What is going on?"

"Mou chan, I did…meet someone," he began carefully. "But it isn't like he thinks."

She was silent for a moment. "What is it like?"

"I told him the truth. He wants me to be this person that he thinks I should be, and I've tried, mou chan—I've really tried—but I can't. I can't be that person. I can't fake it and I don't want to. I know you don't want to talk about it, but—"

"Aiya," his mother sighed. "You told your father these things?"

"Yeah."

"And what did he say?"

Trent hesitated. "He basically told me that if I didn't fall in line, he'd cut me off."

"And is that what you want?"

"Of course not, but—"

"Yunxiang, you must have known this would make your life harder. You must have known from the moment you realized it about yourself." She paused. "You said you met someone. Is that why there's all this talk all of a sudden?" Trent didn't answer right away. "I thought so. And this person, they're going to support you if your father makes you homeless?"

He didn't want to tell her that technically his someone was homeless too. "I just can't lie anymore, mou chan. If he's going to kick me out, then fine. I'll manage." He sounded braver than he felt.

"You should let him overlook this," she pressed. "If you insist on throwing it in his face, you really will be homeless."

"Throwing it in his face? When would he even be here to see anything? I could be giving blowjobs in the street for as much as he's here."

"Aiya, watch your mouth!"

Trent sighed and leaned against the counter. "I'm going to tell him. I'm going to tell him that I'm gay and that's not changing, that I met someone and I want to be with him and it doesn't matter what dad thinks. It doesn't matter what you think, either." He waited for the barrage of noise telling him to reconsider, but it didn't come.

A long silence passed between them before his mother asked quietly, "What's his name?"

Trent was almost too stunned to answer. "Ciaran," he finally said.

"He's not Chinese?"

He laughed softly despite himself. "No, he's not. He's…he's Irish."

She let out a faint sigh through the telephone. "And you're sure about this. This is what you want to do?"

"Yeah. It is."

"Make sure you empty your bank account. Before you talk to your father. I'll put some extra in for you. And take whatever you need from the apartment. Will your Irish friend have a place for you to stay?"

He glanced over at the bedroom door. Ciaran was in no condition to be out on the street, especially when that hunter could still be loose. "Yeah," he lied. "I just…we need a few days."

"Warn me, okay? And let me know where you're going."

Trent frowned. "Mou chan…why are you doing this? After that— after that time, I figured you…felt the same way dad did. You were crying, but you would never let me talk to you."

"Yunxiang," she answered quietly, "I cried because I knew what it would mean for you. I knew this day would come. I didn't want to face it. If you cannot pretend, if you cannot put this aside, then this is the way it has to be. I don't understand you when you say it's who you are. I will never understand, and I can't stop your father. But you are my son. So no matter what he says, if you are ever hopeless, don't think I've forgotten you. You can always ask me for help."

Trent couldn't quite make his voice work. His mother wasn't angry at him. She didn't hate him. She was offering her support, in a weird, dysfunctional way. As small a gesture as it was, it lifted a weight that had settled on his shoulders since that day.

"Thanks, mou chan," he said at last. "I'll let you know before I leave."

He heard her take a single deep breath. "Okay. Well, I hope your Irish friend is worth all this trouble."

"Me too," he admitted softly. She made him promise once more to take whatever he needed when he left the apartment, and then he ended the call, dropping his phone back to the counter with a short sigh.

Trent checked in on Ciaran more often than was really necessary; he tried to distract himself by cooking lunch, preparing a disgustingly sweet meal for when the fairy woke up, and gathering up his textbooks to count how much he would be able to get by selling them back. He was anxious for Ciaran to recover, but just as hesitant at the thought of leaving behind his home and his support system. With Ciaran in his arms last night, everything had seemed perfect and simple, but in the light of day, it was a little more difficult to let go of his doubts. Ciaran had told him before that he was transient; could he trust the fairy not to lose interest in him and leave him stranded and penniless in some unfamiliar place?

He stood from the sofa where he had stacked his books and stepped over to the bedroom door, cracking it quietly to look in on Ciaran's sleeping form under the blanket. There was no point in asking questions like that anymore. Ciaran had come for him. He had put himself right in the hunter's hands when it would have been easier to run, and now he was sleeping peacefully and trusting Trent to take care of him. He slipped into the room and sat at the edge of the bed, his hand moving automatically to touch the fairy's face to test his fever.

Ciaran stirred at the touch, and his green eyes found Trent's frowning face. Trent could feel the tightness in his chest unraveling as he watched the slow smile on the fairy's lips. No more questions. When Ciaran smiled at him, he didn't want to ask them anymore. Trent held Ciaran's cheek to tilt his head and leaned over him, pressing a long, earnest kiss to his lips. He wasn't going to run anymore.

19

Ciaran slept away his fever for most of the day, periodically waking up to eat the food Trent always had ready for him. By evening, his body felt sticky from sweat and his head fuzzy from too much sleep. He crawled out of bed with every muscle in his body aching from the infection in his blood, and he poked his head out of the bedroom door to find Trent lounging on the sofa with a book in his hand. He looked more at ease than Ciaran had ever seen him, and when he looked up, a faint smile touched his lips. Had he done that? Had Ciaran put that soft expression on his face, the unguarded slouch in his shoulders? He wanted to throw the younger man over his shoulder and carry him to bed no matter how he complained—and he would have right then if he'd had the strength. Instead, he gave a longing sigh and gestured over his shoulder.

"I'm having a bath," he said. "If I don't come out after a while, I've probably fallen asleep and drowned."

"Do you want some floatie wings?"

"I think I'll manage." Ciaran grinned at him and retreated into the bathroom, filling the large tub with steaming water and happily sliding into it. He washed his wounds, which looked marginally better than they had last night, and tried to will them into healing faster. He could tell that his fever was almost gone, which was a good sign at least—the iron in his blood wasn't going to kill him. He hadn't wanted to tell Trent that that had been a possibility, and now it seemed he wouldn't need to.

Ciaran scrubbed his face and dunked his head under the water, pushing his wet hair out of his eyes with both hands. He looked up as he heard the click of the door opening, and he chuckled as Trent stepped into the room without hesitation.

"No so shy anymore, are we?"

"I've been thinking," Trent said. He was keeping his distance from the bathtub and his eyes on the fairy's face. "About some things. First, I wanted to ask if it was true that you were with some woman a couple of months ago."

He paused. "Sure. That's how what's-his-face found me."

"And if we're...together, will you still want to—will you still want to be with women?"

Ciaran chuckled. "I like women. I like men, too. Just because I'm attracted to both doesn't mean I'm incapable of monogamy, if that's what you're asking. You were jealous?"

"I *am* jealous," Trent clarified. "In general. I won't compete for you. So if that's the way it's going to be, just tell me now."

"That isn't how I am, Trent," the fairy promised. "If you want me all to yourself, that's the way it'll be."

Trent nodded, and he hesitated before starting again. "I was also thinking about...what you said about everyone asking you for things. I don't want you to think of me that way. But I've decided I do want to ask you for one thing."

Ciaran's heart dropped into his stomach, but he kept his face neutral. "Yeah?" he asked in what he hoped was a casual way, dropping his gaze on the pretense of checking the bruise on his stomach. He always did this. He always got his hopes up, told himself this time would be different. He knew Trent would be giving up his life of luxury by agreeing to be with him, and now here it was—he was going to ask for money, or for some way to stay here without his father knowing, or something. It was fair. He was giving up the life he'd always known and trading it in for nothing but uncertainty. It was fair, but it still turned Ciaran's stomach to be right.

Trent hesitated before speaking. He had his hands in his pockets to keep them from fidgeting. "If you decide...that this isn't going to work out, you have to tell me. You have to warn me. You can't just...disappear. You can't just leave me."

Ciaran looked up at him with a furrowed brow, momentarily too startled to speak. "You...that's what you're asking me for?"

Trent scowled as though the words were being dragged out of him, turning to avoid looking at the other man. "The only thing I want from you is...you. Barring that, I want honesty at least. If you can't do that, then I—I can't do any of this." He gave a short sigh. "And I...really want to do this." He looked back at him with a wary frown. "All of it."

Ciaran laughed. He leaned back in the bathtub and ran a hand over his face, then he waved Trent closer to him. When the younger man approached, Ciaran sat up and tugged him down by the hand, almost bringing him into the tub with him fully dressed. He locked a hand at the back of Trent's neck and pulled him close, unable to keep the grin off of his face. "A thaisce, a chuisle, a rún mo chroí," he laughed. He leaned back only enough to look into Trent's dark eyes. "You will have me beside you until the sun burns out. Geallaim. I promise."

Trent's face flushed slightly, and Ciaran kissed him, pulling him so hard that the younger man had to dunk an arm in the water to keep himself from falling in entirely. Trent broke away after a moment to regain his balance, shaking the excess water from his arm as he straightened.

"I'm—glad we got that sorted out," he said, his cheeks still faintly red. "Then...when you're well enough, I want to go. Wherever you're going."

"It's a deal," Ciaran chuckled. "I'm feeling better already."

Trent turned to leave, hesitated, and then carried on out of the room with a small smile on his lips.

Ciaran stretched in the tub, rotating his injured arm at the shoulder to test his injury. Bearable, and the wound was in no danger of reopening now. It would be worth the soreness later. He finished scrubbing himself with Trent's soap and stepped out of the bath to dry off, rubbing the towel over his hair and shaking out the last of the water. Without bothering with any clothes, Ciaran left the bathroom and stalked into the kitchen, where he found Trent at the counter, cutting a slice of spiced cake to go with the glass of milk he'd already poured.

When the younger man turned around, he gave a slight start and then sighed. "Ciaran, put *something* on," he said, but he was promptly interrupted by the fairy's body pushing him back into the counter. Ciaran's fingers twisted into the hair at the back of his head, pulling him down for an eager kiss that Trent was helpless to fight. He gripped the edge of the countertop as Ciaran pressed into him, a soft groan escaping him at the heat of the other man's tongue exploring his mouth. When they were forced to break for air, Trent reached up to take hold of Ciaran's wrist before he could attack again.

"What are you doing?" he asked, watching the fairy's eyes with concern.

"I don't want to go slow," Ciaran whispered, and he bit Trent's bottom lip and chuckled at the gasp it pulled out of him. "I'll be gentle," he assured him with a sly grin, "but I won't wait anymore."

"You're hurt," Trent said without much conviction as Ciaran's fingers began to work the buttons of his shirt.

"I'm well enough," the fairy countered. His hands slipped over the soft skin of Trent's chest, pushing his shirt back over his shoulders and down his arms as he bent to press a kiss to his collarbone. "Now do you want to argue, or are you going to let me take you to bed?"

A shudder ran up Trent's spine at the low promise in Ciaran's voice. He had very little idea what he was doing. He wasn't exactly innocent, but actual sex was—complicated. And a little frightening, if he was honest. He already couldn't trust himself when Ciaran touched him. Even now, the fairy's hands on his chest and stomach drove him to distraction, threatening to weaken his already severely compromised resolve. He had told himself he had time to prepare for this eventuality while Ciaran recovered, but the fairy seemed to possess supernatural recuperative abilities when sex was part of the equation.

Trent wanted this, no question, but the last thing he needed was to look like an idiot in front of Ciaran so soon after his embarrassing confession, and he had a strong suspicion that he was going to look like an idiot.

"I'm not hearing a no, a mhuirnín," Ciaran chuckled against his skin, nipping a line down his shoulder. "You don't have to be nervous. This is meant to be fun."

Trent took as steady a breath as he could manage with the fairy's fingertips brushing his stomach just above his belt. Ciaran wasn't going to laugh at him. He nodded, and Ciaran grinned at him and pulled him forward with two fingers in his belt, leading him back to the bedroom by the waist. He pushed Trent down onto the bed on his back and crawled over him, capturing his mouth in a heated kiss while his hands worked open his belt buckle.

Trent was hesitant to touch Ciaran in case his injuries still hurt him, but when the other man opened his mouth to him and slipped a hand below his waistband, he gave up caring. He pulled Ciaran close to him, groaning into the fairy's kiss as his hand wrapped around him and gave a tight squeeze. Every time Ciaran touched him, he felt like he could barely breathe—the other man's caress was insistent and firm and burning hot. He couldn't prevent his faint whimper as Ciaran's hips ground against his, but he held tightly to the other man's hair and guided the kiss in an attempt to maintain some semblance of control.

Ciaran broke away from him and tried to focus on removing the fabric obstruction between himself and Trent's growing erection, but Trent wouldn't let him go. He sat up as the fairy pulled away and held him tight, fastening his mouth over one sensitive nipple and leaving Ciaran to grip helplessly at his shoulders as he kneeled over the younger man's lap. Trent shivered at the other man's pleading groan, and he pulled him down into his lap, feeling the fairy's arousal brushing his stomach. Ciaran's hand quickly snaked between them again, gripping Trent tightly and making him jump, and at the fairy's teasing chuckle, Trent gave his nipple a sharp bite.

"Ach, such cheek," Ciaran grinned, and he tugged Trent's head back by his hair and kissed him. Both men fought for dominance of the kiss, but eventually Trent gave in, allowing Ciaran to push him back to the bed and shift down until he could slide the younger man's trousers down his hips. The fairy knelt on the floor to help Trent kick out of his pants, but he paused with his fingers in the waistband of his underwear.

"Now you do seem eager," Ciaran purred, and he nipped at Trent's erection through the straining cotton. "But this is your show, a mhuirnín. You'll have to tell me how you want it to go."

"What—" Trent began breathlessly, sitting up on his elbows to look down at the fairy in confusion. "What are you talking about?"

"Well, I want to make sure you get the full experience, of course." Ciaran grinned up at him before taking the waistband of Trent's boxer briefs in his teeth. He dragged the fabric down with a slowness that made Trent growl with need, and he lifted the younger man's hips up so that he could free him properly. When the underwear was abandoned on the floor, Ciaran touched a single, dainty kiss to the pearling tip of Trent's aching erection. "For instance, do you want this?" he whispered, his breath hot against the sensitive skin. "Or would you rather just fuck me?"

Trent's head swam. He couldn't focus with Ciaran so close to him, could hardly breathe with the fairy's tongue on his hip, scant inches from where Trent really longed for it to be. He knew he was blushing, and he felt the knot in his stomach when he saw those green eyes staring up at him, asking permission to proceed.

"Is that," he started, embarrassed at the shaking in his voice, "is that a real question?"

"It absolutely is."

Trent sighed in frustration, barely able to keep his hips from twitching upwards. Ciaran's hand flattened against his stomach to keep him still.

"If you don't answer, how will I know what you want?" Ciaran murmured as he touched a kiss to Trent's hip. "I'll have to just experiment." He took the younger man into his mouth in one smooth movement, letting out a hum of satisfaction at Trent's sudden gasp. Almost as quickly, he pulled back with a soft chuckle. "That's good then," he mused, seemingly oblivious to Trent's desperate pants. "Good to know." He eagerly returned to his work, groaning as he felt pressure at the back of his throat.

Trent's fingers were in the fairy's hair almost immediately, the heat and friction of the other man's tongue overwhelming him. He wasn't going to last long at this rate. He tried to tell Ciaran to stop, but his mouth couldn't quite form the words. When his grip tightened, Ciaran retreated on his own, pressing one final kiss to the tender tip and causing a satisfying twitch.

"Not yet. We're nowhere near finished, a mhuirnín," the fairy promised, and he crawled his way slowly up the length of Trent's body, kissing and nipping at the skin on his way. He urged the younger man further up the bed and straddled his lap to catch his lips in a kiss.

He felt too light in Trent's lap, barely half the weight he should have been, but it was difficult to think of the fairy as delicate when he was biting Trent's lip and gripping him so tightly. Trent had to gasp to catch his breath when Ciaran broke away from him. Every touch felt like lightning; every breath against his skin made him tremble. It hadn't been like this before. The first time Trent had given in, it had been out of frustration and lust. But now Ciaran smiled down at him, that playful, teasing smile that put small wrinkles at the edges of his pale green eyes, and everything else seemed secondary.

Trent pushed the other man off of him easily, turning him onto his back and pinning him with a kiss. He needed to take things slow. Not just because he was nervous, but because he didn't want this to be over before he had time to thoroughly lose himself in Ciaran's kiss. The fairy's palms were hot against his shoulder blades, and the hard press of his arousal ground pleasantly against Trent's stomach. He savored every sigh that slid from the fairy's lips, every tiny groan as Trent nipped kisses down his neck to touch his lips to every freckle on the other man's shoulders.

He watched Ciaran's breath quicken as he slipped his fingers around him, slowly stroking him until the fairy's cheeks flushed and his lips parted. Ciaran whispered something in Irish that Trent couldn't understand, but the pleading whimper in the other man's voice made his stomach tighten with need. He slipped a hand down to press against his entrance, a low chuckle forming in his throat at the sudden buck of the fairy's hips.

"Stop," Ciaran panted, and he sat up, gripping Trent in a fierce kiss before suddenly breaking away. He disappeared into the kitchen, and Trent heard him banging around in the pantry for a moment before he returned with a slim bottle of olive oil, which he dropped unceremoniously into Trent's hand. The fairy grinned at him and crawled back onto the bed, settling himself on his hands and knees in front of the younger man. "Now carry on," he chuckled with a glance back over his shoulder at Trent's reddened face.

"Wh—but I thought—aren't you...going to...?"

"If you'd rather. Like I said, this is your show."

Trent hesitated, gripping the glass bottle in his hand. Ciaran only watched him with that soft smile on his face, his skin flushed from contact, until Trent longed to kiss him again. He moved forward and grasped the fairy around the middle, pressing fevered kisses up his spine to the back of his neck, only breaking contact to spill some of the oil onto his fingertips. This part, at least, he knew how to do. He smiled against Ciaran's back as he eased one slick finger into him, enjoying the shiver he felt in the other man's skin. Ciaran dropped to his elbows with a faint panting breath and twisted his hands in the blankets as his back arched against his lover's touch.

Ciaran pushed back against him with a pleading moan, and Trent obliged his silent request, slipping a second finger inside of him and gently stretching him until he gasped. The fairy hissed as Trent quickened his pace, pushing into him while he left red marks down his back with every biting kiss.

Trent was momentarily distracted, unable to pull his eyes away from Ciaran's parted lips as he let his head fall to the bed. He wanted to touch him, to kiss him, to have all of him at once and never let him go. He was reminded of his task by the insistent twist of Ciaran's hips, though his pounding heart and shallow breath made it difficult to focus on much of anything. Ciaran pushed against him with a groan that made his impatience clear, and Trent slowly let his fingers slip free to take up the bottle of oil again.

The next step was unfamiliar to him. He struggled to keep his breath steady as he slicked the oil over himself, but his heart was beating too quickly for him to maintain any kind of composure. He didn't know how to proceed. What if he went too fast and hurt him? What if he did the wrong thing? He hesitated with his hand on the small of Ciaran's back, letting out a soft gasp as the other man ground back against him.

"Get on with it," Ciaran ordered grumpily, and Trent's face

flushed.

"Just give me a minute," he snapped, frowning down at the fairy as he turned his head to grin.

Trent took a breath, positioning himself, but then he paused. This wasn't right. He couldn't reach him. He couldn't see him. He pulled away and urged Ciaran onto his back, bending over him and capturing his lips in a kiss. Ciaran's arms wrapped easily around his neck as he shifted, and he lifted his hips to allow Trent to push into him, the younger man's head falling helplessly against his shoulder. For a while, they stayed like that, lying still to let Trent catch his breath and slow his racing heart. The sensation was overwhelming, but Ciaran's fingertips tracing the skin between his shoulder blades allowed him to at least breathe easier.

They moved together slowly at first while Trent adjusted to the sensation of Ciaran tightening around him, the fairy eagerly pushing back with every thrust as he tangled his fingers in the younger man's hair. Trent pressed as close to him as he could, kissing him until he was forced to break for breath. Everything around him was Ciaran—the heat of the fairy's body underneath him, his hands in his hair, the scent of his sweat and the soft panting breath mixing with his as their foreheads touched. He was overwhelming; too close and too warm and too tight around him. Trent moved slowly to try and keep his heart from bursting from his chest, but as he pushed deeper inside the man beneath him, Ciaran gasped and whined and lifted his hips against him.

"God," Trent breathed, his face hidden in Ciaran's neck, and his fingers tightened on the fairy's hip. He stopped moving, his breath coming in shaky gasps. He shook his head when Ciaran ground against him in frustration. "Stop," he begged, the tremble in his voice the least of his concerns at the moment. "I can't—we need to slow down."

"Slow down?" Ciaran panted incredulously. He almost said something biting, but when Trent looked down at him with flushed cheeks and parted lips, his chest tightened, and he drew the younger man's face down to him with a gentle hand. It was easy to forget how young Trent was when he was snapping out insults, but like this, with his eyes shut and his skin trembling, he seemed disproportionately innocent.

"I don't want to rush," Trent whispered against his lips. "But you're really making me want to rush."

Ciaran smiled as he kissed him. "You set the pace, a mhuirnín."

Trent couldn't even bring himself to be irate at being placated. He took a few moments to slow his heart, and as he pushed slowly into the other man again, he moaned into his tender kiss. He rocked his hips against Ciaran at an agonizingly unhurried pace, lost again in the fairy's heat and scent. As he brushed a sensitive spot deep inside the fairy, Ciaran gasped and let his head drop back against the mattress. Trent's stomach tightened at the sight of the other man's lip in his teeth, the soft movement of his Adam's apple as he swallowed. Trent gave one quick, experimental thrust, and Ciaran's hitched moan went straight down his spine.

"Le do thoil, mar sin," the fairy hissed, his grip in Trent's hair tightening almost painfully. Trent quickened his pace automatically, a groan escaping him as Ciaran kissed him and forced his tongue into his mouth.

Ciaran's pleading whimpers and grasping hands were too much for him. Trent pushed against him again and again, his hand moving between them to grip the other man's seeping erection and pump it in time with his thrusts. When Ciaran began to pant and writhe underneath him, his fingernails digging into Trent's shoulders, he could feel the tension coiling in his stomach like a spring threatening to snap. He started to pull away, but Ciaran kept him in place with legs wrapped tightly around the younger man's hips.

"Ná bac leis," Ciaran panted. "A dhéanamh, le do thoil," he whispered, and Trent could hear the begging in his words even if he couldn't understand the meaning.

Trent kept up his pace as best he could, but it wasn't long before he tensed and finished deep inside the other man, his cry muffled by Ciaran's hard kiss as he gave a few last desperate thrusts. He felt the fairy tighten around him, hips bucking as he followed soon after, spilling his climax onto his stomach at Trent's persistent touch.

Trent held himself up long enough to carefully withdraw, but then he dropped to the bed beside Ciaran, tangled in his arms in a mess of sweat and heat. Both of them fought to catch their breath, the process made more difficult by each lingering kiss. Ciaran smiled at him, one hand resting on his neck to let his thumb brush the younger man's jaw.

"Tá mé i ngrá leat, a rún," the fairy whispered, his nose brushing Trent's.

Trent leaned close to press one more exhausted kiss to the fairy's lips. "I love you, too."

20

Julien didn't sleep very well on the sofa, and his wrist ached when he woke up. He tried to slip by Noah, who had fallen asleep on the floor beside him, but the witch stirred at the sound of his step and sat up as Julien reached for the door.

"You can't," he said, scrambling to his feet to get between the hunter and the door.

"I'm just going back to my apartment," Julien promised.

"Shouldn't you...take a break? I mean, your wrist is broken, and you were unconscious, and that's *super* bad for you. Shouldn't you have a rest before you start back with all this fairy crap?"

"It isn't going to stop being dangerous just because I'm injured, Noah."

"But you said he's with that rich kid now. Either the kid's dead already or you've got some time, right? That wrist needs rest, and who knows what kind of lingering effects that sleep might have had on you? So why don't you take a few days off, you know, take a vacation somewhere out of town maybe? We could even go together, like a road trip or something," he rambled, unable to look Julien in the eye. He really didn't want to tell him the reason neither of them would be safe leaving the apartment.

Julien's eyes narrowed slightly, and he looked past the witch at the charcoal markings on the wall. "Is this meant to keep me in?"

"It's to keep people out," Noah answered with a sigh. This wasn't a secret he could keep. He took a deep breath to steel himself as he peeked up at the hunter's glaring hazel eyes. "It's just to hide the door. Look, Julien, something…happened. While you were out."

Julien frowned down at him, his voice low and too calm. "What kind of a something?"

"It wasn't my fault," Noah began, which probably didn't do much to help his case. "I found you lying there, and I went to help you, and then they just showed up."

"Who showed up?"

Noah shrunk slightly at the dangerous tone in the other man's voice, and his mouth went dry. "Cops. Two of them. They said there were gunshots. What are you thinking firing guns in our apartment building anyway?"

"I didn't fire any guns."

"Well somebody did, because the cops sure beat down the door when they got here."

"Noah, what did you do?" Julien asked, scowling down at him.

"I didn't hurt them," he said immediately. "I mean, bruises maybe, but they were fine."

The hunter stepped closer to him, forcing the witch's back against the door. "What did you do?" he said again.

Noah could feel his pulse quickening. He wanted to move—he couldn't open the door if he had to escape, and he didn't like how close Julien was. It wasn't the kind of closeness he had wanted. If the hunter tried to hit him, would he have time to move? "Look, I had to, okay?" He was painfully aware of the tremble in his voice. "You were hurt, and they would have arrested both of us. You can't go to jail. I can't go to jail. It was the only way. Nobody's going to believe them anyway."

"You worked magic in front of them?"

He flinched. "I had to. I only did as much as I needed to get us away."

"Noah, I thought you knew better," Julien growled. "You can't just do whatever you like! You have a responsibility—"

"I was saving your dumb ass from a jail cell or worse!" he countered. "You think the police would have been able to wake you from that sleep? I did that. I did that for you."

"Je m'en sacre! You cannot do magic in front of people! And worse, you used it to attack them!"

"I just—I just pinned them down," Noah said, desperate to calm the hunter down. Julien had never shouted at him before; the normally soft-spoken hunter had turned aggressive and accusing, and it sent a wash of painful memories over him. "They weren't hurt, and it would have worn off in a little while. They probably got right up! I was trying to help!"

"I don't need this kind of help!" Julien snapped. "This is a dangerous road, and if you start down it, you know I won't be able to let you go."

Noah looked up at the hunter's face with a pit settling in his stomach. There it was. Julien might have thought he had a good heart, he might call him his friend, but when it came down to it, magic was magic, and magic was dangerous. Noah was a witch, and to Julien, a witch was no different from a demon, or a vampire, or any other dangerous creature. Not human. "I was just trying to help," he said again, a little weaker.

Julien snorted at him, turning away to pace across the living room. "So now, what, we stay in here and hide? There is more work to be done," he added in an accusing tone as he looked back at the younger man.

"You know they'll be looking for you. They'll be looking for me, too. I've hidden the door, but it won't help if you go out." Noah pushed away from the door and skirted the room to avoid getting too close to Julien, hesitating near his bedroom door. "It's your life, Julien. If you want to go, I'm not going to stop you. But you're welcome to stay until we can figure out what to do. If you can stand to be here," he added softly, and he stepped into the bedroom and shut the door behind him, leaving the hunter alone.

Julien paused, opening his mouth to answer as Noah clicked the door shut, but then he stopped and gave a short sigh. He needed a cigarette. The witch had just been trying to help, Julien knew. But using magic to get away from the police was not something he could condone. He had already let him go too far with the door man the other day. If he let Noah think that he approved, the boy might do even riskier things, and Julien didn't want to be forced to take action. He had to be harsh.

He glanced back at the door and the charcoal markings surrounding it. The police would definitely still be watching the apartment. Noah was right—it would be dangerous to leave now. He needed a plan first, some way to take care of the fairy for good, and then he could leave Vancouver with a clear conscience. Noah might have to move, but it would be easy for him to disappear in the city.

He heard the shower start in the next room and moved over to the witch's bookshelf, scanning the aging spines for anything that might be helpful. Julien had imagined the gean cánach would be more clever than powerful, but the fairy had broken his wrist without a second thought. Even if he was prepared, Julien didn't like his chances with the creature one-on-one after their last encounter. He was surprised he had only been put to sleep, rather than killed. It was possible the fairy was waiting to see how he responded, to see if he had allies who would take his place if he was gone. It wasn't likely that the thing had just been merciful.

Julien ran his fingers along a row of books and plucked one out, resting it on the shelf so that he could flip it open with one hand. It was in Latin. Not much help. Did Noah read Latin? He realized there was very little he actually knew about the boy despite how much help he had been over the last few months. He slipped the book back into its place and paused. Noah had been a great help. A witch who seemed to want to do good, was knowledgeable, and was strong enough to break an enchanted sleep set by the fairy himself. Julien glanced at the closed bedroom door. Maybe the fairy wasn't the only one he had been underestimating.

He sat down on the couch to wait for Noah, listening for the creak of the old pipes as the water shut off behind the wall. Noah reappeared before long, rubbing a towel over his wet hair, and he stopped short in the doorway.

"You're...still here," he said as Julien turned to face him. "I thought maybe you'd run off to hide under an overpass until you could break back into that kid's apartment."

"I wanted to ask you something."

Noah held his damp towel in both hands as Julien approached him, wishing suddenly that he had put on a shirt. "Yeah?" he said, attempting to sound careless, but having the hunter stand so close to him was a little frightening given their recent conversation.

"A few years ago, I was tracking a woman outside Montreal, in Saint-Jérôme. A witch," he added pointedly, making Noah want to retreat from him. "This woman had killed an entire colony of dryads living near her home. She said they were infringing on her garden. I caught up to her just as she was clearing out the last of them, and I saw her use a spell I hadn't seen before and haven't since—it seemed to drain the life out of the spirits in an instant, turning them to dust right in front of me."

Noah swallowed. He knew the spell. It was dangerous to the user and devastating to the victim. He'd never met a witch who would dare to try it, but he'd heard it whispered about in a few dingy apothecaries. It was supposed to be able to kill just about anything, which was saying something in a world where things like dryads could be the least of your worries. It was said to drain the spirit from the victim, emptying it of life until nothing but a husk remained.

"Do you know anything like that, Noah?" Julien asked in a low voice.

Noah instinctively took a step backward. Was this a test? If he said he did know it, did that mean Julien suspected he would use it? He had used some defensive magic on a couple of cops, and now Julien thought he was a killer? Noah had hoped he'd done enough to earn the hunter's trust—had he ruined it just by trying to help?

"I've…heard of something like that," he admitted softly.

"Have you heard of it, or do you know it?"

Noah looked up into Julien's frowning face, watching his hazel eyes for a hint as to what he was thinking. Julien had called him his friend—as painful as that had been, having the hunter think of him as a threat was far worse. He wouldn't lie to him and get himself in even deeper.

"I know it," the witch said. "But it's not—"

"Could you do it?" Julien interrupted him. "Could you cast a spell like that?"

"What? Why?"

"It kills spirits, doesn't it? What's a fairy if not a spirit?"

Noah's eyes widened with realization, and his mouth dropped open for a moment before he could answer. "Are you saying what I think you're saying?"

The hunter gave a grim nod. "It's killing people, Noah. It's dangerous. We can stop it. You can stop it."

"Are you kidding me? Do you know how risky that spell is? Even if you do it right, it can put the caster in the hospital. It's powered by your own energy, and even people who've done it successfully..." He shook his head. "If it backfires—and it's very likely to backfire—it can kill you. Why would I want to do that?"

"Because you're a strong witch, and I believe you can do it. Because you can help me put an end to this."

"But you—" Noah started, and he let out a sigh of disbelief, pacing a quick circle in his bedroom before sitting at the foot of the creaky bed. "You got angry at me just for casting in front of people at all, and now you're asking me to use my magic to kill someone?"

"Some*thing*," Julien clarified. "This isn't a person. It's a monster."

Noah dropped his towel beside him and shook his head, leaning his elbows on his knees. "The woman you were tracking—the one you saw cast this spell. What happened to her?"

Julien frowned at him. "I put her down. She was killing the dryads for no reason; she was clearly insane. She used her magic for personal gain," he added with a pointed nod that made Noah's shoulders slump. "Who knows what she might have done if I'd let her be? Who else would have suffered for an unknowing infraction?"

"You put her down," Noah echoed quietly. He looked up at the hunter with an unpleasant churning in his stomach. "And what about me, Julien? If I do this for you, will I be a monster when I'm done?"

"You'll be doing something *good*," he answered.

"This is crazy. This whole thing is crazy." Noah stood and stepped closer to him, looking up into the larger man's face and trying to force down the lump in his throat. "Why do you care so much about this one fairy? We broke into someone's house trying to get to him, you *kidnapped* some kid to try and lure him out, and you got broken bones out of it! He could have killed you! Can't you just—give this one a rest already?"

"I can't let him go free just because it's difficult," Julien objected.

"Isn't there anything more important to you than killing things? Why is it your problem what this fairy does anyway? The world is full of things that kill other things, and it always has been. Why do you have to kill yourself trying to fight that?"

"You don't understand, Noah. This is what I am. This is what I know. I don't have anything else."

"But you could," he blurted out without thinking. "You could, if you'd just—open your damn eyes." Noah made a conscious effort to lower his voice, but his heart was pounding loudly in his ears. "You don't even see what's right in front of you because you're too stupid to think about anything but this fucking fairy!"

Julien frowned at him, his brow furrowed in confusion. "What are you talking about?"

"Why do you think I'm always asking you to take a night off, Julien? You think I bring you dinner all the time because I'm just so fucking flush with cash that I can afford to pay for your takeaway? You're so—" He paused, running his hands through his hair and letting them drop back to his sides with a frustrated sigh. "I do everything you ask me to because I want to help you, because you're so stupid but you're so—strong, and brave, and you can be so gentle and so kind, and whenever I look at you I think—" Noah shook his head, swallowing the tight feeling in his throat. "I care about you," he said instead of what he really meant, his eyes shut tight to keep from having to look at the hunter's face. "A lot," he added in a whisper.

A long silence passed between them, until Noah was forced to open his eyes and look up at Julien's quiet frown.

"I don't understand," the hunter said. "Us being friends doesn't have anything to do with what I do."

"I don't want to be your friend, Julien!" Noah snapped. "I'm trying to say I—I want more than that."

Julien paused, the full weight of what Noah was saying finally sinking in. He took a small step back, stopping at the pained look his retreat put on the younger man's face. He didn't know how to deal with this. There was always too much work to be done for him to spend any time thinking about his personal life, and a personal life that involved a male witch's affection would never have crossed his mind in a hundred years. He couldn't process it—not with his job still unfinished. Maybe not even after that.

"This has to come first," he said, hoping that would be enough of an answer. "If you want to help me, Noah, this is how you can do it. I want to trust you. So prove to me that you can use your magic for the greater good. Prove to me you aren't dangerous."

Noah dropped back to sit on the bed, running a hand over his face and letting out a small sigh. "I'm not dangerous," he whispered, staring down at the floor. He couldn't look at the hunter. He'd said too much, but it didn't even seem to matter. Julien was barely listening, just like always. "If you kill this fairy—if I help you kill him—what will you do then? Move on to the next thing, the next job, the next obsession? Is it always going to be like this for you? You never take a break, you never live your life?"

"This is my life," Julien answered simply. "I never asked you to live it with me." Julien hesitated at the witch's faint flinch. He didn't like seeing him like this—Noah was calm and casual and had an easy smile. He shouldn't be gripping the edge of the bed so tightly, and he definitely shouldn't be recoiling at the hunter's words. "But," Julien said, offering a small nod as the boy peeked up at him, "when this is done, maybe I'll...take a break. And we can talk. Moé pis toé."

"Talk?" Noah repeated skeptically.

"About everything. If that's what you want. But I can't ignore this creature. Not for any reason, you understand? It has to die."

Noah looked back at the floor and slowly shook his head. "And you really think this is the best way."

"I do."

"And you won't decide later that me doing this for you means that I know too much dangerous magic, or something?"

"Noah, you'll be proving that you're willing to do what you need to do to keep people safe. I can't ask you for more than that."

"People," he whispered. Julien didn't think of the fairy as a person, but he must have walked and talked, laughed and cried, seemed like a person in every way. If a fairy wasn't a person, why was a witch? Maybe he wasn't. Maybe Noah was an 'it' in Julien's mind, too. He leaned his elbows on his knees and put his head in his hands. Despite everything, he wanted Julien to be happy. He wanted him to be able to take a rest, whether that involved Noah or not. He knew it was stupid. He knew Julien didn't feel the way he did and probably never would. He knew he shouldn't get his hopes up. But he couldn't prevent that tiny flutter he had felt in his chest when Julien had said the simple words, 'we'll talk.'

Noah lifted his head to look up at the hunter, and he nodded. "Okay."

21

There was no preventing Ciaran from joining Trent in the shower once they managed to untangle themselves from each other, but Trent didn't mind. He expected to feel awkward or embarrassed or different somehow. As far as he could tell, the only thing that had changed was that he didn't tense up when the fairy slipped his arms around his waist and laid his cheek on his back.

Ciaran pressed a soft kiss to the back of his shoulder and squeezed him tightly around the middle. "You did very well, you know," he murmured against the younger man's skin.

Trent clicked his tongue at him. "Fuck off."

The fairy grinned. "A bit romantic for my taste, but I understand you needing to get it out of your system."

"Do you want to die? Is that what you're telling me right now?"

Ciaran turned Trent on the spot and pushed him back against the tile wall of the shower, giving his chin a soft bite. "This was a favor. Next time I'll make you beg."

"You're assuming there'll be a next time; that's cute."

Ciaran let out a low chuckle, and he leaned up to kiss his lover's frowning mouth. "You are a treat. Doesn't anything put you in a good mood?"

"I mean, you not talking always brightens my day."

"Such a sweetheart," Ciaran muttered, but he saw the faint smile on Trent's face.

They switched places under the hot water until they were both scrubbed clean, occasionally pausing to kiss or tease or trade insults, so that by the time the water ran cold, Ciaran had Trent pinned to the wall with a vicious kiss. They barely made it back to the bed before undoing all their hard work cleaning themselves.

Trent supported himself on his elbow to watch Ciaran doze beside him, idly tracing the pattern in the fairy's gold amulet with one finger. When Ciaran opened his eyes, he turned his head to touch a kiss to the younger man's wrist.

"What is this?" Trent asked quietly. He didn't want to speak too loudly for fear he might break whatever bubble they were in, disconnected from the outside world. With Ciaran in the bed beside him, both of them warmed by the other's skin, he wondered why he ever cared what his father thought of him.

Ciaran glanced down at his chest and lifted the amulet, turning it in his fingers. "Family heirloom, you might say."

"Does it mean anything?"

"Aye. It's the symbol of Anu."

"And who's that?"

"She's a goddess," the fairy said, shrugging one shoulder. "Sort of…our mother. Or so they say."

Trent tilted his head with a skeptical frown. "I thought you said you had children 'the proper way?' So is she your mother or not?"

"The mother of all of us, I meant. Ancestrally, like. You know."

Trent hummed in understanding. "Is it magic?"

Ciaran shook his head. "No. I've just had it for a very long time." He smiled up at the younger man and batted at the jade pendant around his neck with one finger. "What about this one? Any magic in it?"

He scoffed. "Not likely. It's just old—my grandmother's. It's supposed to be good luck, but my grandmother had cancer, so how lucky can it be?"

"But you wear it anyway."

"I've had it since I was a kid. It was still hers, and she still gave it to me thinking it would keep me safe, so I wear it. A family heirloom," he said, mimicking Ciaran's answer.

Ciaran watched him for a moment, and then sat up with the blanket around his waist and reached back, loosening the leather cord around his neck and pulling the gold amulet up over his head. He tutted at Trent to urge him to sit up, and he slipped the cord around the younger man's neck and tightened it so that the round talisman rested at his collarbone. While Trent frowned at him, he unfastened his silver chain and hooked the clasp around his own neck, pausing to watch for signs of disapproval. Trent only shook his head with a small chuckle, so Ciaran smiled and glanced down to inspect the jade around his neck.

"I don't want to forget," he said softly, brushing the pad of his thumb over the smooth green stone. "No matter what, I'll remember this."

"And you said I was a romantic," Trent taunted, and Ciaran shoved him by the shoulder. "So about that 'no matter what,' since you mention it. We can't just stay here. You don't live anywhere, right?"

"Not as such, no."

"So, where were you going to go when you got better?"

The fairy shrugged. "Wherever the wind takes me," he said with a laugh. "Where do you want to go?"

"I haven't really been too many places except here and Hong Kong," Trent said. "We went to Australia one summer."

"Well, spin the globe, a rún, and we'll go. You going to have that chat with your father, then?"

"I'm glad I don't have to do it in person," Trent admitted. "At least this way when he disowns me I can just hang up the phone and throw it away."

Ciaran paused, watching the younger man's solemn face, and he reached forward to gently grasp Trent's fingers in his. "You are going to live well, and fully, and you are going to be so happy that you will wonder why such a small-minded man ever mattered to you at all. I promise."

"Nobody ever made being homeless sound so good."

"So, what are we doing? You want to trash the place before we go, make a bit of a mess?"

"You need rest," Trent pointed out. "You still look like shit."

"You really know how to sweet-talk a girl," Ciaran grinned, but he settled under the blanket beside Trent and quickly nodded off, his breath still sounding slightly labored from his fever.

Trent slipped out of the bed and pulled on some nearby clothes. He would need to pack a bag. His mother had told him to take everything he needed, but what could he really take with him? Some clothes, a coat for when it got cold again, his laptop—he didn't really need anything else. It was freeing, in a way, to think about all the things he could happily leave behind. His Xbox, the rows of dress shoes and suit jackets in his closet, every textbook he'd ever had to lug across the city on a bus. He made a mental note take his more expensive watches, if only to pawn them when the need inevitably arose.

His closet seemed comically large to him now. Why had he needed so many shirts? Ciaran didn't even have any of his own anymore; the one he had bled on had been thrown away, and he'd seemed content to wear Trent's ill-fitting clothes instead. He would buy the fairy at least one outfit that suited him with the money he took from his bank account. Trent idly fingered the gold amulet around his neck as he took stock of what clothing would be best to pack and what could be easily left behind. He actually found himself smiling more often than he was really comfortable with. It hurt his face.

By the time Ciaran woke up again, Trent had filled his unused duffel bag with a few changes of clothes, his laptop, his chosen watches, and a heavy winter coat. The fairy stood quietly in the closet doorway, startling him as he turned away from his newly-packed bag.

"I want to ask you if you're sure about this," Ciaran said. "I'm still waiting for you to come to your senses, I think."

"My senses are fine." Trent slid his fingers through the other man's messy hair and bent slightly to touch his forehead to his. "This is stupid; I've only known you a week, and you've been nothing but irritating the entire time, and if someone had asked me a month ago if I thought that this sort of thing could happen so quickly, I would have thought they were an idiot. Maybe I'm an idiot. Maybe you are, or both of us."

Ciaran chuckled, reaching up to rest his hand on Trent's caressing arm. "As much as I want to tell you that you're an idiot, in this case I'm tempted to say we've been the victims of fate. She does have a sense of humor."

"I didn't even think fate was a real thing. But I'm not going to waste time worrying. You know how to get by, don't you?"

"I suppose I do by now, yes."

"And you're going to take me with you wherever you go."

"Everywhere and anywhere."

Trent smiled faintly and moved in to kiss him, lingering a breath away even after the kiss was broken. "Then it's going to be fine."

Ciaran pulled back to look up at him. "If you're trying to spend the day in bed, you're doing a very good job."

"I'm just hoping to keep you so exhausted that you shut up every now and then."

"Oh, you are going to be so sore when I'm finished with you."

Trent patted the fairy's cheek condescendingly and brushed by him, heading into the kitchen to find some food for supper. The two of them ate on the sofa—Trent's meal substantially healthier than Ciaran's, of course—while the television played catchy intro music in the background.

"Explain to me again what's going on here," Ciaran said with a mouthful of spiced cake, shaking his fork at the television screen.

"Oh my God, it's really not that complicated," Trent sighed. "It's a beauty pageant."

"So they get judged based on how attractive they are, or how much makeup they can get on their faces before it sloughs off in a sheet?"

"It's lots of stuff. Looks, whatever their supposed talent is, how well they answer pre-written bullshit questions, that sort of thing. Half the time it seems they get points just for not falling over."

"But why are they dressed that way? They're children! Who's judging the attractiveness of a four year old?"

"Pedophiles, probably."

"And they put it on television?"

Trent shrugged. "They put a lot of stuff on television."

"Ach," Ciaran scoffed. He slouched back on the sofa and took another bite of cake, pausing to stretch his injured arm and check its soreness.

"We can turn it off," Trent offered, but Ciaran snorted at him.

"Not without finding out if Savannah places," he said as though it should have been obvious.

Behind them, covered by the sound of an overenthusiastic announcer, the front door clicked as Noah turned the handle. The lock slid open at his touch, and he stepped inside with Julien on his heels.

Ciaran sat up with a bite of cake halfway to his mouth as a prickling sensation traveled up his spine. He knew that feeling. He had gotten used to the soft tingling of magic in the apartment that radiated from Trent's family artifacts, but this was purposeful and sharp. He turned to the door and instantly got to his feet at the sight of the two men in the hall, dropping his plate to the floor.

"You don't quit, do you?" he sneered at Julien, and he automatically moved to stand between Trent and the intruders. He tilted his head with a small smirk. "How's that wrist?"

"Don't talk to it," Julien murmured when Noah glanced at him.

"What the fuck do you think you're doing?" Trent spoke up as he stood, but Ciaran put a hand out to keep the younger man behind him.

"Who's this you brought with you?" the fairy asked, his eyes on Noah's uncertain face. Ciaran's lip curled as he took a step forward. "You'll hunt me down for existing, and then you bring a witch into this house?"

"Just do it, Noah," Julien whispered, putting a steadying hand on the smaller man's shoulder. Noah took a deep breath and held out his hands, stopping Ciaran in place.

"You're playing with fire, a mhac," Ciaran growled, pulling against the invisible bonds holding him.

Noah didn't answer him, only shut his eyes and began whispering hasty Latin. He instantly felt the tug in his chest, but he kept going, repeating the phrases he knew by heart. Ciaran swayed in front of him and Trent caught him by the arm to keep him upright.

"What is he doing?" Trent snapped, looking across the room at Julien with panic in his eyes. "What are you doing?!" he tried again when he got no answer. He wanted to call the police, to hit the stranger in the face—anything to interrupt whatever he was doing, but Ciaran seemed to be withering right in front of him. The fairy's face had become gaunt, and he dropped to one knee as he slipped out of Trent's grip.

"You're...mad," Ciaran croaked. "You'll kill us both." His breaths were shallow and labored, and he held on to Trent's sleeve to steady himself. Trent could only kneel beside him and put a hand on his chest, gripping him helplessly. He wanted to do something, but he was afraid of what would happen if he left the fairy's side.

Trent looked up from Ciaran's hollow face just in time to see Julien looming over him, and he was snatched by the back of his collar out of his lover's reach, causing the fairy to lurch sideways. Ciaran barely caught himself on his hands, but he still managed a snarl as Julien forced Trent easily to the floor, pinning the younger man's wrists behind his back with his one good hand. Trent fought the much larger man's weight as his cheek pressed into the cool tile floor.

"Stop it!" he shouted, knowing it was pointless. Ciaran seemed to choke on something, and his green eyes were glassy as he looked over at Trent with a desperate, panting grimace.

Noah grit his teeth through the slow, thudding pain in his heart, his arms growing heavy as the spell flowed out of him and took his spirit with it. He could feel the sweat forming on his brow as he whispered and the trembling in his hands, but it was Julien who noticed the blood beginning to seep from his nose down over his lip. The blood dripped down the witch's chin to the floor, staining his mouth. His brow furrowed against the paralyzing ache in his bones, squeezing tears from the corners of his eyes. He could barely find the strength to keep up his incantation. Noah's legs gave out from under him as Ciaran slumped to the floor, and he dropped to his knees.

"Noah," Julien called out as a warning, his eyes on the fading fairy. "Just a little more," he pressed.

Noah flinched as a weight seemed to hit his chest. He couldn't breathe. He opened his eyes, but his vision was blurred by tears and his head swam from the pain of exertion. He let out a racking cough, feeling bile rising in the back of his throat. He wasn't going to make it, but he could do what Julien asked of him. He could do this for him. Maybe he really would take a break when it was done. And they would never have to have that talk. The witch forced himself to speak the incantation louder until the thread of resolve holding him up seemed to snap, and he fell to the floor in a heap. Julien left Trent where he lay and rushed to Noah's side, lifting the boy's limp body under his shoulders and shaking him while Trent scrambled across the floor to Ciaran.

Trent tried to turn Ciaran on his back and hesitated at the sudden weight of the fairy's torso. He felt like a body, instead of the sprite-like lightness Trent had felt in his arms that morning. He turned him over and held his face with both hands, letting out the sigh he had been holding in as he realized the fairy was still breathing. They were shallow, wheezing breaths, and his head threatened to loll heavily under Trent's touch, but he was breathing. Trent whispered his lover's name more than once, begging him to respond. Ciaran began to cough, twisting onto his side as he curled his knees up to his chest, and a spatter of blood escaped his mouth and dotted the tile floor—red blood. A tremor of panic brushed Trent's spine. Why was it red?

"Ciaran," he said again, his voice wavering. He looked up at the men across the room with a glaring frown.

Julien had his ear to Noah's chest, completely oblivious to the scene unfolding nearby. The boy still had a pulse, but it was weak, and he was barely breathing. Julien whispered to him in French, attempting to rouse him, but the witch was unresponsive. His pupils had shrunk to tiny pinpricks, and a mixture of blood and saliva dripped from his mouth to the floor as his head fell to the side. He looked back at Ciaran with a scowl twisting his lips. The fairy wasn't dead. How wasn't it dead? It was weak now, at least—it would be easy to push the boy out of the way and put a blade in its heart. He could end it. He could put a stop to it for good and make all of this worthwhile. But Noah's body was heavy in his grip, and Julien could feel him slipping further every moment that he lingered. Noah mattered more.

With a short grunt of effort, Julien lifted the witch over his shoulder with one hand and spared Trent one last glance before fleeing the apartment.

Ciaran struggled to breathe, and more blood spilled from his lips with every cough. Trent stayed at his side, touching his shoulder and hair with a helpless persistence.

"Tell me what to do," he whispered, but the fairy couldn't answer. Should he call an ambulance? Would they even be able to help him? Ciaran had no injuries that he could see—there was nothing to clean, nothing to help. He could only kneel beside him and keep him steady, wiping the blood from his chin just to feel like he was doing something, anything to help.

Ciaran went quiet after a while, his breath slowly becoming more even, but he still wouldn't open his eyes. Trent shifted the fairy into his arms, pulling to his feet with significantly more effort than he had needed the last time he lifted him. He was definitely heavier—he seemed an appropriate weight for his size, which was a vast difference. Trent carried him to the bed and laid him down. He stood over him, feeling helpless and frustrated. He had a hundred questions—who had the hunter had with him, what magic had he done that could hurt Ciaran like this, what he should do now to help—and no answers. He was reluctant to leave Ciaran's side, but he broke away from him to shut and lock the front door again, though it seemed to have been little deterrent before.

He sat on the bed beside the fairy and watched him breathe, an anxious tension growing in his chest every time Ciaran shifted or coughed. Trent barely moved for hours, until the lights of the city outside were the only illumination in the room. He couldn't focus on anything but Ciaran. He distantly heard his phone buzzing against the counter in the next room, but he made no move to answer it. He held Ciaran's hand, though it felt cool and clammy in his grip, and he listened to his slow breathing in the silent room.

The sky had begun to brighten outside before Trent realized how much time had passed. He felt stiff and tired. He released Ciaran's hand only to stretch and twist the muscles in his neck. The fairy seemed to be sleeping now, at least, rather than suffering. Trent left him briefly to use the bathroom and wash his face, but then he returned, taking up his place again at Ciaran's side.

The injury on his arm didn't seem bruised anymore. It looked slightly red where the blade had cut him, but the dark veins had disappeared. Trent lifted his shirt to check the fairy's stomach, and the bruise there had all but disappeared. He frowned as he looked back at

Ciaran's face. What the hell had the spell done to him?

It was well into the day before Ciaran stirred, startling Trent out of his drowsy vigil and bringing him back to attention. Trent gripped Ciaran's hand and shifted closer to him as he opened his eyes. The fairy looked up at him blankly for a moment before squeezing his hand and attempting to sit up. Trent urged him back down to the bed, frowning at how weakly Ciaran fought him.

"Have they gone?" Ciaran murmured. "Are you safe?"

"It's fine," Trent assured him, gently brushing the hair out of his face. "Everything's fine."

Ciaran pushed Trent's hand aside and slowly sat up, looking down at himself and seeming to take stock of the situation. "I'm not dead," he said as though it was a surprise to him.

"What the hell was that? You called that guy a witch."

"Aye," he muttered. He touched his stomach with a frown and lifted his arm, turning to inspect the healing red wound.

"Those look better," Trent said. "Why would they be better?"

Ciaran didn't answer him. He lifted his shirt to peer down at the spots of red on his chest and held the fabric out for Trent to see. "Is this from me?" His voice was still faint and weak, as though he could barely find the breath to make the words.

He nodded. "You coughed up a lot of blood. I thought you said your blood was black?"

"It is," the fairy answered with a furrowed brow.

"So, what, it was a spell to make your blood different? That doesn't make sense."

"It should have killed me," Ciaran said, staring down at the stains. "Why didn't it kill me?" He looked back up at Trent. "What happened to the witch? The hunter?"

"The one guy looked like he passed out, and the hunter took him out of here in a hurry."

Ciaran paused. "Maybe he didn't finish? No; that shouldn't have mattered."

"You going to fill me in at all?"

"Sorry." Ciaran shook his head. "That spell—I've seen it a few times before. Very rarely. It's extremely powerful, deadly to just about everything, but it's really a last resort sort of thing. The person casting it is just about as likely to die doing it. I didn't know I was so important."

"Well the other guy didn't look great. Maybe he did die."

"But I didn't," he muttered. "Why?"

"Does it matter why? You're awake and talking. Do you feel okay?"

"I feel...off." Ciaran shifted his weight on the mattress, bouncing slightly. "It's like...I'm without, somehow. That doesn't make sense. I can't quite—" He stopped bouncing and shook his head. "I'm not quite right, I can't—I don't know. I feel like I can't breathe."

"You're heavier. When I carried you in here, you felt like...a person."

Ciaran stopped bouncing and looked over at him. "Like a person," he repeated with a frown. He sat still a moment, staring down at his hands, and then he shook his head. "You're right. I can't do it. It's gone."

"What's gone?"

Ciaran's brow furrowed. "The magic in me. It's all gone."

22

Julien didn't know how much a hospital could do for Noah, but it was definitely more than he could have done on his own. As soon as he reached the lobby of the building, he shouted at the doorman to call an ambulance, and he held the smaller man against his chest to make sure he was still breathing. When the paramedics arrived, they took Noah from his arms and laid him on the floor. One of them began gathering equipment and leaning over the young man to inspect him, but the other blocked Julien's view and snapped his fingers to draw his attention from the boy on the floor.

"You're his friend?"

"Ouais. He's helping, right?" He leaned around the man's shoulder to try to see the paramedic kneeling on the floor.

"He'll take good care of him, don't worry. I need to ask you some things." He glanced down at a clipboard in his hand. "What's his name?"

"Noah," Julien answered, though he had to pause to search his memories for the boy's last name. "Clark. Noah Clark."

"What was he doing when this happened? It came on suddenly?"

"We were...visiting a friend. We were leaving, and he fell in the elevator. Quite sudden." He hoped he wasn't saying anything that would cause them to treat Noah incorrectly, but he couldn't exactly tell them that he was a witch who had been casting a very dangerous spell.

"And was he complaining of anything lately? Any signs you noticed?"

"Not before this, no."

"He allergic to anything?"

"I—not that I know of, no. He never said."

"On any medication?" The stranger glanced down at Noah, clearly taking in his torn jeans and facial piercings. "Legal or otherwise?"

"No," Julien growled. "Nothing like that."

"Any drinking?"

"He had a beer last night. Just the one."

"Smoker?"

"Yes."

"When did he eat last?"

Julien frowned. "Not since last night." Noah had spent the entire day reading and preparing spell components, or shut in his bedroom to meditate. He had done everything he could to prepare his body and mind for casting the spell, and it had still nearly killed him. Maybe it would kill him yet. Julien tried to push the thought out of his head. The paramedic asked him more questions about Noah's history that Julien didn't really know the answer to, and by the time they finished, Noah had a needle in his arm and a tube down his throat attached to a large plastic bulb. The medic slowly pressed the bulb in his hand, helping Noah to breathe as he was lifted carefully onto the stretcher.

Julien wasn't allowed to get into the ambulance with him, but he got on the first bus toward the hospital and sat anxiously in his seat for the entire ride. The thought that the fairy was still a threat barely entered his mind. He didn't know why the spell hadn't killed it, but the creature clearly wasn't in good shape when he left. Perhaps it had already died regardless.

At the hospital, Julien rushed down hallways to the information desk, where he had to restrain himself from barking at the nurse. "Clark?" he asked her, and he let out a sigh when she nodded in recognition.

"Are you family?" she asked him.

"No, I'm...his friend."

She looked up at him with a slightly skeptical look that he didn't appreciate, but she said, "He isn't allowed visitors yet. I'll let them know you're here, and as soon as he's stable, you can go back."

"Que veux-tu dire stable? Is he unstable now?"

"Sir, he's being taken care of; you'll just have to wait until there's more news. Please."

Julien clicked his tongue in frustration and moved away from the desk. He patted his pockets, but he had no cigarettes, so he paced in the waiting area. He had caused this. If Noah died, it would be his fault. It would be because he had been blinded by his need to catch and kill the fairy. The witch had been right—it was an obsession. One that Julien had allowed to endanger someone who he hadn't realized meant a great deal to him.

He had panicked, seeing the boy bleeding on the floor. Noah had known it was dangerous, life-threatening, and he did it anyway simply because Julien asked him to. And Julien had asked knowing the risk. Selfish, stupid thing to do. He had been impatient, and it might have cost Noah everything. He wouldn't make that mistake again.

After what seemed like hours, the nurse from the desk approached him in the waiting room.

"Your friend is stable," she said with a faint smile that was meant to be encouraging. "But resting. As soon as he's awake, I'll let him know you're here."

"Merci. Merci." As she turned to leave, Julien sunk into the nearest chair and put his head in his hands. Stupid. Selfish.

He waited and waited. He didn't dare leave the building in an attempt to bum a cigarette despite how anxiously he was forced to press his hands between his knees. He barely forced himself to walk to the vending machine for a drink, and even then he hurried back to the waiting room in case he missed the nurse's return. He only knew that it was morning by the clock above the nurse's desk; each minute that passed seemed hours long.

When the woman finally reappeared, she offered him a small smile that helped to unknot the tension that had been settled in his stomach for hours.

"He's awake," she said first, "and he's asked for you. Follow me."

"Merci, madame. Merci."

The woman smiled at him and led him down a few winding corridors to Noah's assigned room. Julien quietly opened the door and looked inside, pausing at the sight of Noah in the narrow hospital bed. He'd been dressed in a pale blue gown and tucked into the thin blanket, and he was still attached to the IV bag above him, dripping liquid down the tube into his arm.

Julien clicked the door shut behind him and took a seat beside the witch, tugging the chair closer to the bed. They had removed his piercings. Julien had never seen Noah without the silver hoops at the corners of his mouth, and he somehow seemed younger, more vulnerable without them.

"They said you were here all night," Noah said softly. His voice sounded weak and slightly strained; Julien wondered how long he had needed a machine to breathe for him.

With a soft sigh, Julien reached out for the witch with both hands, gripping his fingers as he brought the boy's hand to his lips. "Je suis désolé, mon râleur," he whispered. He touched a light kiss to Noah's knuckles and shut his eyes with the boy's hand held against his forehead. "Tellement désolé."

Noah froze, instinctively wanting to pull his hand away. He had never seen such an outpouring of emotion from the hunter before, and it embarrassed him, but at the same time, Julien held his hand so gently that his stomach fluttered despite his nausea.

"Of course I was here," Julien murmured without looking up at him. "This is my fault."

A faint frown touched Noah's lips. "I knew what I was doing."

"You did it because I pushed you," Julien sighed. He pulled away, leaving Noah's hand feeling cool in his absence, and he laced his fingers in his lap and shook his head. "I shouldn't have made you think I didn't trust you. I thought I would protect you, and I—used your affection for me to my own ends. I put my obsession before your well-being, and I shouldn't have. That isn't how you treat people you care about. It's been so long since I had anyone I could trust, that I...forgot that." He looked back up to the other man's softly frowning face. "I was wrong. I'm sorry, Noah."

Noah didn't know how to answer. His stomach was still churning, each breath was a struggle, and his vision was blurred, so for a moment he wondered if he had imagined the hunter's heartfelt apology.

"I don't expect your forgiveness," Julien went on, "but I hope you'll let me do what I can to help you while you recover."

"I'm not your responsibility, Julien."

"I am making you my responsibility. I was the cause of this, and I would owe you a lot even if I wasn't. You've done a lot for me since I've been here, and I took it for granted."

Noah felt his face flush slightly, and he turned his head away to avoid looking into the hunter's solemn eyes. "I shouldn't have said the things I said to you. It wasn't the time, it...will never be the time, and I was just so frustrated. So just...forget about all that, okay?"

Julien paused. "Is that really what you want?"

Noah's chest ached almost as much as his stomach. He felt split in two. On one hand, he wanted to tell Julien to ignore his emotional outburst just so that they could go back to the way things were before he embarrassed himself. On the other, he wanted to shout and say of course he didn't want him to forget, that now more than ever he wanted the hunter at his side. That he didn't know what he would do without him now that he knew him. That he didn't trust him not to do more stupid, dangerous things, and he wanted to be there when he did.

Julien tilted his head to catch the younger man's eye, interrupting his rambling thoughts. "We can still have that talk, if you want to. When you feel better."

Noah's throat tightened, but he swallowed it down. "When I feel better," he echoed softly. "Yeah. I'd like that." That would at least give him time to think about what he could possibly say that wouldn't make him sound like a lovesick idiot.

"Do you want me to let you rest?"

"I'd like you to stay," Noah answered without thinking. "Please."

Julien stayed, sitting quietly in the room even after the witch drifted off to sleep. He watched the boy's chest slowly rise and fall with each breath as he rested, and he moved out of the way when the nurse came by to change the bag hanging above him.

"You're the friend who brought him in?" the nurse asked softly, glancing to Noah's face to make sure she wasn't going to wake him. Julien nodded. "Do you know if he's been in contact with anything hazardous? Chemicals, things like that?"

Julien suspected that some of the spell components littering the boy's apartment could be considered hazardous, but Noah knew better than to be careless with anything toxic. Could the dead barghest have passed some sort of venom into him? More likely the doctors were just trying to assign a scientific cause to his magical ailment. If he knew what to tell them, he could lie, but he didn't want to cause unnecessary trouble.

"No," Julien answered in a whisper. "I don't think so."

She eyed his bandaged wrist and watched him skeptically for a moment, but then she nodded, marked something off on Noah's chart, and left the room. The beeping machines attached to Noah's skin made the only sound in the room above the witch's soft breath. Julien slouched in the uncomfortable chair, folding his arms across his stomach to rest his injured wrist. It felt much better than before, doubtless thanks to Noah's healing poultice, but it was still sore and stiff in its makeshift splint. He probably should let them look at it. He anticipated spending a lot of time in the hospital over the coming days anyway.

Noah stirred some time later to find Julien dozing in the seat beside him, his head slumped forward. He felt his heart thump uncomfortably. Noah hadn't expected the hunter to be so guilty or so attentive. He had gotten used to being ignored, teased, or brushed aside. Julien had been kind to him as long as they'd known each other, but he was always at arm's length. Always working, always focused. Having his full attention was intimidating.

Noah stared around the stark room in the silence, clutching his hands together in an attempt to control their slight tremor. The doctor had told him he seemed to have been poisoned, and though they couldn't identify the chemical specifically, he was showing all the right signs, and his response to treatment had confirmed their suspicions. Noah had assured her that he had no idea what he could have come into contact with, and she seemed to have believed him. Alone in the room with a twisting in his stomach, fluid in his lungs, and a mercilessly throbbing headache, he felt pretty poisoned.

The spell Julien had asked him to cast was universally acknowledged to be a bad idea—though the reason why was less readily explained. It worked so well on supernatural creatures because it stripped them of their spirit, their soul. Without that, most magical beings were little but dust and bad intentions. As for why it affected the caster so, he couldn't guess. But his head felt too full, and his chest beat out of time with itself, and he just felt—strange. Like there was too much of him. He lifted the hand that wasn't attached to machines and put it to his head, wiping away the thin film of sweat that had formed on his brow even in the cool room. Distantly, like a whisper at the end of a long hall, he thought he could hear voices, but he shook his head to push them aside. He didn't need hallucinations on top of everything else.

A slow weight squeezed around his heart, and he put a palm to his chest and tried to breathe through the crushing pain. He could hear voices, but he couldn't understand them; he could feel fresh air, but there was none.

Rolling hills, and a lake shore dotted with trees. The earth is green and soft but trembles with the footsteps of armies. The air off of the still lake is clean, cool, a gentle caress on his cheek before the storm. A weight touches his shoulder; a friendly hand that shifts the heavy blade at his hip. "Bid co féchsanach muigi. Ní frith ní fuigébthar brithem bas fíriu cathroí."

He shakes his head, feels the smile on his lips. "Ferr síd sochocad."

Noah was pulled out of his dream by Julien's hands on his shoulders. The machine at his bedside gave off an angry alarm, and the nurse that rushed into the room checked his pulse, looked into his eyes, and turned the valve on his IV to increase the flow of medicine into his arm. When he could take a steady breath, he turned to look at Julien, who frowned at him and gently wiped away the tears streaming down his cheeks.

"This isn't right," he whispered, but he wouldn't say anything more until the nurse was satisfied and left them alone. "This shouldn't be—there's more of me," he rambled despite Julien's warm hands on his cheeks and the gentleness of his quiet shush.

"You're safe, Noah. Don't get worked up. What are you saying?"

"There's too much of me," he sobbed, pressing his eyes with the balls of his hands. He took a labored, rasping breath and looked up at the hunter standing over him. "The fairy, he's dead? It's done?"

Julien hesitated. "No," he admitted after a moment. "I don't think so. It wasn't dead when I left."

"Why?" Noah pressed. "Why didn't you finish it?"

The hunter's brow furrowed. "Because you were dying, Noah," he said with a soft frown.

"You should have killed him," the witch sighed, his breath hitching into a racking cough that brought blood and bile to his lips. "You should have killed him. He's still here. He's here." Noah put his hands to his head and turned on his side, curling his knees to his chest on the bed. "He's still here," he whimpered.

23

Ciaran had been looking at himself in the bathroom mirror for at least an hour, leaning against the counter and inspecting his face. He felt too heavy. The marble counter dug into his hip as he leaned on it, and his hands seemed clumsy and numb. He turned his head this way and that to check his reflection—touching the small points of his ears, peering into his pale green eyes, scrunching his face at the freckles on his nose and cheeks. Everything was in place, but it still wasn't right. Red blood ran from his forearm to pool on the smooth countertop, the result of cutting himself with Trent's safety razor to test the color. That was still wrong. The magic was still wrong. He had tried every simple magic he knew from teleportation to illumination, and nothing had worked. It was as if his battery had run out after four thousand years.

Trent leaned against the bathroom door and tilted his head. "Are you done? What are you expecting to see?"

"Hoping something will jump out at me," Ciaran murmured, then he sighed and pushed away from the counter, stumbling slightly at the unexpected momentum of his weight. "I'm a bit foggy," he said. "I feel fine and not fine. I can't feel the iron in my blood anymore—blood that apparently is red now."

Trent clicked his tongue at him and stepped forward to lift his bleeding arm. "What the hell is wrong with you?" He snatched a hand towel from the ring on the wall and held it to the fairy's cut.

"I don't know; that's what I'm saying!"

Trent sighed. He glanced up at Ciaran's puzzled face and reached to touch his cheek, turning his chin up to look him in the eyes. "I'm just glad you're not dead," he said softly, and the fairy chuckled.

"It'll take more than that to kill me. Apparently," he added with a laugh.

"So what do we do now? Are you fine or are you not?"

"I don't know." Ciaran shook his head. "I want a nap."

"So have a nap. I'll have something for you to eat when you wake up."

The fairy nodded and slumped himself back to the bed, pulling the blanket up over his head to block out the light from the fan above him. Trent clicked it off on his way out of the room, but he left the door open so that he could listen for any more coughing. He had a sick feeling in his gut; he didn't know what the spell had done to Ciaran, exactly, but it was clear that he wasn't himself. Could magic change what a person was? Was he even a fairy anymore?

Trent paused in the kitchen, the thought stopping him in his tracks. That wasn't possible, was it? But he was heavy like a human now. He bled like a human, and the iron didn't seem to poison him anymore. He couldn't use his magic. If the spell had been meant to kill him, was it possible that it had half killed him? He glanced back at the open bedroom door with a frown. It didn't make any sense, but not much had since the fairy had shown up in his apartment. Illusions and hunters, witches and spells, not to mention the completely nonsensical developments between the two of them personally—none of it should have been happening in the real world. If Trent could believe that a fairy had been staying with him for the past week, that he had finally stood up to his father, that he had said the words "I love you" aloud to another living person and meant them, why was it impossible for that fairy to then have become human because of a vengeful witch's magic spell? It seemed to make perfect sense in the context of what Trent's life had become.

Trent hadn't had time to fully comprehend the depth of his decision to enter into a romantic relationship with someone who was apparently immortal. If Ciaran really was human now—or a close enough facsimile—the realization that he might grow old was sure to be jarring. It would be a huge adjustment for him. Trent stood at the kitchen counter and looked down at the plastic dome covering what was left of Ciaran's chocolate cake. He probably shouldn't be eating that anymore. This was assuming that Trent's suspicions were in the least correct, which he fully expected they wouldn't be. He knew absolutely nothing about the way magic worked, and he was prepared for Ciaran to laugh at his idle theories. At least the fairy seemed as puzzled as he was in this case.

He ate some leftovers out of the fridge while he waited for Ciaran to wake up, and he was startled by the sound of the fairy crashing into the dresser in the next room. Trent rushed to him, but Ciaran was already supporting himself with both arms flattened against the top of the dresser. He was breathing heavily, and he was still just as pale as he had been the night before. He was functioning, but not recovering.

"Shut up," he said before Trent could comment. "How do you function like this? I feel like I've got anvils strapped to my feet."

"How do I function while obeying the laws of gravity?"

"Didn't I say shut up?"

"You asked me a question."

"Well who told you to answer it?" Ciaran snapped, glaring over his shoulder at the younger man. He turned grumpily away from Trent's offended scowl and gave a small huff, winded by the exertion of his shout. He released the dresser once he was sure he was steady on his feet, and he stalked by Trent into the kitchen. He needed to eat something. That was why he felt so weak, surely. He needed to eat, and then he would feel better; then he could think and figure out this problem. He squeezed an inch of honey into the bottom of a glass and filled it with milk, downing the whole cup in a single breath. He took the entire cake with him to the sofa with a fork and dropped heavily into the cushions while Trent watched him from the doorway.

Trent considered taking the moment to tell Ciaran his theory, maybe even suggest that he not eat half a chocolate cake in a single sitting, but he was less inclined to be helpful following the fairy's outburst. He watched with his arms folded across his chest while Ciaran devoured the cake, counting the seconds in his head until the other man gave a pained groan. He pushed the cake to the edge of the sofa, frowning at it as though it had betrayed him as he curled up on his side.

"I don't know if you should be eating so much cake, by the way," Trent offered helpfully.

"I don't know if you should be talking," Ciaran countered. He buried his face in the cushion and held his stomach.

Trent sighed through his nose and stepped over to him, setting the cake aside to sit near the fairy's head. "I think maybe that spell changed you. I mean...actually changed you."

Ciaran grunted into the sofa without looking up.

"Is it possible that you're...not you anymore? That you're not what you were?" When the other man only gave a rough cough as an answer, Trent reached out to lightly touch his hair. "I don't know anything about magic, but you seem very human to me."

Ciaran rolled over onto his back, frowning upside-down at him. "Human," he murmured. His brow furrowed, and he stared up at the ceiling in silence for a few moments. "That spell the witch used—I've heard it's supposed to destroy your spirit. Maybe it worked after all, and without my magic I'm...this?"

"Your spirit? As in, your soul? Do you not have a soul anymore?"

"I'm not sure what a soul *is*," Ciaran said.

"You said before that you feel like you're missing something. What are you missing?"

Ciaran paused, and his fingers lightly brushed his chest over his heart. "Something," he mused. "Things that were close before seem far away. I'm missing...I can't remember what. It's like there was so much of me before, and now there's only this. Only right now."

Trent did his best to hide the worry in his voice. "Do you...still feel the same things you did before?"

Ciaran looked up at him for a moment and then sat up to face him. "You're asking how I feel about you?"

Trent scoffed in an attempt to appear cavalier. "How should I know how it's affected you? Just tell me now. It won't change anything, but I deserve to know."

The fairy narrowed his eyes skeptically, and he touched Trent's cheek to draw him close, pressing a soft, lingering kiss to his lips. When he broke away, he looked into the younger man's dark eyes with a faint smile. "There's only this," he said again. "Only right now. So there's only you."

Trent sighed at him, shutting his eyes and letting his forehead fall lightly against the other man's. "You really need to decide if you're going to be sweet, or if you're going to be irritating," he muttered.

"Why?" Ciaran chuckled. "Have you made that decision yet?"

Trent pulled away from him, their fingers lacing on Ciaran's lap. "So what do we do now?"

Ciaran gave a small sigh. "I don't know how to fix this. If it even can be fixed. But I can't go on this way." His shoulders hunched, and he released Trent's hands to cover his deep cough. He could feel the younger man's hand on his back as he weathered the coughing fit, and when he pulled his hands away from his mouth, his palms were spotted with red. He could taste the blood on his lips, a metallic tinge that was unfamiliar to him. "I need to see someone who can tell me what's wrong with me."

"You have someone in mind?"

"Maybe," Ciaran muttered. He frowned down at his bloodstained hand. "I'd hoped to avoid it forever. I suppose that was foolish."

"Avoid what?"

The fairy shook his head and sighed through his nose. "I need to go home."

Trent's brow furrowed. "Home?"

"To Tír na nÓg. Where my people are."

"You need to go...to fairyland?"

Ciaran sighed. "Yes. To fairyland."

Trent paused, watching him for a few moments. The other man was trembling slightly as though he was cold, and every breath seemed to be difficult to draw. He was right. He couldn't carry on like this. And Trent had made him promise to take him with him, wherever he was headed. He reached out to touch Ciaran's hair and leaned forward to touch a kiss to his temple.

"Then I suppose it's a good thing my passport's up to date."

ABOUT THE AUTHOR

T.S. likes to write about what makes people tick, whether that's deeply-rooted emotional issues, childhood trauma, or just plain hedonism. Throw in a heaping helping of action and violence, a sprinkling of steamy bits, and a whisper of wit (with alliteration optional but preferred), and you have her idea of a perfect novel. She believes in telling stories about real people who live in less-real worlds full of werewolves, witches, demons, vampires, and the occasional alien.

Born and bred in the South, T.S. started writing young, but began writing real novels while working full time as a legal secretary. When she's not writing, she reads other people's books, plays video games, watches movies, and spends time with her husband and daughter. She hopes her daughter grows into a woman who knows what she wants, grabs it, and gets into significantly less trouble than the women in her mother's novels.

Made in the USA
Columbia, SC
30 March 2019